MERCY
ROAD

OTHER BOOKS BY ANN HOWARD CREEL

The River Widow

The Uncertain Season

The Whiskey Sea

While You Were Mine

The Magic of Ordinary Days

MERCY ROAD

A NOVEL

ANN HOWARD CREEL

Text copyright © 2019 by Ann Howard Creel
All rights reserved.

No part of this book may be reproduced, or stored in a retrieval system, or transmitted in any form or by any means, electronic, mechanical, photocopying, recording, or otherwise, without express written permission of the publisher.

Published by Lake Union Publishing, Seattle
www.apub.com

Amazon, the Amazon logo, and Lake Union Publishing are trademarks of Amazon.com, Inc., or its affiliates.

ISBN-13: 9781542041980
ISBN-10: 1542041988

Cover design by David Drummond

Printed in the United States of America

This story is based on real events, and although the author has striven to stay true to history, this is primarily a work of fiction and the characters are of the author's imagination.

*The chauffeuses . . . were manifestly ladies of the
new school . . . not sitting in balconies, gazing at
sympathetic stars and longing for the hero to return.
No, indeed, they were following him in a motor car.*

—Esther Pohl Lovejoy, MD, Chair of the
American Women's Hospital

Chapter One

Paris, Kentucky

March 1918

Tornado and I jumped the stone fence and landed, fleet-footed, in our far meadow. I let him run the way he had when he'd been a racehorse and so often placed first. Tornado exhaled ribbons of steam into the silent morning as the sun crested and our pastures glistened with dew in this, the bluegrass country of Kentucky. His gallop drummed the ground so beautifully, like a beating heart, and his black coat pulled in the dawn light and reflected emerald and gold as we left Favier Farm behind us and skirted the dense woods, where deer often appeared and disappeared like phantoms. We flew beyond the limits of our land, into the blue, and on to forever.

It was but a dream, of course. Tornado was our most prized breeding stallion, a fierce Thoroughbred with a regal nose and wide-set eyes, whose contracts for siring live births able to stand and nurse right away were the most valuable assets of Favier Farm. Risking an injury to a stallion such as Tornado was foolhardy, and my father might have allowed an occasional careful canter, but galloping at full speed and jumping fences were out of the question.

In the dream, Tornado finally tired, and I trotted him back toward the green-and-white stallion stables, complete with steeples, where my father stood outside in the tall and distinguished way he had about him, waiting and watching, a lit Gauloise cigarette in his right hand, its rich scent reaching my nostrils as Tornado lifted his head in response to approaching his master.

But something was wrong. My father's face, lined but still handsome, looked drawn and filled with loss, his eyes exhausted, as if he'd been searching for something—questions, answers, peace—that he would never find.

A burning scent seeped into my brain. I opened my eyes to sudden consciousness. Tornado was dead. The dream vanished, along with its dozens of sensations, but the smell of cigarette smoke—or some other kind of smoke—was still there.

Someone screamed.

It was the middle of the night.

I sat up straight, threw aside my covers, and hit the polished walnut flooring at a run. Flinging open my bedroom door, I recoiled as a fumid haze hit me. Throat burning, my eyes stinging, I whirled toward the staircase, then Papa's face appeared out of the vapor, an ashen oval marked by the two dark smears of his wide-open eyes. Wearing only his dressing gown, he'd taken no time to don shoes.

He spoke my name in a surprisingly calm voice, "Arlene," as he grasped my arm. "The house is aflame. We must leave at once."

"What?" I sputtered. *The house is aflame,* he'd said . . . so calmly as if giving me a report about the weather. "Where are Maman and Luc?"

"They are here. Now let us move."

I blinked and saw Maman, who must have been the one who screamed. She'd managed to slip a peignoir over her nightdress and now clutched the banister as she crept down the mahogany staircase. My brother, Luc, wrapped in a burgundy silk robe, followed.

On the first floor, a dense blanket of noxious fumes seized my throat. Maman and Luc coughed desperately, overcome by the smoke, too. Gasping and choking, I stayed close to Papa. Only he seemed unaffected by the onslaught, or perhaps he pretended to be immune, showing strength for the three of us.

Maman had to stop and lean over her knees, wheezing and hacking, her lacy nightcap trembling with the effort. Papa grabbed her arm, and with Maman and me pressed to his sides, he steered us into the center hallway. As I turned to make sure Luc stayed close behind us, I glimpsed through the smoke a scarlet inferno burning in our kitchen. Papa said, "Move away. Keep moving. Quickly, quickly," as he shoved us adamantly down the hall toward the front door.

A heavy, seething cloud billowed in, so fast, so impenetrable. Yes, we had to get out now. I groped for Maman—she would need my help—but the heavy vapor clogged my lungs. I could barely see. I tried to breathe, my throat spasming in revolt. Papa gripped my arm and thrust Maman and me forward, together as if one, then pushed us through the front door onto the porch, Luc on our heels, Papa the last to exit. We sucked in the clean air and stumbled down the porch steps, then came to a dazed halt on the gently sloped green lawn in front of our house. I turned and stared back in stunned disbelief.

"What has happened? How has this happened?" asked Maman in a wretched voice.

No one answered. Instead we watched it burn—our beloved white Colonial home with its two-story columns standing tall across the front, its wide veranda adorned with white-painted chairs, blooming flower beds below. My father had built the house after relocating from Montreal as a young gentleman to begin his own horse farm. After he married my mother, she decorated it in an elegant but warm style. Now this adored family home was afire, with tongue-like flames bursting through the windows and walls on the kitchen side and licking at the second floor.

Papa raked a hand through his perpetually pomaded salt-and-pepper hair. Even after awakening in the middle of the night and fleeing a fire, he had a commanding presence. His calm came partially from his nature, but on that night, it also aimed to arrest the panic rising in the rest of us. "It appears to have started in the kitchen," he said over the roar of the fire, now spitting sparks, then asked us to please step back farther.

"How could this have happened?" Maman asked helplessly, as if she could keep asking the same question in a slightly different way and receive a different answer. "How could this have happened so quickly? While we slept?"

Although we kept domestics for housework, they went home every night unless we were hosting out-of-town guests. With our bedrooms located upstairs, we Faviers were sound sleepers. Until then, our lives had been so pleasant we'd had no cause to suffer from insomnia.

Luc, always a straight shooter despite being one of the quietest people I knew, finally said something. "The house is gone." His quiet demeanor and gentleness in manners had made some people wonder if my brother might be simpleminded, but he wasn't.

Frantic now, Maman lifted her hands in the air. "Can't we do anything?"

Before fleeing, we hadn't had time to call on the hallway telephone, and any water we might have lugged in buckets to douse the flames would have amounted to a pitiful attempt at the impossible. It was too late for the house now. Our horses could hear and smell the fire—they whinnied wildly in the stables—but the building sat far enough away, out of danger. I listened, closed my eyes, and found, thankfully, that no wind blew that night, the air beyond the house eerily still. But if even the slightest breeze stirred up and blew sparks close to the stables, I would've immediately dashed there to set the animals free.

Instead I watched the house, now full of strange colors appearing in the flames, the fire brighter and bigger, its heat burning the skin of my face and hissing and spewing and forcing us to take more steps backward. Trying to let it all go—our furnishings, wardrobes, family photos, art on the walls, brasses of horses, Maman's china and crystal, our heirloom rugs, our feather beds. What terrible pain, but I had never coveted inanimate possessions. People, my family, our horses, our land—those things meant everything to me. Even then I could whisper a tiny prayer of thanks for our escape.

"How did this happen?" Maman asked the air again, and God help me, I found myself growing the tiniest bit annoyed. I loved my mother, but I was Papa's girl, and he and I had never had to speak to understand each other. I could almost hear his thoughts: *Arlene Favier. You must be kind. You must keep yourself together for her. The house is—was—her domain.*

But instead Papa looked faraway for a moment, trapped in another realm, frowning and shaking his head, as if he might rid himself of the fire's mystery the way dogs shake water off their bodies after emerging from a pond. He whispered through a forlorn and removed sigh I'd never heard before, "We may never know . . ."

It startled me, but I thought he meant that we may never know how the fire had started. Later I came to wonder what else he might have meant. What else would we never know? His expression revealed devastation and a sad acceptance, the same way he and other horsemen and horsewomen knew that a lame animal must be put down.

I turned back toward the house, and an image of the fireplace mantel expanded in my head. In a leather frame, a photo of my father taken after he'd won his first race. Another showed my grandparents posed in front of their horse farm outside Montreal, where they'd lived since immigrating to Canada from France. Baby photos of Luc and me, and Papa's lucky horseshoe, polished to a silver sheen. My parents' wedding portrait. And above the fireplace, an artist's rendition in oil of Provence, which Papa had brought back from a trip to Paris and given to Maman upon their engagement. On either side of the painting, mirrors in gilt

5

frames. The fireplace flanked by side chairs shipped to us from New York City, their leather upholstery as soft and warm as butter. All gone now.

And then a pitiful gasp jerked my attention toward Papa. He lurched forward while shooting a demand back at us. "Take yourselves farther away. I must go inside."

A moment of stunned, perfectly horrible silence. Then "NO!" Maman screamed, and panic hit me like a whip.

Papa darted a severe look at Luc and, pointing his finger, yelled in a fierce and fraught voice I'd also never heard before, "Do *not* follow me, and do not *let them.*"

"Papa!" I said, but he had already started sprinting up the porch steps, two at a time, and then he vanished inside the gaping hole of our front door.

My eyes searched the door for his quick return, my last glimpse of him splitting into hundreds of pieces as though he had walked through a broken mirror. Little did I know that those fragmented images would accompany me for the rest of my life.

Moments felt like hours, a battle raging inside my head, and my mouth so dry I could not swallow. The house now reduced to a skeleton, pieces of timber began to fall with immense guttural groans, fangs of flame thrashing like evil spirits, and cinder showers exploding and drifting downward like so many falling stars.

I broke free of my puzzled trance. "Papa!" I screamed, all fury and fear let loose and coming out in animal-like panting and shooting tears. "He's not coming out. He can't get out!"

I lunged forward, but Luc grabbed me from behind. My younger brother, only sixteen, already had Papa's strength. He held me even as I struggled and found myself in the middle of the blackest nightmare, and I couldn't writhe away. Luc would not let me go, even as his tears dropped on my head and the back of my neck. Luc would never disobey an order given by our father.

Falling through the crust of hell. *Papa.*

As a girl, I'd sat on his lap while he braided my long auburn hair. He'd taught himself such little motherly duties so I would sit with him longer, but finally he'd allow me to leave his lap for visiting the brood-mares or running with colts or winding ribbons into the manes of fillies. A few clucks would escape from his lips, and then he would smile and say, "Go along, *ma poulette.*" *My little chicken.*

Papa always groomed his small mustache and wore a clean, starched shirt with pressed trousers every day, even while working with the horses. Born in Paris, France, he'd mastered English, but he still retained that lovely French accent. I adored the way he said *"feesh"* instead of "fish" and *"poe-leece"* for "police." He taught Luc and me to speak his native lan-guage at the same time we learned English from Maman and at school.

Trying to breathe. My eyes would not close as the fire continued to burn, a rage of flames, sparks, bursts, and collapsing explosions finally engulfing the entirety of our home, taking my father with it.

That night I learned the most brutal lesson of my life: The devil could poke his finger through the earth's ether to tinker with any of us at any time. He could play a sinister trick just because he wanted to. He could change the very fiber of us in only a matter of moments.

More screaming, whereas I had no awareness of even existing. Maman kept crying and wailing louder than the sound of the fire. I blinked, and then the scream, which had been large and loud and ring-ing in the air around us, moved backward toward me and slipped back into my mouth.

Maman on the ground now, weeping, Luc silent. And still I strug-gled. I didn't stop fighting until help arrived and two of our closest fam-ily friends held me still, swept me up, and took us away. With the house still burning, a partially standing carcass, we drove off the land in an ash-covered Maxwell automobile, and Papa's friend Charles Bentwood covered my eyes with his hand and pushed my chest down into my lap, at long last suppressing the screams that I hadn't swallowed after all.

Chapter Two

Papa's funeral took place in the Methodist church, and then the remains of Beaumont Favier were laid to rest in the town cemetery. Dressed in black crepe dresses loaned to us by others, mine hitting just above the ankle and Maman's floor-length, we clung to each other, and my brother, wearing a borrowed black suit, tried to remain composed.

This day marked the beginning of the end of all we had known. I would never be young and carefree again. My innocence had vanished.

We had been a fortunate family, not excessively wealthy, but comfortable, not only financially but because we did what we loved. Papa, Luc, and I devoted ourselves to the horses—Papa and I knew their breeding, their blood, their speed and strength, while Luc had gifts more attuned to the animals' daily needs, their physical manifestations, and even what he believed went on in their minds. He spoke on their behalf in the world of the language-speaking creatures entrusted to care for them. And Maman had her home, her friends, her little soirees, and her tame place in society.

While in high school, one of my classmates lost both of his parents, one from an accident, the other from a mysterious fever only a few months later. Jimmy was all boy and a humorous scold whom everyone liked. Suddenly left homeless and destitute and all alone, he needed help; therefore Papa hired him for after-school and weekend work in our stables. Away from school, where boys usually played with boys, and girls usually played with girls, he and I took to each other almost immediately, but Maman discouraged my growing friendship with Jimmy, claiming that we moved in different circles and it was best to keep it that way.

On the funeral day as a cool breeze washed over the town of Paris, Kentucky, the only home I'd ever known, I remembered Jimmy. Now I understood the losses he'd suffered, and I wondered what had happened to him. He no longer lived in Paris, and when I first learned he had moved, I wondered what would make someone take his leave of this land, such a genteel place, the perfect landscape for breeding horses, sipping bourbon, and growing sweet green things.

Papa had discovered Paris as a young man after striking out on his own. Located seventeen miles north of Lexington in Bourbon County, Paris had taken its name in tribute to France's help during the Revolutionary War. The pretty little town, lined with filigreed two-story buildings, must have attracted my father because it shared a name with his birthplace, but it also happened to be in the middle of the best horse country anywhere. The rich soil full of limestone strengthened the bones of racing giants. Here Papa had raised a house, horses, and a family.

I had expected to get through the funeral by placing myself in something of a fog, but instead everything stood out in etched detail, from the leaves on the trees to the deep-brown contours of Papa's casket as it was lowered into the ground. Maman wore a crepe-trimmed mourning bonnet with heavy veiling. Behind the veil, her face appeared skull-like, pale as bone, eyes like empty sockets.

No one would see her shed a tear, but I had chosen to face the day open and exposed. For the first time in my life, my father would go somewhere important without me. He went back to the ground and to his maker, alone.

Many townspeople attended, as my father had treated everyone from our stable workers and hired help to the equestrian elite with the same kindness and goodwill. His intuitive way of choosing stallions to stand at stud had become legend; he had produced many race-winning legacies. We opted to breed our own mares from time to time and occasionally raced a horse simply for the joy of it. But Papa had focused on stud service; stallions provided our bread and butter.

As I struggled through the tarlike mud on our way out of the cemetery, my mind seized on a single heart-wrenching question, one that now haunted me and had turned my peaceful slumber into a nightly war: Why had Papa run back into a burning house?

Two days later, wearing our borrowed black attire, Maman, Luc, and I drove into town. Since the fire we had stayed with the Edwards family, who owned a large Victorian house and bred racehorses on their farm only a mile or so away from ours. They assigned us a separate wing of their home, sent servants to attend to our needs, and began gathering clothing, shoes, hats, and other essentials so we could still go about our days and pretend to be living.

Every meal a feast and every one of our physical needs met, still we could find no help for this. I could hear Maman weeping in her room across the hall every night. But the silence coming from behind Luc's closed door proved even more traumatizing. Luc, like most young men, chose to suffer alone.

Today we had an appointment to meet with Papa's attorney in town. At least for a few hours, I would have to abandon my helpless search for something logical and comforting in the midst of so much misery. So far I'd found nothing, no semblance of reason, no answer to help me even begin to comprehend what had happened to us.

In town, posters urging men to sign up and notices about war bond drives hung everywhere. Knowing his homeland was now a brutal battlefield had tortured Papa. Although we'd never discussed it specifically, I was sure he had donated generously to the cause.

At our appointed meeting time, we waited outside the door of Mr. Gary Patterson's office in a wood-paneled reception area under a shining, punched-tin ceiling in the heart of Paris, a city famous for its lovely courthouse and charming Main Street. It seemed an interminable wait; however, we knew what to expect. Papa would have left everything to Maman with some extra dispensations to Luc and me. Only the day before had I begun to think of rebuilding. It was almost unbearable to imagine a home without Papa, but I told myself we needed our own roof over our heads again.

Mr. Patterson emerged and ushered us into his office, where he had set three upholstered armchairs to face his desk. A stout man with cherubic cheeks and a mustache that curled into almost perfect circles on both ends, Mr. Patterson had always made me smile.

Today he wore a solemn expression, and the sadness in his eyes looked real. We barely spoke and simply sat before him while he read the will laid on the desk. As I'd expected, my father had left the bulk of his estate to Maman but had requested money set aside for Luc's education, and he left matters concerning our sire service and business to my control.

"Your father wished for you to attend university," Patterson said to Luc.

I glanced at my brother. He didn't have to flinch for me to feel his discomfort. As of late, this topic had been a bone of contention between my father and Luc. Although well aware of Luc's particular gifts with the horses, Papa had wanted him to receive a more formal education.

Luc caught my eye, and I blinked a signal he was sure to receive. We did not need to take this up with Patterson. Now the three of us would make decisions, and this one could wait. Besides, Luc still had one more year of high school to complete.

Patterson, who should have left well enough alone, said to Luc, "Your father and I discussed this once." A small, sad smile curled his lips. "As nature might have it, you're too big to become a jockey, and riding is much too dangerous anyway. Your father knew you hoped to train and race your own horses in the future—"

"Yes, sir," said Luc.

"But he wanted you to have a broad base of knowledge. Mathematics, art, music, fine literature. So that later in your life when you travel—"

"My life is here," Luc said.

He hadn't meant to sound disrespectful, but still I sent my brother an admonishing stare. All of us exhausted from lack of sleep and the ravages of grief, we would wither in the face of more tension, especially Maman.

"We understand," I said to Patterson.

Patterson put a finger between his neck and collar, loosening its grip. I sensed a shift in his posture and affect. "I need to let that wish of his be passed on; however . . ."

I straightened.

"Now," he said and looked down as though hesitant to speak. Then he brought his gaze up and focused on me, not Maman or Luc. He wove his hands together on top of the desk. "If I may be so bold, I must tell you that I've spoken with your father's banker, and . . ."

A blur, like tears, bloomed in his eyes, and a dark sense of knowing ran across my brain. I sat up even straighter but remained unruffled and said, "And what?"

Muscling his words together, he said, "I'm sorry to say . . ." A long pause and then his face filled with compassion. "That your father's bank account is almost empty."

Maman gasped, but I did not. It had to be a mistake. "I'm sorry?"

Patterson composed himself. "Yes, I'm afraid you've heard me correctly. The bank account . . . well, apparently your father . . ."

"My father . . . what?"

"This is a delicate matter, but I must relay the truth." His voice lowered, but in the strained silence of his office, each word fell like a bomb. "I'm sorry to say that perhaps some recent decisions, er . . . it appears as if your father's finances have suffered as of late."

I made myself pull in air and breathe, guardedly, as a strong sense of foreboding transformed into a painful dawning. Ever since Tornado's sudden death, our stud service had been less lucrative. But we had endured some slower business times before, and never had it affected our lives. A careful man, Papa would have planned ahead and never left us in peril. This I knew on some instinctual level, but my training to take over had not yet extended to handling the business's bank account.

"Most assuredly not," I said calmly. "There must be other accounts."

Patterson darted a glance aside, then focused on me again. "My first thought, too, but I've worked on this solidly for the past week. I hate to tell you that I've not been able to uncover anything else other than a small life insurance policy."

"Life insurance?"

"Yes," he said and paused. "At one time, Mr. Favier had a fire policy on the house, but he canceled it a few months ago. According to Mr. Cross at the bank, Mr. Favier had been engaged . . . in a struggle . . ."

"Impossible," Maman whispered in a way that sounded like a hiss, although she hadn't intended to aim any anger at Mr. Patterson. My mother walked about now as though a cruel plot had been hatched against her, and it took every ounce of her willpower to push through each hour of each day. She turned to me. "Your father would've told you. Hasn't he trained you in the financial matters? Haven't you seen the accounts?"

"No, Maman," I said in a whisper, all I could muster at the moment. Since finishing high school five years ago, I'd studied and worked with Papa and had learned most of what it took to run our business, although I'd failed to glean his inexplicable way of knowing stallions. Many times

Papa chose neither the biggest of the sires nor those that had won the most races. Instead he watched the horses in their paddocks, the way they moved, how they held their heads, and how they snorted and whinnied, and he could see things others couldn't.

Once, at a horse auction, he crouched down next to me and turned me to face a stallion he was considering buying, then said, "Just watch and wait for something inside you to respond. Ask yourself if this stallion has a spark, something which you feel . . ." He put his fist gently on my chest, and continued, "In here, in the heart."

Papa and I were so alike and loved horses so intensely, of course I wanted only to follow in his footsteps. But though I'd been given more and more authority to make decisions over the years, I still had not, as of then, chosen a stallion on my own or made any major financial moves.

I answered Maman, "I've taken over many duties, but I've not made a deposit or withdrawal. Papa wanted me to know the day-to-day operations like the back of my hand . . . first." The words died in my throat. Perhaps Papa had not given me access to the money for a different reason. Perhaps he hadn't wanted me to see a bank balance going down and down. But my mind yelled *Impossible!* in almost the exact tone as Maman's.

"If you please, surely, there are things he hadn't shown you yet," said Maman with a bit of desperation. Of course by *things* she meant more money, more accounts, more assets.

Patterson clenched his hands together. "Your father made a large withdrawal on the day he died, almost everything left. According to Mr. Cross, to purchase a stallion . . ."

Of course. Papa and I had made it our mission to replace Tornado, although he'd never truly be replaced. We owned several fine stallions, but Tornado had been our biggest success story, siring many fine racehorses. We not only respected what he had done for us; we loved him. And so when one morning six months earlier, Luc discovered him dead in his stall for no apparent reason, it shook us to the core. Horses are unpredictable animals, and sometimes even during their prime years, a sudden ailment or call from the heaven of horses takes them. But Tornado had seemed invincible. Luc, despite his instincts and attunement to our animals' every need, had intuited nothing, and his devastation became unending. Even Maman, who normally kept her life separate from the horses and only indirectly understood what we did, felt the painful loss.

But we owned other profitable animals. I still couldn't fit my thoughts around what Patterson had said. It couldn't be . . . but yes, as I considered this news, I realized that it was true; we hadn't acquired as many stud service contracts lately. Chicory hadn't had a good year, producing for our customers fewer mares in foal and fewer live births. Another of our stallions had developed a visual ailment, and we'd had to put him down. But the result couldn't be an almost empty bank account.

Pieces began to click together. Papa and I had chosen a gray stallion to replace Tornado. The young Thoroughbred, named Cotton Coat, was costly because of his rarity; he had lineage to Pink Star, a Bourbon County racehorse that won the Derby in 1907. Pink Star had developed a fever later in his career and never went to stud. Cotton Coat, his much younger cousin, seemed like an excellent choice. But more importantly Papa had seen that special quality he always looked for in a sire of champions. He'd planned to pick up CC, as we'd affectionately dubbed him, on the day following the fire.

Now it came back to me. Papa had planned to take me along when he picked up the stallion. By then everyone knew I was immune to the call of a traditional woman's life. When given my first doll, I had liked her, but she didn't move or breathe or whinny or bark like my other friends, and soon I cut her hair short and stripped her down to her pantalets so she could ride atop Tornado like a boy.

Papa had laughed out loud when he saw her, but Maman had wrung her hands, turned on her heels, and stomped away from the stables, where I played every evening until forced inside by one or both of my parents. Although considered attractive (my papa had said *"bu-tee-fool"*) and already twenty-three, I'd never taken to courting. Maman had eventually come around; she saw that my destiny lay in breeding. Papa had been preparing me for life as a horse breeder, as the head of a family business that meant more than just business; it was our dream.

As I sat in Patterson's office, the truth came to me fully formed as another scream I would not let escape me. My father had raced back into a burning house for the cash, for money he would never have told anyone, not even me, meant so much. All to no avail, and all causing us to instead suffer the biggest loss of our lives.

Luc would not continue his education at a university after high school, because we had no money for it. I would not purchase Cotton Coat and revive our stud service, because the cash had burned in the fire. And Maman would not rebuild the house she'd so lovingly decorated and managed, because we had no insurance to pay for its replacement. And none of us would ever again know the inexplicable joy that came from my father's very pores, the peace and pleasure he brought everywhere and to everyone, especially the three of us.

If only he had left the money to burn!

But that was not Papa. A gentleman with a quiet and calm demeanor, he also possessed the will of a fighter. One did not cross the Atlantic to bring back a painting for his fiancée, one did not leave a farm he might have inherited to make his own name, and one did not discover stallion kings using only his gut instincts without a fighter's way and will. He had protected us from the truth; instead, he'd planned to take a leap of faith with CC. I'd had no idea; the purchase of the new stallion had struck me as nothing less than a joyous event.

Yes, Papa had tried to save us. But as it turned out, nothing could do that.

Chapter Three

The next day, Luc drove the two of us to the farm in our 1914 Chevrolet Baby Grand, one of Papa's prized possessions. Parked by the barn, both the Chevrolet and our old converted Model T had survived the fire and had suffered nothing more than soot on their hoods. Neither of us spoke during the short drive, and once we arrived, Luc headed to the stables, whereas I faced the house and took my first hard look at the remains.

The smell of charred wood emanated, even though the air held still. Other than the remains of two stone chimneys, nothing stood but pieces of beams and the twisted limbs of the staircase, and among them, blackened piles of stinking rubbish that would someday turn to dust. Now that I knew we would not rebuild anything, the sight of it nearly blinded me with disbelief.

I'd always believed that like the horses, I would sense a change in the wind, that I would feel something ominous on the horizon coming our way. So many times, I'd witnessed the way a horse perks up and flicks its ears forward a second or so before any sign of danger. Horses intuit impending storms, approaching animals, even the birth of a foal nearby. Inexplicably they go on alert. I'd thought something of that horse sense dwelled inside me, too. Now, I knew better.

A faint haze of ash still floated in the air, or maybe I imagined it. I brushed my shoulders anyway. I had to take special care of my borrowed attire. Olive Taylor, a friend from school of similar tall and lean build with small hands and feet, had loaned me two everyday calf-length dresses, one suitable for church and business and a more practical one for wear at home. Today I wore the casual one, sunny yellow with a cinched empire waist and puffed sleeves. I stood grayly within it.

After the fire investigation, friends of ours had searched the wreckage and found nothing save one small brass statue of a jockey from the upstairs fireplace mantel in Maman and Papa's bedroom. It must have fallen far enough away from the inferno to survive in a blackened but intact shape. Maman kept it, her only remaining memento of Papa, at her bedside. I grasped the small gold baby locket I wore on a delicate chain around my neck—the one thing I had from the house other than the nightdress I wore on that night. It held a tiny photo of me as an infant that my father had placed there.

So far, I'd made no arrangements for cleanup. On the night of the fire, Papa had said, "We may never know . . ." A prophetic statement. No one, not even the fire investigator, could determine the exact source of the fire.

Turning away for a moment, I gazed over our rich land gently rolling in all directions, so in contrast to the pile of what was left of our home. When I looked toward the remains again, my chest tore open. I closed my eyes and wished for the cauterized rubbish to fly away on some errant wind. I never wanted to see it again.

Then a split second of desperation took me two steps closer to the rubble. Could Papa have placed the money in a safe or fireproof box I might still uncover? But that amounted to foolishness, and I stopped still. Papa had hidden everything about his troubles from us. He'd always promised to take me to France, and about a year or so before

18

the fire, I'd asked him about going over. He, of course, reminded me that a war raged in his home country, but now I wondered if money had worried him even then.

A flock of sparrows took flight from a nearby tree and scattered to the heavens as though they, too, had given up on finding something below.

I returned to the stables, where the scents of horses and hay gathered and Luc stood grooming Chicory. Our stable boy was around but out of earshot. Maybe now Luc and I could have the conversation we needed to have. Luc waited for me to start, while Chicory gave off one of those snuffle-snort sounds only horses make.

"What now?" I asked.

People outside our family rarely asked Luc for his opinion. He continued to brush Chicory but glanced in my direction. "We'll begin again."

I held my tongue. I hated to shatter his remaining dreams. That day, Luc wore loaned work pants and suspenders, no hat, and even with the wrinkled light that came through tiny cracks in the grooming stall, his clothing and blondish hair appeared dull, as if the ash outside had made its way here. He had pomaded his hair and slicked it back this morning, but his normally straight part on the side ran a bit crooked. Papa would've laughed, play-punched him, and sent him back inside the house to fix it. I opened my mouth to speak, but something swelled my throat and stole my breath.

He said, "We'll rebuild the house. A smaller one. I'll take care of the horses."

"Luc." I swallowed and tried to fortify myself. "We have no money to rebuild a house, not even a smaller one."

My stomach churned acid. Worry about money was new to me; I'd never had to concern myself about it. In fact, I'd never faced a serious problem, especially one that only I could solve. I had to push all the pain and loss to the periphery and put practicality in the center.

I said, "We need a different plan." Luc sighed and then held still for a moment. "We still have Chicory."

He was correct about that, of course, and we probably had breeding contracts in place for the next month or so, but Papa's schedule had burned in the fire, and no one had made contact. Our customers most likely thought it kind to breed their mares elsewhere and not bother us during this sad time.

I said, "We need a place to live. We can't count on the Edwards family's charity much longer."

Mr. Patterson had whispered to me before we'd left his office: "Let me give you a small but important piece of advice. Don't tell anyone about your situation unless you have to."

I'd turned to him in shock. What others would think hadn't even occurred to me. And yet a certainty in the truth of his words coursed through me then. Patterson knew what he was talking about.

He probably thought we'd sell the land and move on, most likely to Montreal to Papa's family, and that we'd make haste without revealing anything other than a desire to live closer to family now. But both my grandparents had weak hearts and hadn't had the strength to make the journey to see their son buried. We had visited them in the past, but their house felt nothing like our home. And I had no knowledge of their finances; since retirement my *grand-père* and *grand-mère* had probably lived on savings. Besides, Papa would never have wanted his parents to know he'd left his family destitute. Maman's parents had died early, before Luc and I ever knew them, and she had only one brother, who was but a clerk in Lexington.

Luc turned to face me, leveling a questioning look that seemed to ask *What?*

Even though I hadn't handled the bank accounts, I'd placed orders and calculated fees. I'd gone to the feed store and tackle shop. I'd paid for business luncheons. I'd done enough to know what things cost. Luc and Maman knew nothing. I braced myself and said, "We might have to . . ." Then I couldn't say the words. It had never occurred to me that I'd do anything other than live and work here.

Luc must have thought the same thing. "We aren't selling the horses." By then we owned only one stallion and three broodmares. "We can still stand Chicory at stud and breed the mares." One of our mares, Mary Blue, was in foal, but most likely this would be her last time.

I kept my voice steady. "And what do we live on until then? Chicory's fees have fallen, and even if Mary Blue's foal is a beauty, we won't get much for it. If we breed the others, they won't foal for a year. We won't have enough . . ." I glanced back toward the house's remains. Although painful to look at again, they showed the truth—the truth I wanted Luc to accept, too.

Both hands clenched on his hips now, he said, "Maybe we can still get the stallion."

"CC?" I shook my head. Still too young, he couldn't see what I'd started to see.

"Can we get a loan?"

I shook my head again. "The banks ask for collateral. And we have nothing."

"Dash it all! We're not giving up what's left of Papa's dream!"

I'd rarely known Luc to raise his voice. His dogged determination came close to desperation. My brother had rarely known friends. Our society looked down on those like him, who lacked some skills, such as the ability to make small talk and play silly games required at lawn parties, and who would rather face the gallows than dance. He fit here and only here. He said, "You and Maman can stay with friends. I'll stay with the horses. We won't even need a stable boy."

That gave me pause. I moved closer and stroked Chicory's face, then looked into the black depths of his eyes as though I might find answers there. But I saw only the kind of boundless spirit that all horses hold inside.

Luc's idea had not occurred to me as an option. But Papa had once built some small living quarters back behind the mares' stables; our help had slept there during busy seasons, especially when we expected a mare to foal. A woodstove inside kept it warm during winters. Luc could live there like a stable boy . . . and his suggestion made sense.

As I pulled in a deep breath, what remained of my childhood self floated away. *You're the oldest,* I told myself, *and you will have to make the hard decisions.* "Luc, listen. Friends will grow weary of us. People will pass us around like a bad cough. I need to move Maman into a room in town. That takes money."

"What about the life insurance?"

"I don't know when it will arrive. For now we have to sell something."

"Not one of the horses."

"Then what?"

He gestured with his hand and cocked his head toward the door. Outside, the Chevrolet stood. "The motorcar."

I supposed we could sell it.

He said, "We'll still have the Lizzie."

I'd always preferred the old girl myself. Papa used it as a farm truck and had taught me to drive it as soon as I could reach the pedals and peek over the steering wheel. But even if I sold the car, the money from its sale would run out. The life insurance money would run out. The bank account would empty. We had to support ourselves. I couldn't imagine Maman working, and Luc had to stay in school. I would have to work, although I would surely face opposition. People spoke of women *working* as though it were a curse word. But I had to move past those beliefs; I had to graduate from the school of societal expectations.

So I would get a job, and if Maman and I took a room downtown, I could walk to my place of employment. I wondered if Patterson would employ me in his office. Perhaps Luc and I *could* continue working with the horses, but I needed income we could count on while waiting for stud fees to come in or for a mare to foal.

"You'll have to come out here," Luc said, "to help me sometimes."

I'd never known that Luc had such a persuasive side. Of course he could handle most of the work on his own, even though as the summer heat approached, the chores would intensify. Horses sunburned easily and needed frequent watering to keep flies off. The stallions and the mares could never mingle; always they must keep to their own stables and fenced pastures. The mares usually went out in the morning, and the stallions went out at about 1:00 p.m. and could stay out until dawn on quiet nights.

But we had to move the horses inside if storms came. They had to be groomed, fed, and watered. We ordered hay from others, and those people weren't going to give it to us for nothing. Furthermore, it took four men in our breeding shed to bring a stallion and a mare together safely—two to hold the mare into submission and two to handle the stallion as he mounted. Even with my help, we would have to hire men during breeding season, which typically ran February to July.

I said, "I'll find some work in town."

"And I'll start getting contracts to stud Chicory next year."

I wondered how much demand would remain for Chicory. Now we could be perceived as bad luck.

"What kind of work?" he asked.

At a loss again, I lifted my hands. "What a very good question."

I had received a good education, but I had never worked outside the stables. I had never taught a class. Maman played the piano and had wanted to teach me, but I'd never let myself be bothered. So instructing in a school or teaching music, perhaps the most reputable of the female professions, stood outside my reach. I had no secretarial skills. I had no medical training. What could I do?

Luc must have read my mind. "You're a horsewoman, Arlene."

Yes. I loved the animals and rode expertly. But I'd never trained a racehorse—typically men took those jobs and possessed those skills. I'd observed the breeding process but had never assisted. The process was rather brutal; the men had to tie up the tail and one of the mare's legs so she wouldn't instinctively kick and injure a valuable stallion. Papa had padded the walls inside our breeding shed because maidens often fought. My father hadn't wanted me directly involved. I could care for horses as well as any stable boy, but I wasn't a stable boy. No one would hire me for that, and besides, Maman would be mortified at the thought.

One thing, however, became clear: the townspeople would definitely know of our plight, even if Cross and Patterson remained silent. I relived my last conversation with Olive, during which she'd pulled dresses from her armoire. When she suggested we visit the tailor in town to order me a new wardrobe, my heart seized. Of course she had no idea.

Growing up as fortunate girls about the same age, our companionship had evolved rather naturally. At one time, we'd dreamed of marrying brothers or cousins so we would share a family. I pretended to like her dolls, and we pledged to have babies at the same time so our children would grow up as friends. As teenagers our friendship involved taking the Paris–Lexington Interurban, an electric railway, to Lexington for lunching and shopping, or playing tennis wearing our lacy dresses and button boots on her family's court. Our time together had been enjoyable, but I'd eventually returned to my horses, and Olive started courting, married early, and married well. Looking back, I couldn't remember feeling truly close to her. But she thought we were. "What is it, Arlene?" she'd asked me with worry lines across her forehead.

"N-nothing," I'd stuttered and placed my hand on the back of a chair. "Forgive me, but I can't imagine doing something as frivolous as buying a new wardrobe right now." Although that was true, it wasn't the entire truth. I no longer had money for clothing and needed to make the small amount left in the bank account last as long as possible.

She said, "I understand; of course I do. I've always cared for you, and I always will."

I looked her squarely in the eyes. "No matter what?"

She appeared confused. "What do you mean, 'no matter what?'"

My thoughts returning to the present, I looked up at Luc and shook my head. I wondered how many friends he, Maman, and I could count on after I became a working girl.

You're a horsewoman, Arlene, my brother had said, as if the declaration alone held the power to pull me back. But for the time being, I could no longer think of myself as a horsewoman, and my heart took a leaden fall at the thought. I lacked the courage to borrow Olive's equestrian attire, so I hadn't ridden a horse since the fire. My friend was handsome and smart but not always attuned to others. She meant well, but I would have to ask for everything. And so I didn't.

I said to Luc, "I'll come up with something."

Looking relieved, he nodded. "Next time we come, I'm staying put." He pointed behind him. "You wouldn't believe what's stored in there. I'll make do."

Fine, I thought, but he had to have provisions. Food for him and feed for the animals. Veterinary care. Gasoline for the farm truck. Maintenance on the stables. I looked down at my feet. Dust and pieces of straw stuck to the very thin and supple leather of the lace-up boots that didn't belong to me. "I'll sell the car. Even though Papa loved . . ." He had called it *"mon bébé."*

Luc lowered an eyebrow. "He loved the horses more than he loved that car."

I nodded. Sometimes Luc and I could communicate with simple gestures—talk exhausted him eventually—but this day begged for spoken words and decisions. "You're right. You stay here, and I'll see to Maman. And some job will materialize for me." I really had no reason to believe that. The automobile's popularity everywhere had put liveries, wagon makers, blacksmiths, coachmen, and teamsters out of work. Even with more men joining up for the war every day, many skilled male workers had lost jobs and sought new ones.

Luc turned away, then started stroking Chicory again.

On the drive back, he reached over and touched my cotton-gloved hand. His version of an apology or a gesture of support. I glanced his way and witnessed the beginnings of the kind of strength Papa had. But I also noticed his lip quivering.

Three days later in Maman's bedroom at the Edwards residence, I told her the plan Luc and I had agreed to. I also told her I'd sold the Chevrolet and let a room for the two of us in town at the Fordham Hotel. She surprised me by offering no resistance. Standing in front of a window that streamed light through its sheer curtains, she looked like a dark angel with her back to heaven. She quickly swiped at her face with a linen handkerchief and asked, "When shall we go?"

"Tomorrow," I answered. "They keep a piano in the gathering room. You might play it sometimes." Maman missed her music; now and then, her fingers fluttered like wings in her lap as if she played the keys. I thought the piano would make her feel better, but she didn't respond. "As soon as I get you settled, I'll look for work . . ."

Her face paling, she finally asked in a pained whisper, "Is our situation that loathsome?"

Slowly, I made myself nod.

She pulled in a shaky breath. Her eyes held the stunned blur of a stolen life, but I could see resignation there, too. Before the fire, my mother would never have stepped outside the front door, even to sit on the porch, unless her dress looked perfect, her hair meticulously styled. No longer a pampered wife, was she angry with Papa?

I never asked.

"What will you do?"

I told her I would inquire at the town's numerous bakeries and confectioner's shops. I would talk to Mr. Patterson and visit the city and county buildings. The banks didn't hire women, but we had our own Bourbon County telephone company—it employed women as operators—and a store in town, Varden and Sons, that might need help.

She sighed heavily. "Your father will turn over in his grave . . ."

Lifting my chin just a bit, I said, "He would've seen what I see."

She nodded once. "Yes, he would. He'd see the resilient young woman you've had to become, but he would hate the idea of you working in any of those places."

We hadn't even mentioned the whiskey distilleries and saloons, as Maman would probably disintegrate if I found work in one of those establishments. "Look on the bright side," I said, deliberately lightening my tone. "In town all the time, I might be able to nab a nice little husband."

It was the farthest thing from my mind, but Maman would appreciate my sarcasm. Everyone knew I had always loved my horses and father too much to ever leave them, and a marriageable suitor would want his wife to be by his side and take care of *him* instead. Eventually I'd convinced Maman that a man would never put up with me.

I detected a tiny smile on her face, the first one I'd seen since Papa's death. "Not when I've already given up hope!" she said, but her smile soon faded.

I moved forward to hug my mother, and when she held me, I could feel the strength that remained. Shaky strength but strength nonetheless. Maman came from a comfortable home, but no one had spoiled and kept her until she met my father. I'd always thought she held inside a quiet, untapped fortitude, evident in her firm jawline. Surely she had suffered at some time during her life, and maybe now she relied on that old way of faring.

Besides, we had to face the facts. Perhaps someone would train me as a secretary. Perhaps I'd help in the Windsor Hotel or the telegraph office. Paris was the county seat, so maybe I could work for the county or the city. My father would've never wanted me to do any of those things. But I cared almost nothing about what that menial work would do to me, and as to the damage to Maman and Papa's reputation . . . well, I could do nothing about that. I hated to sully my father's legacy and embarrass my mother, but I could not bury our secret like a rock in the ground.

She released me, and I stepped back.

"How long do you think we'll have to live in town?" she asked. "It won't be . . . forever?"

"I hope not. If I put away every extra cent, then maybe we can save enough to rebuild—"

Her face brightened. "Rebuild the house?"

"Not as before," I answered and then tried to sound hopeful. "But maybe a smaller house. Maybe we can also rebuild our stud service. Luc can handle the horses for now, and someday, I can do what Papa did. I *do* know most of what he did, Maman. He taught me well."

"I see," she agreed. After a moment, lilting her voice, she said, "Look on the bright side . . ." Mimicking me, she showed a tiny flicker of her old sense of humor. "He didn't teach you about handling the money, but it's not a problem now because we don't have any."

Until then I'd never known smiles could be so sad. I thought our conversation had ended, but as I reached the door, her voice drifted over . . . "Arlene?"

Turning back, I prepared myself for just about anything—she'd worked hard to stay in control, but now I could imagine her crying, or worse . . . Instead she stood tall and said, "Thank you."

I stood still, too. For the first time, Maman looked at me as if I'd entered adulthood, and I wondered how many steps it took to enter another life. The next one beginning now. And with that thought, taken with the faith in me written on my mother's face, a heavy thing that had pressed on my chest since the fire finally stepped aside, I released a long stream of breath. Despite all we had lost and how much our lives had changed and would continue to change going forward, we would survive.

Chapter Four

After the Edwards family drove us to town, I thanked them, as did Maman. Earlier I had agonized over what to say and then had given Mr. and Mrs. Edwards a brief version—we had much less money than we'd thought, and I would need to find a job. I witnessed a powerful, stunned new awareness in these fine friends, and then inevitably came the pity. The shock on their paling faces made me feel momentarily like nothing, or something ephemeral—a passing ghost—but so be it. Very soon, what I'd told them would filter outward, and everyone would know. At least I wouldn't have to repeat the story.

At the back of the hotel, the room Maman and I would share must have once housed servants before, but the hotel owners had made improvements for us. Some inexpensive artwork hung on the walls, the windows gleamed, and the furnishings consisted of an iron bed, a good mattress, some small tables, and one chair. A worn rug patterned with pink cabbage roses covered the floor.

Maman sat on the edge of the bed and said, "Well . . ."

I sat down next to her. "Yes . . ." Though always close, we had never shared a room, much less a bed.

She sighed. "I do hope it won't be long."

"That reminds me." I pressed my hands onto my knees and stood. "I must prepare for tomorrow. It's about time to call upon some people."

"Oh, Arlene," Maman said. Her strength waxed and waned, and I never knew what mood she would evidence. "I'm so sorry this has happened to you. I know you made a joke about nabbing a husband, but I've always pictured you giving in and marrying someday. After you've worked in this town, however, like . . . like . . ." She knew what she wanted to say but searched to find a softer word.

"Common folk?"

She nodded but looked ashamed of herself. A kind person, she nevertheless sometimes fell victim to the beliefs of her generation and society, one that often divided and classified people. She gathered herself and went on. "Once you've worked in this town, no real gentleman will want you."

I almost laughed as I walked to the window, where I threw open the curtains. I placed my palms against the sun-warmed glass. "Let me worry about that."

"You won't worry about that. You'll ruin your youth and looks by worrying about money instead."

The next day I walked through town to inquire about available positions. I called on Papa's friends and business associates. Inside his office, Mr. Patterson spoke tersely with concern. "I thought you weren't going to tell anyone about your . . . situation," he said. "I've already heard people on the street gossiping about it."

"And what am I to say? That I'm seeking employment and living in a room in town with my mother because I think it will be fun?"

He shook his head.

For days I talked to managers at the stores and hotels and to our friends, all to no avail. Instead of receiving support, I experienced something like a shunning. Almost a shaming. Then again, some people believed others' bad luck could rub off on them. Maybe I now trailed tragedy behind me like the train of a soiled gown.

I missed Papa so much I felt hungry all the time, but when food was put in front of me, I could scarcely touch it. Before then, I hadn't fully conceived of the idea of death; I hadn't wanted to believe that it walked the path of our lives at our side and could so suddenly take away anyone, even a person most precious to us.

Next, I inquired at the telephone company, and for the first time, a manager ushered me inside and granted me a real interview. But after talking for a while, he informed me he had no current openings. Once he'd shown me to the exit, I stood back on the street letting yet another disappointment sink in. Someone ran up behind me.

"Arlene, Arlene, wait up," she called out and stopped me. One of the operators, but I didn't know her. "Are you looking for work?"

Then I recognized her. Bethany Masters. We'd gone to high school together but had never known each other well. As Maman would've put it, we traveled in different circles. But I remembered her because in our small class, she and I were the only redheads.

I answered, "Yes, I am."

Breathless from running, she said, "Look, you won't find anything in this town. Even lots of men are out there seeking work. I landed this job two years ago in a stroke of luck. Once we get on, we don't quit unless we get married. But they're looking for women factory workers in Cincinnati. They pay a lot more up there."

My shoulders sank. "Cincinnati?"

"Yes, it's a distance, but you'd get to live in the city and get away from all . . . this," she said and blinked. Her eyes, bright and utterly clear, told me exactly what she meant. Even she had heard about my father.

On the streets earlier that day, I'd come quietly upon a group of gentlemen and overheard, "Who knew he didn't have sense when it came to money?" Those words like broken glass against my skin. Sometimes fates simply changed, but people would forever blame him.

Another man said, "Those poor women and that boy. They'll never recover."

Back in the moment, I told Bethany, "You're right. I've found nothing in town. So perhaps I can work in Lexington and ride the Interurban every day back and forth."

"You won't find much in Lexington, either. You'll make a lot more money faster if you head up to Cincinnati. Lots of us working girls want to go, but most of us can't."

I mulled it over for a moment. If I made the kind of money paid in a city, then I could perhaps have a real shot at rebuilding. And if I left, Maman would have the room at the Fordham to herself, Luc could take care of himself on the farm, and I could make our dream happen faster. Too bad, though; I couldn't go that far away from Maman and Luc after all that had happened.

Besides, I'd never left home and had considered it only once before, when the US entered the war almost a year before. I'd mentioned volunteering for the Red Cross to my parents, even though it would've hurt my heart to go away, even temporarily. But my father rather adamantly shook his head. Papa had also forbidden Luc to even think about joining up, citing his age, but plenty of boys were lying about their age to get into the army.

But as more days went by and then a week and then another, during which the people who did the hiring turned me down in place after place, both in Paris and Lexington, the idea of Cincinnati returned to me. One afternoon I took a walk to clear my head before having to tell Maman that I'd failed to get a job yet again.

When I reached a place to view Stoner Creek, I gazed down at the rushing water. Due to spring rains, the creek ran muddied and mad, but powerful. I'd always had a penchant for moving water—rivers, streams, waterfalls, and creeks. Never stagnant, they always flowed onward to other places. Like a horse at a full gallop, the flow was smooth and lovely, strong and unstoppable.

Three days later, the time had come for me to go. Now I had to tell Maman and Luc.

Chapter Five

Cincinnati, Ohio

April 1918

Exactly one month after Papa's death, I embarked on the first leg of my journey. I boarded a steam locomotive on the Louisville and Nashville Railroad in Paris that would pass through Cynthiana, Falmouth, and smaller town stations on its way to Cincinnati. So far, I'd spent $2.10.

As I walked the aisle of the carriage, my thoughts drifted to my conversation with Maman during which we'd talked about this plan. A resigned look on her face, she'd said, "You have to go now; I see that."

The life insurance money had finally come, but I used most of it to pay off the funeral home. I'd given the rest to Maman for the room. After selling the Chevrolet, I gave all the money, minus ten dollars, to Luc. Olive had given me some more clothes, shoes, hats, and an overcoat. She also loaned me a traveling satchel. I took the ten dollars with me.

Before I left, Maman had handed me something. A photo of Papa with someone I knew—a much younger Mr. Edwards, my father's friend who had taken us in after the fire. Maman said, "He came by earlier today after he located it in his things. It was taken almost twenty years ago, when you were but a toddler."

In the slightly faded and yellowed photo, my father and Mr. Edwards faced the camera and stood with their arms draped across each other's shoulders. They both wore big smiles, and in the background, one could see a racetrack.

"The Edwardses' horse had just placed in the Derby. Mr. Edwards knows we have no photos of your papa . . . I want you to take this with you."

Still entranced by the photo, I hadn't yet registered what she'd said. Papa so young, so happy, so handsome, so lovely. And his smile! Finally I looked up at Maman. "No, you must keep it. This treasure should stay with you."

"I insist," Maman said. "Take it, please. Your father would've wanted that. After all, Luc and I have each other, but you're going onward alone."

Grateful beyond words, I nodded and then placed the photo in my traveling satchel. As I mulled over the things I still had to do, I felt Maman looking at me in a strange way.

When I met her eyes, she said, "I can see that you're worried. But you'll learn. You'll adjust. Just remember why you've gone away, and always remember to set your own sails; otherwise it won't be your journey. And it *will* be your journey, my dear, one that I hope eventually brings you back to us."

I said, "Of course I'll come back."

"Come to think of it, you already know how to set your own sails."

I shook my head. "What?"

"Look at you. You're doing it."

When I'd told Luc I planned to leave to find work, he cried. What a terrible thing to witness—a young man weeping despite all he'd been taught about male conduct. Now came the real end of innocence, the dissolution of all we'd ever known, and, cruelly, so much of what we also loved.

I had looked away so he could have his moment. "I'll take enough for train fare and a boarding room until I get a paycheck. I'll write as soon as I have a place, and then you and Maman must keep in touch. Write me anytime, and let me know how you and the horses are doing."

When Luc had calmed, he blew his nose into a handkerchief. Sticking to the business side of things on purpose, I supposed, he'd asked, "How am I to stand Chicory without you?"

"You'll have to hire help. Every week or so, I'll send money. I'll send money as soon as I can."

Now as I left it all behind, I wanted more than anything to bolt and run back for safety. Until I remembered that I was my mother's hope and my brother's keeper, and my father would've expected no less of me. And so I took a seat.

The train was nearly full, making me wonder why others were traveling on this day. A cluster of children who smelled warmly of milk sat in the rows in front of me, overseen by a matron wearing a ribboned and netted hat who kept them in control. Other than a few couples, the other travelers looked like businessmen in their suits. One man wore evening attire complete with a tie pin and a smartly buttoned vest. He held a bouquet of red roses, and on occasion their scent drifted my way.

My breath made a dewy circle on the window glass as I gazed beyond it. The journey took half the day, and each time the train clacked across another bridge or huffed up and over another hill, my former life fell farther behind me. Others on the train looked relaxed and maybe even bored, whereas I couldn't stop doing sums in my head and wondering where I would sleep that night.

The evening before, I'd saddled Chicory, hiked up my skirt, and ridden that beautiful animal, allowing him to do as he pleased. He galloped for a little while, then cantered, and finally paused to tear at some new spring grass emerging in the pasture. With only stars as our ceiling overhead, I buried my head in his mane, wrapped my arms around his neck, and felt him breathe. I had no idea when I would return. I had no idea when I would ride again.

Most of the terrain I saw from the carriage felt familiar until we reached the Ohio River. Thereafter my gaze went adrift in that vast waterway. Whitecaps curled along the surface the way I imagined they did in the ocean. Even barges below felt so small. I'd never seen so much water before, had never been to the ocean or the Great Lakes, and it moved me. It seemed like a signal that my luck would soon change.

The station in Cincinnati was called the Pennsylvania Depot, and for a moment I feared that I'd arrived in the wrong state. But as I stepped away from the depot into bright sunlight, I saw a newsboy selling copies of the *Cincinnati Enquirer*, and I breathed a sigh of relief. The sun warmed me, and all the people bustling about gave me a small burst of unexpected energy. Some good daylight hours still lay ahead, and my instincts told me to search for a job first, then find an inexpensive room later on.

So I parted with some of my dear coins, bought a copy of the paper, and soon spotted what I had hoped to find—several ads calling for women workers. Before I left home, Mr. Patterson had advised me to look for industrial work, as it would most likely pay the best. One ad called for women workers in a machine shop. It paid eleven dollars a week to start, more than I had expected. The factory was located in Oakley, however, a place I'd never heard of.

Carrying my small case of clothing, I began walking down the street. I found the heart of the city a dense jungle of stone, brick, and concrete; it was as if I'd staggered into a maze. Dozens of buildings, all of them at least four stories tall and a great number of them taller, and so many automobiles in one place, sharing the roads with clacking electric streetcars. People walked briskly about on the sidewalks, hopped in rumbling taxis, and ducked into stores and restaurants as if on important missions. They evoked ease and purpose, and I envied them; they knew where they were going.

A man on the street told me Oakley lay on the outskirts of the city, and I would have to take a streetcar to reach the factory. The prospect of figuring out the streetcar system was daunting, and I worried I'd never find a place to stay if I ventured so far. So I went back to the newspaper, where another ad caught my eye.

It called for French-speaking female drivers. I had no idea what kind of company would seek French-speaking female drivers and why, but curiosity drove me to ask a woman on the street for directions. She told me how to get to the address, only a few blocks away. I brushed down my overcoat with my hands and started walking in that direction, telling myself to do this, that I could be brave, but I felt like a sparrow fallen from her safe little nest into the vast unknown world of the ground below.

When I reached a nondescript office building and found the suite, a note taped to the etched-glass window in the door caught my attention. It read *Applicants please return tomorrow at noon for an interview.*

I considered taking the streetcar to Oakley but didn't want to spend the money. I filled out an application at Cincinnati Bell, but a secretary told me it might take a week or more before they could set up an interview and testing. I didn't have time for what sounded like a lengthy application process; I needed to start making money now. Then I began to worry where I would stay the night. Checking the paper again, I found rooms to let—"near streetcars and factories," the ad read. Back rooms went for $3 or $3.50 a week. Front rooms for $4 or $4.50, depending on size.

Already the numbers came together in my head. A three-dollar-a-week room would cost me over twelve dollars a month. But I had to stay somewhere. After asking for directions again, I walked to the boardinghouse, a drab and forlorn-looking three-story building constructed of brown brick with faded red awnings. I took the three-dollar-a-week room in the back. Looking out at my view, I could see only concrete, bricks and mortar, and wood-framed glass windows. The bed squeaked and the mattress was lumpy. The landlady had promised good steam heat in the winter, but the room felt drafty. I had my own sink and toilet but would have to share a bath down the hallway. Even so, I told myself it would do.

I remembered my old room on the farm with its tall windows, canopy bed, paintings of horses on the walls, and photos of Tornado and Chicory on my bedside table, and a clotting sensation entered the back of my throat, until I swallowed it away.

How would I get by until I had a job and a paycheck in hand? Once a day I could eat bread, tinned sardines, or soup. I could walk everywhere. If I ran out of money, I could sell my gold baby locket—I'd hate to have to do that, but I would do it.

I propped the photo of Papa and Mr. Edwards against the lamp on the table, then watched a line of ants climb the wall near the window and listened to street sounds that traveled all the way to the back of the boardinghouse. I told myself I wasn't alone, I had a plan, and I would succeed here. But in less than one day, I'd already spent too much money. Just five dollars remained.

I wished I could tell Maman and Luc about my first day in the city. Maman would sit closely at my side and brush out my hair, and Luc would hang on to every word, a curious interest in his eyes. They both loved to hear me talk and tell stories. But these thoughts brought on such an aching loneliness inside, I had to push them away.

I stepped back downstairs and told my landlady, a matronly woman who wore her hair in a bun enclosed with a net and on her face a dour expression, that I had come to the city looking for work. She almost recoiled. "I assumed you already had a job; else I might not have rented you the room."

"I'll get one soon," I quickly said. "Probably tomorrow."

She shook her head ever so slightly but noticeably. "What kind of work are you looking for?"

"Factory or secretarial work, I suppose."

"You suppose?" she asked. "Have you ever worked in a factory or an office?"

"N-no, not yet."

She shook her head again. "Good luck to you. You're probably going to need it. Sure, some of the factories are looking for women, but probably not your type of young woman."

I thanked her, for what I didn't know. And then, hoping she hadn't seen how stinging her words left me, I strode through the front door and began to walk the street. What had I expected? So determined to make money, I hadn't really contemplated how it might feel to live in a big city where I knew no one and I had no connections to help me land a job.

The sun at my back sinking between buildings and the dusk coming on, I noticed small groups of women walking together, laughing, smiling, some arm in arm as they reached the streetcars and boarded. I imagined most of them suburban gals—probably heading home, back to mothers and fathers, younger siblings, cats and dogs. I imagined the smells emanating from their mothers' kitchens and their fathers' pipes, the sounds of younger children laughing or slamming the door as they ran outside.

Something broke open inside me then, and I grasped the fabric over my wounded heart in a fist. How had my life turned into this? Alone in a big city, counting every penny, responsible for my mother and brother.

Go see the river. I hadn't yet stood on its banks and studied its mighty flow.

So I walked faster then, forging onward with a fierce determination to push away pain. I had to zigzag around the depots and train tracks. I peered down side streets and finally spotted a public landing. The water rather dingy and brownish, the river impressed me anyway with its power. I kept walking along the bank. Weakened by eating so little and having to concentrate on where I stepped, I lost track of time.

Before I knew it, complete darkness had closed in. Just as I turned around to head back, rain began to fall. I hadn't noticed that clouds had gathered, and I'd come with so few dresses, I couldn't ruin the one I wore. I decided to leave the riverbank in search of cover, and huddled beneath the awning of a quiet building until the rain stopped.

In completely unfamiliar territory, I walked again, past smaller and darker buildings than those in the heart of downtown. I found myself in an area of industrial plants, boarded-up storefronts, and bars. A few men standing on a corner took note, and one of them wolf-whistled. I picked up my pace and headed in the direction I thought I'd find the streetcar.

But blocks later, everything looked wrong. The night had turned the shadows of the city midnight black, and warm yellow lights ablaze in the upper windows of a building seemed to mock me. Hunger gnawed in my stomach, but its intensity could not match the longing for my former life. I should've stayed near the boardinghouse. I didn't have the luxury of getting lost.

The streets I walked now emitted a sense of warning from alleys and empty buildings, and the air was cooling. But I broke out in a sweat. I almost entered a small store to ask for directions, but the man behind the counter stared out the open door and gave me a wolfish smile, so I changed my mind.

I made a turn and tried a different direction. Then another. And another. But I'd set myself hopelessly adrift on the inside and outside. The rain began to fall again, and I found myself in an even heavier industrial area. I made a fist and bit my knuckles. My dress soaked, my drenched hair falling from its pins, I had no idea where to turn or how to get out of this bind.

Calm down, I told myself, but as time ticked onward, panic set in.

Nothing looked real, the buildings like the fake sets at the back of a stage during a play. They had no hearts, no souls, so many almost the same. Then I realized I had inadvertently come around in a circle. I could scarcely believe it, but I'd walked this street once before. Tangled in a mess I couldn't escape and with no idea where to turn next, I plowed onward.

Someone began to follow me. I glanced back to see a man carrying a brown paper bag that appeared by its shape to hold a bottle. He looked huge, and I looked tawdry. I started walking faster, not caring any longer in which direction, just going. *Keep moving away.* I turned a corner and ran right into something, a person, which froze me with fear. The man took me by the shoulders and held me at arm's length.

He wore the uniform of a police officer, and I burst into tears. "Now, now." Young and baby-faced, no older than me, he said, "What have we here?"

Between sobs I managed to say, "I don't know where I am. I'm new in town. I don't know anyone. I'm—"

"Now, now." He stopped me. "I'm willing to bet it's not that bad."

I remembered very little of what other kind words he said to me, but I finally stopped crying.

"Let's get you home," he said.

After I told the young officer my address, he took off his jacket and gave it to me for covering my head, even though I was already soaked, and with rain pouring off the brim of his hat, he walked me to the boardinghouse door. Shaking and so terribly cold by then, I couldn't remember if I ever thanked him.

Some people stood about in the parlor, a few women seated. I looked a fright. Dripping water on the wood floor, I darted for the stairs and ran up to my room, where the flood that had already started continued to pour out of me. Tears streaked down my face and mixed with the rainwater that still leaked from my hair. I sat on the bed, even though my wet dress might stain the coverlet. I didn't care. I let loose all of what I'd been holding inside, and then my eyes landed on the photo of my father with Mr. Edwards.

Papa. He was responsible. He had done this to me, to us. I stared into his eyes, and then with the room going gray and blurry, I grabbed the photograph, crumpled it in my fist, lurched to the window and shoved it open, then tossed the photo out. Still sobbing, I sat again until the fractured image of Papa entering a burning house came back to me, followed by the most horrible guilt, followed by love.

I dashed down the stairs, ran past astonished faces, and flew through the door. The rain had stopped, but a heavy fog had floated in to replace it, and I could barely see in front of my face, the same way the smoke in the house on that awful night had blinded us. I sloshed through puddles until I reached the faint outlines of the back of the building and guessed where I thought my window was situated above. There I found the photograph, wet but intact. I picked up the image of my beautiful father, flattened it as best I could, and held it to my chest, then retraced my steps back inside the boardinghouse, aware that my fellow boarders, perhaps even my landlady, had been watching and now stared agog at me as if I'd turned into a madwoman.

So much for making any friends here.

Chapter Six

In the morning, I put on my damp dress, smoothed it out as best I could, asked my landlady for a slice of bread for breakfast, and set out. With the wind blowing viciously, sending war posters, newspapers, and trash sailing down the street, I closed my eyes and imagined Favier Farm during the green, green summers.

I filled out applications at two factories but did not gain an immediate interview. At noon I walked back to the closed office I had found the day before. A polished-looking brunette secretary asked me to fill out an application. The waiting area, spartanly furnished with nothing on the walls, had a temporary feel, which struck me as a bit disconcerting.

On the application, I gave my name, age, and schooling. I had nothing to report concerning previous employment, but I wrote that I had worked with horses and knew how to drive a Model T. Then the secretary invited me to sit in a chair before her desk. She looked down at my application. "And you are Miss Arlene Favier?"

She said Favier with the *r* sound at the end, but even as I opened my mouth to correct her pronunciation, the words screeched to a halt in the back of my throat. And I had clenched my hands together; I forced them apart. "Yes, ma'am, I am."

"And you're interested in becoming an ambulance driver?"

I blinked. Ambulance driver? The ad hadn't said anything about that. It had mentioned needing drivers but not *ambulance* drivers. No matter; I had to jump on any opportunity or at least find out more. "Yes, ma'am, I am," I said again.

"Miss Favier"—again with the *r* sound—"where are you from, and why are you seeking employment?"

I had decided to keep my explanations truthful but brief. "I'm from Paris, Kentucky, and I'm seeking employment in order to help my family after an unfortunate fire."

One eyebrow lifted. "Brave girl." She took my application, glanced at it, and sighed—I could only assume because of its incompleteness. She appeared about forty-five, a bit heavyset. Probably a widow or never married—she hadn't introduced herself.

At home, such women were pitied, but here she had a profession and a position of authority. I couldn't stop watching her smooth movements as she proceeded to measure my height and weight. She tested my hearing and eyesight, too. She recorded everything but made no attempt at small talk. I was a horse at auction, scrutinized and judged and hoping someone would purchase me.

"You're of a different social status than many of the girls who come in here," she said and perused my face after we sat again. "I have little doubt you can master the necessary skills, and we will train you thoroughly. But a girl like you is sure to meet a nice man in this city. I worry we'll pay you, train you, and then you'll meet a man and leave us."

I gathered my thoughts together quickly. "My goal is to return to Paris, Kentucky." I stopped, realizing that I might be making a mistake. "That will take many years, of course, but I won't fall for a man here, because I wouldn't want to stay here."

She gave a small laugh. "The other day, one of the doctors suggested we look for unmarriageable girls."

I hadn't a clue what would make a girl "unmarriageable," and I had to rummage around in my brain for a quick response. "But I *am* unmarriageable," I said.

"And why is that?"

I slightly cocked my head and summoned my sense of humor. "I like horses more than I like men."

"That so?" she asked, the hint of a smile in her eyes. "But there are horsemen around here, many of them. You could have a husband and horses, too."

I wasn't about to tell her what I'd pledged to Maman and Luc. No matter what, I would return to Paris. Whether I succeeded at finding work or not. "Perhaps, but in my brief experience with matters of the heart, I've found that men don't fare well taking second place."

She laughed heartily, then stopped. "How much experience do you have driving?"

"I can drive a Model T."

"How much do you know about the engine?"

"I assisted my father many times when he worked on our motorcar. I know how an engine runs—well, the basics."

Gauging me differently now, she appeared to have seen something she liked. "I'm not sure if Dr. Rayne can see you at the moment."

I rose and extended my hand to thank her.

"Miss Favier." She almost laughed. "Hold your horses."

I couldn't believe she'd used that old saying. *Hold your horses.* That was what we Faviers were trying to do: hold on to our horses and our way of life.

With no idea how I had done it, I seemed to have passed a first test. Five minutes later the secretary ushered me into an office to meet with Dr. Beryl Rayne, a *woman* in her forties. I was taken slightly aback. Of course I had heard of female doctors; I simply had never met one before. Dr. Rayne appeared fashionable in her traditional tailored suit, which contrasted with her more modern-looking hair, cut to chin length and waving about her face. It looked naturally blond with a few streaks of white flowing from her temples. She wore no jewelry other than a wedding band.

We sat in chairs and scooted them to face each other. An immediate sense of safe harbor emitted from the doctor. She had a generous mouth and smiled easily, although a sad weight in her eyes seemed to reveal evidence of an enduring grief. Her face moved softly with each change of expression, but her sturdy jawline made her appear as if she held something urgent inside—ambition or purpose, it seemed to me.

After asking me some facts about myself, she looked over my application.

"I see you have some driving experience and have even done a few repairs. How well can you speak French?"

The ad had said something about French-speaking drivers, and a slow dawning came over me. They were looking for women to drive ambulances *in France*. I couldn't reveal I'd only then figured it out. "My father was born in Paris—Paris, France, I mean. While my mother taught my brother and me to speak English, Papa taught us French."

"Would you say you're *fluent*?"

I smiled. "Papa would have never said that; he always wanted us to speak as if we were born there, but yes, I can speak French."

Then she inquired of my stamina.

"I've worked on my feet with horses for many long hours since I was a girl," I answered without hesitation.

"Yes," she said. "But I'm talking about stamina of a different sort. Once in France, we'll focus our efforts primarily on the villagers and refugees, but don't expect it to be easy. I've toured the area, and let me tell you, even though I'd thought myself prepared, it came as a shock. We'll enter a razed countryside peopled by impoverished villagers and those forced from their homes under the worst of wartime conditions. We'll face food shortages, see destroyed towns, and you'll have to traverse barely passable roads. We'll witness typhus, dysentery, and tuberculosis. People will die; children will die. If you're squeamish or suffer from the vapors, don't bother to come."

I nodded. My mouth had gone as dry as paper. Before everything changed, I'd once wanted to go to France as a volunteer, but both Maman and Papa wouldn't hear of me being anywhere near a war zone. And now this opportunity had fallen into my lap. "My father's family is French. Some of those people you refer to could be distant relatives of mine."

"Your French is a fine advantage. And it doesn't hurt that you're a pretty girl." She glanced away momentarily.

I didn't know how to respond. The way she'd said *pretty girl* didn't sound like a compliment. So I kept quiet with my hands folded in my lap.

She reached for a pair of glasses on a table nearby and placed them on her face. Her keen eyes and scrutiny intensified as she assessed me through the lenses. I became a specimen on a petri dish.

"We're an all-female team raising money to go overseas and start a hospital in France. The military won't take female doctors, other than a few contract surgeons, so we'll go on our own, probably with the help of the Red Cross." She paused. "We have the education and the skills, but the powers that be still exclude us from the good ole boys' club. We need drivers we can trust, who know how to fix things, and who won't flinch when faced with illness, injury, and death."

I raptly listened, further amazed by everything she had told me. I'd not heard of any female teams heading to France.

She continued, "Our leader is a skilled surgeon, but in many ways she's still a woman of the old order. Our nurses, drivers, and aides must not join us with the purpose of fraternizing with soldiers—or any men for that matter. Personally, I don't care what someone does with her time while off duty, but Dr. Logan does. If I choose you to go with me as my personal driver, you must promise not to embarrass me." She paused, I presumed for effect.

Nodding again, I found it hard to believe she might consider me for her personal ambulance driver.

"So why—besides your family history—are you so willing to go over?"

Dread poured over me then. "I must tell you something. I need to work for money. I'm not a volunteer. I wish more than anything I could be, but I'm not able."

She stared hard.

I continued: "My family lost everything, including my father, in a fire, and I'm doing my best to earn enough money to build a new house for my mother and brother. I need to make a good amount of money."

She looked slightly amused. "A good amount?"

"Yes," I said while almost squirming.

"Relax," she said. "I'm not as intimidating as I might appear. And I like the way you present yourself." She rubbed her chin. "How much are you making now?"

"I'm not employed yet. I only just arrived, but the factories are paying eleven dollars a week," I said and then quickly added, "plus bonuses and sometimes extra shifts."

She seemed to like me; her voice softened as she said, "The Red Cross will pay our salaries for overseas hospital staff, and it will come to much more than that, I can assure you. We're looking for specific skills, and we know it."

I exhaled with such relief I feared she could hear it.

She proceeded to relay the requirements for acceptance—an interview with the Red Cross to make it official. Then I would receive vaccinations, and I would have to provide loyalty letters, proof of birth within the United States, and a passport. No persons of German or Austrian heritage would be accepted.

"I understand you need to start working now, and it so happens we've just received good news; we'll leave soon. We can hire you and set you up with a mechanic for further training right away."

Could I do this? I had come in search of a job, but I'd never imagined this. Some would say it could be the adventure of a lifetime, in addition to a chance to see Papa's homeland, albeit now decimated by war.

But it was France. Notre-Dame and the Seine. The Eiffel Tower and the Louvre.

But also trench warfare, maimed soldiers, and shelled villages. The war reports horrified me. I wanted to help, but now that the opportunity had presented itself, I wondered if I could really do it. I would have to cross an ocean and work in a battle zone, and I had only driven Papa's car down lazy country roads. I tried to imagine what it would be like to drive an ambulance in a foreign country. I tried to imagine what Maman and Luc would say.

I'd never thought of going so far away, across an ocean. Maman and Luc might feel as if I were abandoning them. My parents hadn't wanted me to volunteer in France, but our lives had completely transformed since then. Maybe this was a touch of fate like a whisper in my ear.

Arlene, il faut bien écouter, it said. "Arlene, you must listen." And then the old French saying, *Sans destination, il n'y a pas de destinée.* "Without destination, there is no destiny." How many times had Papa said those things to me . . .

Snapping back to the conversation at hand, I smiled at Dr. Rayne. "I can't tell you how happy I am to hear that."

Leaning forward with her elbows on her knees, a curious look on her face, she asked, "So . . . what happens after the war?"

I took in a sharp breath. "I hope I'll have enough money to rebuild our lives, beginning with a home."

"How much will that take?"

Before I'd left Kentucky, I'd studied the Sears & Roebuck catalog and found a modern home for sale for $872. Since we owned the land back home, and I assumed that Luc and I could put the house together with some hired help from others, my goal was to save at least nine hundred dollars before I returned home. But my nervousness wouldn't allow me to ask for that much. "I need about eight hundred dollars."

Slowly she leaned back in the chair again. "I have a proposition for you: if you make it to the end of the war, I'll reward you with a bonus."

I waited, holding my breath.

"Let's make it an even one thousand dollars."

I gasped. "That's too generous."

"Many donors have given generously to us, and many of us can pay our own way. It's not too much if I say it isn't."

"I'm honored, of course. And of course, I'll stay till the war's end."

She placed her hands on her thighs and seemed about to stand. "Now that that's settled . . ."

"I can't thank you enough."

She stilled then, and her gaze held something much more pressing than appraisal now—a sizing up to the highest degree. "Don't thank me so hastily. You haven't been over there yet."

My mouth had gone even drier, but I managed to say in a brave, sure voice, "I can bear it."

She extended her hand. "I hope so. I'm trusting you." I could see her mollify a bit. "So, we have a deal? A thousand dollars in your pocket when it's over?"

I hadn't imagined anything this auspicious; it was too much to hope for, but I could see that Dr. Rayne had made a completely serious offer. Perhaps I did have much to offer, too. But a thousand dollars? A dream come true. Papa would've said, *Quelle aubaine.* "What good fortune."

Dr. Rayne waited for my answer. "Most assuredly so," I replied, then shook her hand; I found her handshake firm, like a man's. We stood, and she ushered me out to the door.

There she stopped and said, "Come back tomorrow dressed for work in a shop and prepared to start studying with a mechanic. And Miss Favier . . ." Her eyes razor-sharp and blue, she finished, "Remember what I've told you. All of it."

Chapter Seven

New York City, New York

May 1918

In the middle of May, we embarked on the first leg of our journey by train to New York City. The organization formed by the women doctors, the American Women's Hospital, had raised two hundred thousand dollars by then, enough to send the first team to France.

When we arrived, we gathered at the AWH headquarters, 437 Madison Avenue, in rooms donated by Otto Schlesinger. After final plans and many speeches, tailors measured us for our uniforms—a mid-calf-length woolen skirt, topped by a single-breasted, belted long-sleeved jacket with both chest and hip pockets, a blouse and tie, and then a rather mannish brimmed hat. Those of us who couldn't pay for uniforms received aid from donors.

In June, the entire AWH team departed for the docks, where the Model T chassis that we would rebuild into ambulances overseas were already waiting for us, and boarded an army vessel transporting soldiers to Europe.

I'd had three weeks of training with Cass Frank, a woman of about thirty and the leader of the ambulance drivers. A little heavyset, she wore her hair in an unflattering bun and wore mechanic's overalls stained with grease. I could easily see why the AWH had hired her. She projected an air of competence, and she owned her own car, something almost unheard of for a woman.

In a bay loaned to us by a mechanic's shop, Cass and I had worked on her Ford engine for so long, so intensely, that a line of grease lived under my cuticles, my knuckles stayed constantly chapped, and my fingers ended at chipped nails. Cass said we had "man hands," but neither of us cared. She taught me how to take the engine and practically the entire vehicle apart and put it back together again.

When three newly hired drivers joined us, Cass had to train them even faster than she did me, and I often helped her. Talk of maintenance and repairs consuming us, we'd had no time for talk of our lives, no time to get to know one another as friends.

But now on a journey to cross the ocean for twelve days, we had little to do.

On board, the sea of khaki green on deck spread as wide as the midnight waters beyond the ship's railings. The men, just boys really, amused themselves with pranks and laughter. They struck me as unprepared, likely still at the naive stage of being excited to participate in an adventure. Had anyone warned them about what they would see, as Dr. Rayne had warned me?

The AWH Team Number One consisted of an all-female contingent of ten doctors, a dentist, six nurses, five *chauffeuses*—as everyone had started calling us—and three volunteer aides. With Cass and I assigned to share a cabin, it soon became clear we would spend lots of time together.

Bundled up against the cold sea and spray, we walked the decks for fresh air and exercise, and she asked me why I had joined the team. Facing the open sea that dampened my face, I gave her my pat answer about the fire, losing Papa, and needing money to rebuild. Just that morning I'd written a letter to Luc and enclosed as much money as I could spare. Breeding season would soon end.

She listened, watching me with empathetic eyes.

"Once the opportunity presented itself, I realized I could not only earn money but also go to France and be of some help. My father was born there, and he always intended . . ." I had to clear my throat. "To take me there someday."

Cass stared at me, her head slightly cocked in a curious pose. "My God, Arlene . . ."

"My father used to say *'Petit à petit, l'oiseau fait son nid.'* It means 'little by little, the bird makes its nest.'" The tiny smile I wore froze. I could see Papa's face, gentle but forceful love in his eyes, on the day he'd first said this to me. *Petit à petit, l'oiseau fait son nid.* And I could see his smile.

"You must miss him."

I nodded, grateful she'd asked me only a yes-or-no question. Thoughts of Papa always made me mute.

A few minutes later, I managed to say, "Thank you for training me."

"My pleasure." We stopped at the railing and looked out over the sea. "You've gained the necessary skills, and you'll have that plus a special advantage over there." I knew what she was going to say. "You speak—"

"French."

"Exactly."

I learned that before the AWH hired her, Cass had worked as a matron at a factory. She and Dr. Rayne became acquainted over the course of setting up physicals for the new female hires. After a while Dr. Rayne mentioned taking Cass overseas.

She said, "When I learned it would be an all-woman team, I had to join."

I nodded. Even after only a few weeks in Cincinnati, I had witnessed what women could do. On the streetcars, I'd met many women workers—widows and mothers, girls without marriage prospects, and wives whose husbands were sick, injured, drunks, or just lazy.

Cass sighed. "We're living in a world that still doesn't know what to do with free-thinking, smart women. This is our chance to change that. The British, however, have sent female doctors and ambulance drivers to France from the war's beginning."

"I didn't know that."

She continued: "Our doctors are a new breed of women with their own ambitions. They've fought hard to go overseas on their own. I admire their pluck."

I told her more about Maman, Luc, the horses, and the land. "I have to work and earn money—it's not a choice now. Without my income, we'll have to sell the horses and the land just to survive. So I understand the doctors' determination."

The ship began to lift and surge, and a spray of seawater hit us. "Enough of this," Cass said. We slipped back inside and brushed the droplets from our coats. "I know what we can do. We both need haircuts."

I was puzzled. "Haircuts?"

"The bob is all the rage in New York, and it probably came from Europe."

"Do you know how to cut hair?" I asked.

"No. Do you?"

I shrugged. "No. But how hard can it be?"

"Precisely," Cass replied. "After all, we can fix engines."

I nodded. "And take them apart and put them together again."

Smiling with either forced or real confidence—I didn't know her well enough yet to say for certain—she stated resolvedly, "We can do this."

"I agree. Do you have some scissors?"

She scoffed at me. "Of course I have scissors. I have everything."

"One question," I said. "Why do we have to be in style?"

"Except for me, have you noticed they hired only young, pretty drivers?"

I shook my head. "Why?"

"Gasoline will be in short supply, and it's controlled by poor Frenchmen. Dr. Rayne says the ambulance drivers must be pretty to talk their way into getting fuel."

I was still puzzled. "But you said these were a new breed of women."

"Yes, but they're also practical."

"So we're to be pretty and stylish."

She nodded. "And besides, all this"—she touched her bun—"is just going to get in the way."

That night we washed each other's hair and then cut it while it was still damp. We laughed as we spilled long locks everywhere and used curling rods to create the waved bob of the day. When the evening ended and I climbed into my bunk, it seemed I'd made a friend. Cass was so affable and strong—who wouldn't like her? Only then did I realize she'd told me nothing about her personal life, while I had told her just about everything concerning mine.

Over the next few days, Cass and I chatted with just about everyone on the AWH team, except the lady in charge, Dr. Herberta Logan. Assigned her own small stateroom, she rarely emerged except for meals.

We shared some polite conversations with the nurses, two of whom were obviously hired by Dr. Logan; they were as old-fashioned as could be. Nurse Helton and Nurse Carpenter, unmarried and devoutly Catholic, prayed the rosary together daily on the deck. The others kept themselves apart, too.

The other three ambulance drivers—Lottie, Kitty, and Eve—were young and adorable in their red lipstick and lacy gloves, their hair flying free of any pins and combs. They wore high-heeled boots—Kitty's sported bows—which they would have to put aside once we began working. Lottie rolled her eyes at the nurses, but she and the others did nothing more than share passing nods or simple greetings with the men on board. Apparently they'd received the same stern warnings I had. We were on a mercy mission, and there would be no hanky-panky.

Dr. Rayne whispered to me when Dr. Logan finally arrived late and pale at the dinner table one night, "Seasickness." We ate in the dining hall, where, despite the war, some niceties still existed, including decent food. Like Dr. Rayne, Dr. Herberta Logan appeared to be in her forties, but her statue-like face, white and smooth, evidenced no lines or crinkles about the eyes—although I had heard that she, also like Dr. Rayne, had come into a life of service due to personal tragedy. Both were widows who had lost a child. Dr. Logan emitted a powerful presence similar to Cass's air of competence, only hers was loftier and more commanding.

I strained to hear the conversation across from me and could make out only some mention about our setup in France, where we would establish a *hôpital mixte*, serving civilians and, to my surprise, soldiers, too. From what I could gather, everything centered on business and no pleasure.

Cass, who sat on the other side of me, whispered, "I wonder if Dr. Logan wears a corset in the operating room." She kept her face deadpan. "And in bed, as well."

I hid my smile beneath my gloved hand. "Please!" I touched my neck and the ends of my hair, amazed by the feel of it, so short. Cass's bob still surprised me every time I saw it, too. It did make her look more stylish, younger as well.

I could barely tear my eyes away from Dr. Logan. Whereas Cass discerned something unyielding in her, I saw our leader as a woman of quiet strength and graceful determination. So far, I'd had no conversations or personal meetings with her—I'd received only a short introduction, during which she pierced me through with unflinching but not unkind eyes. To me, she was something of a puzzle, and I hoped someday to get to know her, as I'd gotten to know Dr. Rayne.

Our small groups stuck mostly to themselves. But Dr. Rayne rose exceptionally above the rest of us. A friend to everyone, she flowed like a river around and between our separate islands.

On the thirteenth day at sea, we docked in Liverpool, England, and the next day we boarded a train for Southampton. We arrived just before midnight. The next evening we pulled out of the harbor at dusk to cross the English Channel by night on board a hospital ship.

I would never forget the feeling of cutting a path through the surge as an uninvited storm battered the prow and lurched the ship to and fro. As we plunged onward into an impenetrable black abyss, I could hear some of our American boys singing hymns. *Rock of Ages, cleft for me . . .*

As the first red splashes of dawn appeared in the east, lights flashed at us from shore. Scores of men in uniform pushed up against the railing and cheered the red, green, and white beacons on land. After our dark crossing on an unlit ship, those lights felt like the jewels of heaven, and as the sun began to rise, dozens of ships came up from the west, bound for France, carrying our men into the jaws of war. Closer to shore the bulky American transports bounced through the chop, coming toward us.

Cass and I hugged each other hard, congratulating ourselves for making it over, even though our safe almost-arrival had nothing to do with anything we'd done.

We debarked on one of the big docks at Le Havre, and I was finally in France.

On the slow train to Paris, Cass gave me the window seat so I could better enjoy my first glimpses of Papa's birthland. On the second day, we began to see farmhouses, fields, small woods, and tiny, compact villages with the traditional tall steeples in their centers. Soldiers stood guard at tunnels, bridges, and major crossings, and faster troop trains carrying soldiers to the front passed us over and over. As we chugged through villages, we saw blind men being helped to walk furtively down the narrow lanes. Children dressed in dark breeches, dresses, and aprons raced along the track, reaching out their hands. Cass and I longed for something to toss to them.

Everywhere, women did the work of men. Wearing head scarves, they tended to the fields. Dr. Rayne, who had insisted I start calling her by her first name, Beryl, told us the men were either dead or fighting. Now the women had to mend fences, handle heavy farm equipment, and corral livestock. Many wore black, and we heard no laughter or music.

I'd not expected to see such wartime effects so far from the battlefield. I'd imagined the front line with its muddy trenches, shell bombardment, grenades, and barbed-wire traps, but I hadn't anticipated a country engaged in war in every way. That was the battered France we entered, however, as we joined the war on our own.

Chapter Eight

PARIS, FRANCE

JUNE 1918

When we debarked in Paris under a gray sky, my first impression was that the city functioned in full-blown denial of the war. As we headed to our quarters by bus, concierges smiled and chatted on sidewalks in front of hotels. The sun broke through the clouds, and the city came more alive. We passed beautiful cars and beautiful girls wearing impossibly fashionable little hats, walking impossibly adorable little dogs. With their doors propped open, the cafés hosted many well-dressed women sipping espressos at their tables as if they had nothing else to do. Many of them wore uniform-style looks with tailored blazers adorned with braids. Beryl told us the fashion of the day was called "military chic." I noticed some female factory workers, but Paris swarmed with military uniforms, ranging in color from a grayish, heathered blue to almost-black navy. Mixed in we saw the happy reds of the Turks' tunics, and of course America's khaki. French soldiers on leave wore tin hats, muddy uniforms, and worn boots.

Of course Paris could not altogether deny the war. Paper tape crisscrossed shop windows, sandbags protected the bases of most monuments, and nailed-on boards covered the priceless stained-glass windows of cathedrals. I spotted the Eiffel Tower from afar, but we couldn't get close. It now served as a radio transmission station and was therefore off-limits.

But nothing could diminish the excitement of arriving in Paris, the city of my father's birth. We got off the bus and filed into the grand lobby of the elegant art deco Hôtel Lutetia on the Left Bank. All of us, including Dr. Logan, had reservations to stay there.

Rooms in Paris had become scarce, and Cass and I thanked our lucky stars for our assigned front room, which we would share, while the other three drivers would have to cram into a single room near the back.

Standing in the lobby, Beryl said, "By the looks of it, you'd think Paris was immune to the war."

I later learned that the Boche had gotten close enough to fire on the city with a huge weapon called the Paris Gun. Really a cannon, it could unleash the power of nine million horses with explosive strikes and had hit the church of Saint-Gervais in the Marais, a very old district, killing eighty-eight people and reminding Parisians that they did indeed live in harm's way. They simply didn't act that way.

After we'd settled in, our leaders told the team we could rest for the remainder of the day, but on my first day in Paris, I had no intention of lounging in a hotel room. Cass and I took a walk to the Champs-Élysées and the Arc de Triomphe, some of Paris's grandest attractions, which thrilled us. Finally I soaked in the sights of my father's Paris, dazzled by the elaborately fronted stone buildings, with their slate roofs, rows of splendid tall windows, and handsome wrought-iron railings. We strolled through narrow side streets lined with tiny shops, apartments above them, and we crossed the gleaming Seine on ornate bridges and gazed down on charming, toylike riverboats. Above us potted flowers on balconies occasionally let loose a petal or two, and we gazed up in awe at lovely clock towers, steeples, and domes.

How I wished Maman and Luc could see these same sights. I longed to be an artist who could capture it all on canvas and bring it back, just as Papa had once brought back a painting of Provence to his fiancée. I could imagine my father as a youth running the lanes here with his friends, riding a bicycle, and climbing the hill to Montmartre. Once he'd told me he grew up *bourgeois*. A horse expert, my grandfather had made a brave move to Canada in order to have a farm of his own. My father had done the same thing when he started from scratch in Paris, Kentucky, and I filled with pride for being a Favier.

Darkness had fallen by the time we returned to the hotel. Adjacent to the lobby we spied a bar, where Lottie, Kitty, and Eve sat together and talked to some American soldiers—officers, I gleaned by their uniforms. With their backs to us, the men held themselves up straight and tall, side by side, but stayed in motion—jangling change in their pockets, smoothing their jacket fronts, and preening for our girls.

Cass said to me, "We should watch over them so it doesn't get out of control. You and I cannot drive three ambulances twenty-four hours a day."

Back in New York we'd found out we would open our hospital with only three vehicles, but with promises of more ambulances and drivers to come. I inclined my head toward the bar. "And it's a good excuse to go inside and get a drink."

"Hallelujah."

We took seats at the bar; behind it glass shelves lined the mirrored wall with spirits and wines. The other drivers sat around a table to the right and back of us, but we could check on them by simply glancing at the mirror from time to time.

Don't you dare think of leaving with those soldiers, I pleaded with them in my mind. It was alright to converse in the hotel bar, but going off with the men would be a different story. We had much to do before we left Paris, and we needed their help.

The bartender suggested I try a French 75, a drink named after a French field gun, served in a flute. The main ingredient was Champagne. He recommended that Cass order a sidecar. We'd already heard that liquor was being reserved primarily for the French soldiers, the *poilus*, so the hotel staff had warned us that drinks might disappoint. Mine didn't. It fizzed in my mouth and went down like silk.

Cass utilized the time to tell me more about the maintenance required on the modified version of the Model T we would soon drive. At least twenty high-friction areas needed regular greasing, and we would have to check our oil levels once a day.

After Cass excused herself to the ladies' room, someone slipped down beside me. I glanced over and into the face of a man that held me in a grip. His eyes bluer than delft pottery, his face tanned to a beautiful shade of doe brown. A straight nose drew my eyes down to his well-defined lips and dominant chin.

He said in a low, husky voice, "Now, do tell me: Why is a pretty girl like you sitting with the old maid and ignoring me?"

Incensed by his words about Cass, it took me a moment to realize that he might consider this flirting. *Old maid?* "I'll have you know my friend is not an old maid. She simply has better things to do than chase men." This I didn't really know, because Cass had still told me nothing personal. I imagined that she'd lost someone she loved dearly and had never tried to replace him.

He smiled, revealing teeth as white as piano keys. Looking him over, I regarded his hair, a magnificent mix of lightest brown and darkest blond, like buff sand mixed with golden sand, and his uniform, in perfect condition with not one loose thread. He held up his hands. "As you say, as you say." Then he dropped them once more and lowered his voice. "But you haven't answered my real question: Why are you ignoring me?"

I shot a glance at Kitty, Lottie, and Eve, who remained enthralled by the other American officers, minus this one at my side. I said, "You were otherwise engaged."

The bartender came over; I turned to him and said, *"Un autre, s'il vous plaît." I'll have another, please.*

"Ah, you speak French," the lovely officer said. "The most beautiful language, and the most romantic." He paused, I supposed for me to respond. His eyes roamed all over my face; I could feel his gaze like a warm breeze that smelled of the spicy aftershave he wore. "You know, you could pass for a Parisian woman. The girls here are all slim, no thick ankles, and they have the loveliest look about the eyes. Their mouths are full, and they wear red lipstick so well." He focused on my lips then, and I found him overly confident and too direct.

I couldn't believe it; he was flirting with me, even though I was obviously no Parisian woman. It seemed the captain had made the same mistake as other men had in the past. Those who'd once wanted to court me had assumed I wanted romance and marriage and didn't register how I differed from other women. Then they saw the dirt under my fingernails, smelled something of horse when they got too close, and came to realize I would never love them as much as my horses, my family, and our land. But here the stable dirt had finally washed away, along with my *parfum de* horse.

"Do you speak French?" I asked.

"No, just admire it." He leaned closer.

"My father taught me to speak his native language."

I thought he might ask me about that—most people thought it interesting—but to my surprise, he said dismissively, "But let's not talk about French any longer." Then with a sly grin, "It appears as if you're still trying to ignore me."

Yes, indeed, I found him perhaps the most handsome man I'd ever encountered. "I am not. But my friend will return any moment now, and we have much to discuss."

"Do you now?"

"Yes, we'll soon drive ambulances for the American Women's Hospital. She's the better mechanic, and she's giving me some final pointers."

"And that's more important than me?" he asked with a roguish half-smile.

I slowly smiled. "At the moment, yes."

"You've hurt my feelings," he said and then winked.

Finding it difficult to swallow, I managed to say, "We're here to work."

He leaned back, obvious disappointment on his face. Then he turned to face the bar, and I thought our conversation had ended. But he tilted his head as if catching his reflection in the mirror. He ran a hand over his hair, then said, "A lady who's hard to get. I like it."

I went mute. This man could easily sweep any woman off her feet, and with one mistake, any of us could lose our position and be sent home. I could handle his advances, but Cass was right; we really did have to take care of the other girls who might prove unable to resist him.

Cass finally reappeared.

He stood and introduced himself to her. "Captain Felix Brohammer, at your service, ma'am."

Cass, bless her, seemed unfazed by his looks and charms. Flatly she said, "You don't say."

"And you are . . . ?"

"Cass Frank. Pleased to meet you." Still as flat as a concrete slab.

He turned to me then, and I knew what he wanted. I said, "Arlene Favier," before he could ask me.

"Arlene Favier," he said in an even lower, softer voice. "I'll remember that." Then he strode away and out of the bar.

Cass sat down and turned to me. "What was *that* about?" she asked.

I almost snorted out a laugh but got a grip on myself. "I honestly have no idea."

The next morning, carrying a list of automobile supplies Cass and I had compiled, I stepped downstairs to the hotel lobby in search of coffee. We hadn't brought all of our tools and materials overseas—it was too impractical—so now we had to supply ourselves here before we left for our final destination.

I spied our leader, Dr. Logan, out front on the sidewalk, embroiled in what looked like an animated conversation. I decided to skip the coffee, as by then pulverized chicory root had often replaced the real thing, and Dr. Logan appeared to need some help.

I pushed through the door. Dr. Logan spoke with a small weathered Frenchman via a translator, whom I recognized as the doorman. They talked about the ambulances, and as that was my area, I decided to intervene.

The man said in French, "The vehicles have to be taken to our shop, on the outskirts of Paris, to build the bodies."

But the bellman/translator said in English, "The vehicles are outside Paree with the bodies."

Apparently the doctor had tried and tried to make sense of the situation for quite some time, but I could see she always maintained her composure, and not one flush of color had risen in her cheeks.

I stepped up. "Perhaps I can be of assistance." I looked at Dr. Logan. "What the other man actually said was that the ambulances must be taken to his shop, on the outskirts of Paris, to *build* the bodies."

She allowed herself to sigh. "Well, that's a relief. So there's nothing wrong with them?"

I checked with the Frenchman again; he reassured all was well. The customization had to take place in his shop. I conveyed the information to Dr. Logan.

She expressed her appreciation for my help and then said, "You must be the multitalented driver I've heard about."

"Arlene Favier," I said, even though we had met before.

"I'm Dr. Logan."

"Is there anything else I can do?"

Dr. Logan looked me directly in my eyes when she spoke, and I sensed no airs from her, although Cass called her Dr. Snob behind her back. "What *can* you do?"

My mind went blank. Frankly intimidated for no reason other than her education and reputation, I suddenly felt that I had little to offer. "Other than speaking French, nothing out of the ordinary."

"I doubt that," Dr. Logan said very pleasantly. "I've heard you're quite the gal about town."

By that time, the Frenchman wanted to know if he could proceed. I gave him all the information, translated from Dr. Logan, as to where he could find the ambulance chassis, and he said he would arrange transportation for an extra fee, which Dr. Logan accepted.

That night I told Cass what had happened on the sidewalk. "I'm confused by a comment Dr. Logan made. She called me 'a gal about town.' You don't think she could've heard about that little talk I had with Captain Brohammer in the bar, do you?"

Cass sat on the bed already dressed in a nightgown, even though it was only ten o'clock. "I wouldn't be the least bit surprised."

I shook my head. "But she seemed pleased. I thought we weren't supposed to fraternize with men."

Cass held a comb, which she started to rake through her hair. "If the men happen to be American officers, believe me, they'll look the other way."

"Why? Are you joking?"

"I am not. The officers are college-educated. But the enlisted men are just your average boys from some hard city streets or dusty little towns."

I sat on the bed beside her. "How do you know this?"

She almost laughed. "It's common sense—horse sense, you might say. The doctors already like us. Well, the others besides Dr. Snob do. But it appears as though even *she* likes you." She stopped combing. "They just want the best for us. It's quite Victorian, but if one of us happens to snag the affections of an American officer, they would bend the rules."

"Are you joking?" I asked again.

And she followed suit: "I am not."

I pulled out a note I'd hidden under the lamp's base. It had come earlier that day from Captain Brohammer; he'd left it at the hotel desk. In it he asked me to join him for dinner the evening of the next day. After I passed the note to Cass, a case of nerves came over me. I hadn't anticipated any of this.

She took the note and even before opening it said, "Oh dear." Then she read the message and looked at me with unblinking eyes. "You should do it."

I shook my head again. "But we aren't supposed to—"

She smirked. "Are you going to ask the doctors for permission?"

"Maybe I should."

Cass guffawed. "You'll do nothing of the sort. You're a grown woman, and as I said, they'll be pleased even if they don't show it."

"But I could tell you didn't like him!"

Cass threw her hands in the air. "Not hardly. It wasn't him. I was a little chafed because something I knew would happen was already happening."

"What are you talking about?"

"Forget it."

"Oh, for heaven's sake. You can't keep me in the dark. Just tell me."

She looked a bit dejected, and all of a sudden, I knew what she was thinking. Her chances of meeting someone over here were slim. Cass was thirty years old, and many men, even older men, probably considered her a hopeless spinster.

She said, "I always thought you'd meet someone over here."

"Well, I wish you'd told me so I could've at least prepared myself."

She gazed away wistfully. "How could you prepare yourself for someone who looks that devilishly good?"

I pressed my palms against my cheeks and paced the buffed floors. "He *looks* great, but I'm not sure I like him, and I don't understand what made him like me. I didn't even treat him very nicely."

"Maybe it's a man-woman thing, Arlene. It's happened in the past; you know, attraction, magnetism . . ."

I shrugged. "I didn't feel anything."

She sighed. "Well, if one would ever allow herself to relax, one might be able to feel something."

"I haven't had time to relax."

"So now you're getting a rare opportunity to do just that."

Recalling the conversation with him, I murmured, "I don't know . . ."

"Why not?"

I wasn't about to tell her the captain had called her an old maid. "He looked at himself in the mirror."

"So, he could be somewhat impressed with himself. One can usually count on military officers for that. It doesn't mean anything."

"I don't like vanity in a man."

She shook her head as if saying *This is ridiculous*. "Please. If that's his only vice . . ."

I crossed my arms and finally stopped pacing. "I don't know . . . if there's more to like."

"Go out with him," Cass insisted. "Otherwise you'll never know."

Chapter Nine

The next day, Cass and I took a taxi to automobile supply houses and procured the necessities and tools for all three ambulances. The doctors had trusted us to stock the vehicles and equip them for anything we might encounter on the roads ahead. After we'd dragged back or arranged deliveries for everything we needed, we took a couple of hours to visit Notre-Dame, the gardens of the Tuileries, and Napoleon's tomb.

Eve had apparently tired of Kitty and Lottie's company, or maybe she wanted to see more of France's sights instead of its shops, because she asked if she could join us. A diminutive blond whose freckles covered her face all the way to her hairline, she could've passed for a schoolgirl, although she was twenty-three, like me.

As we walked the boulevards and parks, Eve tended to fall a few steps behind us, and I couldn't figure out if she liked to lag behind or if she lived for the most part in her own world. She had purchased a small Paris guidebook, and she read as she tagged along.

I could've remained on the Pont Neuf for hours looking down at the smooth flow of the river that calmed my nerves about the date coming up that night, but we had much still to see, and we also purchased postcards to send home.

We took a taxi to Montmartre, where Papa had told me the artists congregated, but a waiter informed us that the artists' turf had moved to the cafés of Montparnasse. Therefore we splurged on another taxi and headed to Café de la Rotonde, which according to Eve, Pablo Picasso frequented. There, Eve finally joined the conversation. "Did you know that when the Tuileries gardens first opened to the public, they barred some people? No beggars, lackeys, and soldiers."

"Heavens," I said.

"What are lackeys?" asked Cass.

"I think it's the service class, such as servants and footmen," Eve answered.

"Footmen?" Cass asked, then chuckled. "Maybe yesterday's footmen are today's drivers."

I laughed. "Yes, perhaps we wouldn't have been allowed. But I don't understand banning soldiers."

Indeed, the American soldier in France commanded a lot of respect. Whereas the French and British soldiers often appeared war-weary, like haggard ghosts of themselves, the American soldier wore a clean uniform and polished boots and smoked prized American-made cigarettes. He knew he would encounter danger, but he kept everything light with jokes and laughter. Other soldiers looked up to him, girls flirted with him, and children followed him around.

That thought swept me away for a while, the American soldier Captain Brohammer on my mind. I had guessed his age to be about thirty-one or thirty-two; he seemed like a youngster to have already reached the rank of captain. His dashing appearance made me think of Swedish warriors, and I could imagine him in a former life slaying dragons and sea serpents with a shining sword. My hands started trembling, and I put them under the table in my lap. I hadn't gone on a date since high school.

Cass's groans brought me back to the moment. Eve pointed at her guidebook and told us that France had always been a war zone. She talked about Charlemagne, William the Conqueror, and Joan of Arc. "This part of the country has been the site of sieges, marches, battlegrounds, and the war camps of France's enemies going back to the beginning of recorded time."

Cass looked around the café. "Does anyone have some paper?" she asked the air. "I seem to have wandered into a class on French history, but I forgot paper, and I need to take some notes."

I held my breath, but Eve, a good sport it turned out, only smiled and continued talking.

Cass held up her hands. "Wait a minute. Are you always like this?" she asked Eve.

"Most of the time," Eve answered.

Turning to me, Cass said, "If we ever have to ride doubled up, she's going with you."

I laughed.

Eve wove her hands together on the tabletop and leaned in. To Cass she said, "If you and I ever have to ride doubled up, I'll do the driving."

I liked this girl.

Cass gave a little whoop. "Not on your life."

"I'll wager I'm better."

"Behind the wheel?" Cass shook her head. "What foolish fancy."

"Speaking of fancies, do you race?"

Cass paled, obviously astonished. "Are you challenging me to a race?"

"Now, girls," I interrupted them, but the smile wouldn't leave my face. I hadn't shared a laugh with friends in a long time.

That night I wore my best dress from Olive, and it gave me a small sense of pride to think that a dress—and a girl, for that matter—had made it from Paris, Kentucky, to Paris, France. A bit too frilly for my tastes, the dress didn't come close to the military chic of the day. I walked down the steps to the lobby, where the captain waited for me, holding a small bouquet of flowers.

The sight of him almost squeezed the air out of my lungs. He looked freshly shaved and combed, and that spicy scent emanated from him. But that bit of unease, like a tiny warning—the same way I'd felt in the bar—was still there. Handsome, yes, but in a superlative, sort of impenetrable way.

After thanking the captain for the flowers, I asked one of the bellmen to take them upstairs to my room so they wouldn't wilt over the evening. "Do you mind?" I asked Captain Brohammer.

"Of course not. As you wish."

So polite and gentlemanly.

We took a taxi to a restaurant. Because of the war, portions were small and menus offered soups and *ragoûts* rather than grilled or roast beef and pork. I drank my first Bourgogne that night.

Felix requested that we communicate on a first-name basis, and over dinner he told me much of his life story. Raised on Long Island, he had excelled in athletics and then attended Yale with the idea that someday he would go to medical school. But his father's military service nudged him to apply to West Point, and he graduated with an officer's commission. Discovering he liked the military life, he'd eventually decided to become a career army man.

"I'd rather wear a suit of blue than a white surgical gown," he explained.

"The doctors I'm going to be working with are so dedicated. I admire them greatly. They've had to fight every step of the way to get here on just plain moxie."

He leaned back in his chair. "You're a serious one, aren't you?"

In his eyes I registered something that felt soulless, and it muted me for a moment. I didn't know what I wasn't seeing, but something about him seemed missing. I thought he'd want to know more about the doctors' story, and his lack of interest rattled me a bit. "Not always. But this is serious business for them . . . and for me, too."

He scoffed. "You've just arrived. You're in Paris. Enjoy yourself for a while. You'll see the front soon enough."

Funny, earlier that day I'd done a lot of laughing and teasing. So why did Captain Brohammer have this effect on me? I said, "I'm trying."

He reached across the table for my hand. I found his own large and big-boned but soft to the touch. No calluses. He perused my eyes. "Try harder. Please."

I had no idea what to say. His face unreadable, I had no idea what he expected. "I'm not very experienced with dating. I suppose I'm not good at it."

His eyelids lowered just a tad. "Are you a virgin?"

I couldn't believe it. But he *had* said it. He'd asked the most private question I could imagine. I pulled my hand away. "My dear sir. What a question."

His face, a mask. "It has been known to happen, and if you are, it would explain a lot."

Still stunned, I couldn't speak again for a moment. I found it difficult to believe that the modern, well-educated man spoke this way to a woman. But I had led a sheltered life; perhaps I didn't recognize acceptable conversation any longer. After the outrage faded, I began to doubt myself. Was I old-fashioned?

"You're probably scared, and that could explain . . ." He glanced about the room, then looked back at me. "I'm not accustomed to the rebuff, you know."

"Are you talking about our meeting at the bar?"

"Of course I am." He took my hand again and began to lift it to his lips.

Too fast, everything transpiring far too swiftly. But I let him brush his lips across my knuckles, then I slipped my hand away again. I couldn't make sense of this tête-à-tête, and I couldn't relax around him. "You don't mean to tell me that every girl you show interest in drops everything to turn her focus on you?"

He gave a low chuckle. "I mean just that."

"They must not have valued their friends very much."

"Not necessarily. They just valued me more." He leaned closer. "But not you. You want to make me work for it."

My mouth had gone dry. I sipped the wine, and moments later my mouth went dry again. The same feeling I'd had at the bar crept over me. He disturbed me, but maybe I just didn't understand the norms. The captain had taken me on a real date, and in Paris. What he'd said rang true; I had to find a way to enjoy myself.

"In case you're wondering, I will work for it," he added.

I smiled and decided to play along. "Will you succeed?"

"Of course I will."

I made myself laugh. "I guess there's nothing wrong with confidence, but you're rather impressed with yourself, aren't you?"

He sat back a bit. "Why shouldn't I be?"

Like acid in my stomach, that uncomfortable feeling turned to something more noxious. I'd told Cass I didn't like vanity in a man. This went far beyond vanity. I should've followed my instincts. Felix Brohammer was a cocky braggart and a cad. He disgusted me, and I didn't want to spend the rest of the evening with him.

The conversation stalled. The captain's eyes filled with disappointment, but I detected a hint of outrage, too. "When you said you weren't good at this, you weren't kidding."

"And you, sir, despite thinking so highly of yourself, surely do not know how to sweep a girl off her feet."

He sat still for a long and tortured moment, then he burst out in laughter. "So you've done it," he said. "You've made me laugh. Now I like you even more."

Had this man recently escaped from an insane asylum? I scrutinized him then, in awe of his gall.

"Let's start over," he said as he leaned forward again.

I didn't want to start over. I wanted to leave. I wanted out of this date. We'd finished the main course, but most likely Felix Brohammer had dessert in mind, perhaps followed by a stroll along the quay. Maybe I could feign a sudden illness. Or plead fatigue because I'd walked around all day.

In the end, I didn't have the nerve. So I went through the motions, and every moment lasted for eras. As we walked, he told me about his unit—he commanded an engineering battalion that worked alongside the infantry building bridges and roads and so on. He said his men had once built a bridge in three hours.

Night began to fall; the streetlights turned off at ten o'clock, the darkness a safeguard against attacks from the Boche Gothas, German heavy bombers.

At long last I could tell him I had a curfew and must return to the hotel before midnight. He steered me there, and before we reached the hotel doors where slabs of light leaned out onto the sidewalk, he took me around the waist and pulled me closer. He gently took my chin in one hand and lifted it toward his face.

I turned my head.

Brohammer let his hand fall away from my face and stood perfectly still for a few long moments, then he dropped his other hand from my waist. "I see," he said.

"I-I'm sorry."

A long, unbearable silence ensued. I studied my shoes and soothed myself with the idea that soon I would go inside and leave his presence. Brohammer lightly took my upper arm and started walking again. He led me to the hotel entrance, and I began to thank him for a lovely evening. Maman had taught me to do this, no matter what, when someone had shown generosity toward me.

But he interrupted me, saying, "You can stop now."

And so I said good night and slipped inside.

Finally I could breathe. All night long my dress had felt too tight, although it fit me perfectly. Brohammer had never asked me one thing about myself. Then I realized that the dress hadn't constricted me; the captain's presence had.

The next day, two of the ambulances arrived from the shop, where they'd been equipped with all-wooden bodies, electric headlights, and rolled canvas windshields instead of glass ones, which could easily shatter. The third ambulance wasn't ready yet, but we could no longer wait. We five drivers had to get started painting the ambulances and stenciling "American Women's Hospital" in an arc on the sides. We would finish by painting large red Geneva crosses on the roof.

Before we got started, Kitty and Lottie ran up to me. "How was it last night, you lucky dog, you?" asked Kitty, bouncing on her toes.

And Lottie practically squealed, "It must have been dreamy. Tell us all about it."

I put my hands on my hips and faked indignation. "Now, you know a girl isn't supposed to kiss and tell."

The night before, I had told Cass all of it, and for a long time she'd merely sat, listened with rapt attention, and pensively looked around our room.

"If I were you, I'd say nothing about it. I doubt the evening was pure torture, and those three girls," she said, meaning the other drivers, "would give anything to be in your shoes. To others, his interest is the highest of compliments, and you'll seem thorny if you don't even give him a try."

"Thorny!"

"You're sprouting them now as we speak! Even some of the doctors and nurses might find your resistance a little laughable. Best to keep it under wraps."

I'd been pacing the floor but stopped. Cass never ceased to surprise me. She stretched and then finished, "Besides, you'll probably never see him again."

I managed to shirk the girls' questions and stuck to the work at hand. After painting, we filled our handmade boxes and storage lockers, along with a third oblong driver's box that would stay inside the cab. In the latter we stored chains, rope, spark plugs, and tire chalk, and we stocked the exterior running board boxes with extra tire inner tubes, a bucket, and a pump. On the rear we strapped spare water and cans of reserve gasoline, oil, and kerosene. The back of each ambulance accommodated two stretchers on the floor and a third one centered above them; they slid in on rails installed by the shop and attached to the crossbeams above. In the event of an emergency, though, the vehicle could squeeze in ten sitting or standing passengers if the stretchers were taken out or moved aside. Other passengers could sit squeezed in the cab next to the driver.

Now we would do what we'd come for, and we prepared to leave Paris.

Cass and I awakened before dawn the next morning to drink strong, bitter coffee and do some final engine checks. When the day broke, it was time to go. I placed my hand over my upper chest where my baby locket lay under my blouse. I had decided to wear it always, for luck.

Our convoy consisted of two completed ambulances, a few automobiles to deliver the doctors and nurses, and one supply truck. My ambulance would take the lead, as I could converse with the French along the road and also with the guide who would accompany us. As I bent over to crank my engine to life, I sensed a presence. I took note and stood up straight, then looked toward the hotel door.

Brohammer stood on the sidewalk. Why was he here? He mouthed something to me. I stared, dumbfounded, and read his lips as he mouthed it again: *I forgive you.*

Suppressing a shudder, I concentrated on the task at hand. When my engine began turning over, I had to jump into the driver's seat, right the gas and spark by fine-tuning the steering column levers, and swap the ignition from the battery to the magneto. *Please don't stall,* I begged.

Soon all the vehicles rumbled, idling, ready to go. I kept my gaze averted from the sidewalk, not wanting Brohammer to distract me again. So angry he'd come here, so flummoxed by him and his attention, I nevertheless had to let it go and stay focused.

Lottie shouted from the street just before she jumped in back, "Look, Arlene, it's your beau!"

Then I had to do it. I turned and lifted my eyes. Brohammer, still standing there, smiling. A cold, unfeeling, untouchable smile.

I didn't dignify him with a response.

Moments later, we started on our way. Lottie, Kitty, and one of the aides sat in the back of my ambulance. A woman from the village where we would work sat in front with me. She would guide us to Neufmoutiers-en-Brie, in the Seine-et-Marne, some twenty-five miles from Paris. Utilizing a small château assigned to the AWH by the French Sixth Army, we would treat not only villagers and refugees, but also the military in the area, as need be.

All the months of preparation had come down to this moment.

Nervously, I squeezed the steering wheel as we navigated the vexing narrow lanes of Paris in our precious Fords, then drove beyond the city limits. Though our ambulances could traverse any topography and could attain speeds of fifty-five miles per hour, a flat-land steady speed of thirty miles per hour was ideal.

Each ambulance had cost the outrageous sum of $1,600, which included the chassis, overseas and overland shipping, early maintenance, and a customized body. The responsibility for my vehicle landed squarely on my shoulders. The ambulances had monetary value, but even more important, they were truly the means to save lives.

After leaving all signs of Paris behind us, we drove through an area destroyed earlier in the war. Everywhere we went, we witnessed a wasteland of crumbled brick and stone, pockmarked roads, and underground dugouts. The earth smelled foul. Most of the trees had fallen from the effects of bombing and shelling, and some people had stuck dead branches up along the sides of the roads to look like trees, hiding the road from the Germans. Some trees—olive and fruit-bearing varieties—had barely survived and were scorched and stripped of their leaves.

Entire villages decimated and much of the farmland charred and pitted with shell holes, the countryside looked unlivable. I was stunned when we saw people—dazed and weak and with hopelessly haunted eyes and rail-thin bodies. Amid the walls left standing in the villages, a curl of smoke sometimes drifted upward from a lean-to or cellar, showing us that people did somehow live in the rubble of war. In one village, I spotted an old man walking with a stick; in another, some children building play towers with fallen chunks of debris. They stared at me as though they'd never seen a woman driving a car, but they always waved and shouted, *"Vive l'Amérique!"*

Desolation seemed to ride along with us as we crossed the land; I hadn't envisioned it this terrible. Papa would've hated to see this, and I heard no sounds from the back. Everyone in the ambulance must have been astounded, too. Such widespread devastation, such downtrodden and defeated-looking people. Those safe in the United States had no idea.

Even so, occasionally Brohammer entered my mind. *I forgive you.* What did that mean? I didn't know and had to shake it off; I had a huge responsibility here.

We could hear the dull thunder of distant shells, lest we forget that the war still raged close by. Cemeteries lined with small, plain wooden crosses also provided a constant reminder. The roads twisted and rose and fell, showing me why the agile Model T had been chosen for our ambulances.

The village woman, Camille, who would become one of our kitchen maids later, said in French, "Up ahead, a sharp turn at the bottom of the hill."

I spotted the curve and braked to take it slowly. I steered around the bend, where the road fell off even more, and then my ambulance nose-dived into a shell crater.

After a few moments, Camille said without emotion the French equivalent of *whoops*.

A cloud of dust fell all around the ambulance like dry rain.

I coughed and tried my door, which wouldn't open. We'd landed close to the crater wall on my side. "Is anyone hurt?" I asked.

Camille wiggled out on her side and worked her way around back, then moved up to her door again. "All are well." She looked inside the cab at me. "Funny thing," she said, her gaze roaming to the crater wall in front of us. "When I came through here yesterday, this hole was not here."

Chapter Ten

NEUFMOUTIERS-EN-BRIE, FRANCE

JULY 1918

When I got out, the back wheels, suspended in the air, still spun. With the help of some rope, chain, and Cass's ambulance, we pulled my vehicle out of the crater. I had to change the inner tube in the right front tire, but the ambulance had suffered no other damage. No one seemed upset or angry about my mistake.

Cass, of course, had to say, "And they put you in the lead?"

I gave her a hideous glare.

Beryl walked up to Cass and me as I changed the inner tube. She said, "When you're in front, you're bound to make the first mistake."

My hands hopelessly covered in grease now, I'd also ripped a portion of my jacket hem while I crawled out of the ambulance on the passenger side. Already I'd learned to expect anything around a bend. "I won't make this one again."

Soon we moved on. We passed groups of *poilus*, French infantrymen. Obviously exhausted, their faces unshaven and grimy, they looked toward us, their weary eyes posing a question, *Can you give us a lift?* But most of them asked for nothing. At one point a soldier did ask for a ride, and Camille responded, *"C'est interdit."* *It's forbidden.*

The *poilu* replied, *"Merci quand même."* *Thanks all the same.* In his eyes, no guile, no blame. Just acceptance of a sort that I found more woeful than resistance. The war still raged, but both the land and the people appeared already conquered.

I drove onward, a sick feeling in my stomach. A few moments later I asked Camille in French, "Who has forbidden us to help these soldiers?"

"The *médecin-chef.* She said if we stop for one, we have to stop for all, and if they don't look injured or sick, we must carry on. We must arrive before nightfall since you can't turn on your lights."

I gripped the steering wheel. Of course by *médecin-chef* she meant Dr. Logan, and I did have to yield the doctor's point, but I found it painful to simply drive past those unsung heroes.

In between areas of devastation were some untouched farmhouses, fields, and signs of normal village life—old men gathered together talking, children playing, and women hoeing gardens—while not far away a desperate battle was likely being waged. Often the ground rumbled, and biplanes and monoplanes swooped over our heads. Soon we came to an area beyond the reach of German shells, a green pastoral land with copses of great spreading trees, patchwork fields, and small villages, charming if not modest and mostly poor.

When we came upon an American company marching overland, Camille, looking over her shoulder, told me that the car carrying Dr. Logan had pulled over, so I braked and pulled over, too. Apparently our leader had decided we should witness this show of military might. Everyone got out of the vehicles.

Ammunitions wagons, machine-gun battalions, a great artillery company, and long columns of infantrymen marched toward the front. Clean-cut officers rode astride on horses, and other men carried the flags and banners. Last came the ambulance and Red Cross groups.

For the first time, I thought of our safety. The enemy wasn't supposed to target ambulances and those in convoy with them, but we'd heard of casualties among medical teams.

Soon, children with dirty faces appeared on the road, as if they had materialized from the ground, and gave us flowers. They asked us about America. We also saw a decrepit village woman carrying a baby and then more villagers on the move. Before we could become distracted, Dr. Logan ordered us on our way again.

With our journey slowed considerably by the stop, road conditions, and my little accident, six hours had passed since we left Paris. At last we arrived in Neufmoutiers, a small village that consisted of a church and about fifteen houses set along the street running down from an obelisk. Assigned to a small château, we entered it through a lovely stone arch. A two-story building made of beige and gray stone, our new hospital had high ceilings, large rooms, a massive fireplace, and regularly spaced, heavily framed windows. Inside, it smelled of time gone by.

Before we went to work, Dr. Logan gathered us together and told us that we would do our work without any consideration of gender, age, rank, nationality, or financial or social status. We would set up a hospital in this building, which had never been intended for that use. Food and water might be in short supply.

"Let us not fail, my ladies. Let us do more, always do more than we think we're capable of. As we embark on this journey, ask yourself now and every day—every bad day, every good day—if you have done your best." She paused; then, as she slowly swept her gaze around our little assembled entourage again, she said, "Ask yourself even now—especially now—as in the words of the poet Edgar Guest, 'Have you earned your tomorrow?'"

No one moved; I think we all held our breath. For the first time, it completely sank in. A great honor had been bestowed upon me; I stood here with the likes of her.

Ann Howard Creel

Never before had I done something this important.

Although the village was small, families living there hosted about 60 refugees from the war zone in the Aisne, and within a twenty-mile radius of the village, 360 more refugees were spread about. With all the French doctors now at the front, no one had received any recent medical care.

How had the French endured this for so long? No wonder the villagers were tired and irritated about having to house and feed refugees for so long now. It didn't help that the refugees came from a more prosperous area in France, and the classes would not have otherwise mingled. Who could blame the villagers for the exhaustion and strain caused by this seemingly never-ending war?

Every member of the AWH team pitched in to set up the hospital with the help of a squad of *poilus* loaned to us, and we emptied four large rooms of furniture and rugs and then set them up as wards, which would give us a capacity of fifty beds. The servants' dining room, with its painted walls, tiled floors, and running water, would be the operating room. Some of our supplies, including the surgeons' instruments, had not arrived. The Red Cross had no furnishings to spare, so Dr. Logan had purchased fifty regulation French Army hospital beds while in Paris. Thankfully these had been delivered, so we quickly set them up in the wards. We carried in the autoclave and many white enamel tables and worked late into the night to prepare a hospital for immediate use.

Finally we had to stop to sleep.

After a restless night, I awakened to a hospital already full of villagers and refugees needing medical care—some moving about on crutches or with their arms immobilized in slings, others sitting quietly holding babies and sick children too listless to move about or play. Cass and I received orders to drive to the surrounding villages in search of those who couldn't get to the hospital on foot. Quickly we downed our coffee and stuffed our mouths with a few bites of bread and readied ourselves to leave, then we heard shouts from outside. We flew out of the building to find a villager shouting and pointing at smoke in the sky and a plane circling overhead.

We were told that a German Gotha had dropped his load on a neighboring village, and the pilot cruelly continued to fly about, surveying his dirty work. We jumped in our ambulances and headed toward the wide plume of smoke. The winding and narrow road had room for only one ambulance to pass through at a time. As we drew nearer, my heart raced, I breathed in a burnt scent, and I sensed the imminence of death in the same way a horse can sense fear in a rider.

I clenched the steering wheel, but I would not show weakness. Ever since I'd lost Papa, tears welled up easily, but now I had to prove myself worthy of Cass's and Beryl's faith in me. It was time for courage to come calling.

Cass took the lead and drove to the edge of the bombed village, where dense black smoke billowed upward, and I had to squash the uncontrollable memory that flashed in my mind—our house burning.

The air floated choking dust and filled with screams and shouts. I could see that the village had once been a dear place of poplars and small homes, with a stone bridge over a creek and a Catholic church. The bomb had scored a direct hit on a market area, where apparently many people had gathered. We had to dodge collapsed walls and lumps on the ground—dead men and women. Some people still crawled out of the ruins, covered in whitish dirt and dust, coughing and holding on to injured limbs or bleeding heads. Haggard, smoke-smudged, and stunned-looking villagers left standing quickly took note of our arrival and immediately began to ferry the injured, a few hastily wrapped in bandages, to our ambulances.

They loaded mine with three people, among them a young girl of about thirteen with half her chest caved in. The stooped, white-haired man who placed her on my stretcher shook his head, signaling to me a sense of hopelessness. He said, *"Vite."* Hurry. The girl, beautiful with a thick mane of silky black hair and dark eyes, gazed at me with fright, with pain.

Cass waved me off. As I drove away, I noticed a village woman propped against a wall, her skin black with soot and her neck hitched to the side in an unnatural manner as though her spine had snapped. I doubted she was alive. And now we had to leave many more villagers behind. How many would cling to life until we could come back for them?

I drove back as speedily as I could on the narrow, rough road, but the girl's labored, raspy breathing, audible at the start, had stopped. I almost stopped breathing, too. Now she had joined *les morts*. The dead. I had to bite back a scream. No doubt someone's loved and precious child, a girl on the cusp of womanhood with her life ahead of her only this morning, she was now dead. I had seen her alive, the last person to do so, and I hadn't even known her or comforted her.

Beyond the sound of my engine, a silence like no other and an unfamiliar scent made sure I'd never forget this moment. Death drifted in the air and forced me to inhale it, much the way I imagined the poisonous gas discharged in combat overcame its victims. It lay on my skin, but instead of an urge to brush it off, I knew this death-air would surround me in France and maybe forever.

My other two passengers, still conscious and roughly bandaged with strips of cloth, held pressure on their wounds. They said nothing I could hear, only occasionally crying out when we juddered over an especially rough patch in the road or when the ambulance lurched jerkily down an incline crosshatched with exposed tree roots that made for a dreadfully bumpy ride. I cringed all the way down.

Cass pulled up at the château-turned-hospital a few moments after me. Dr. Logan had located and purchased an operating table in Paris, and luckily it had arrived. Our surgeons began operating on patients using the assembled pocket kits they'd brought with them. I'd just started to catch my breath when I received orders to embark on an urgent mission to the hospital in Tournan in order to borrow some desperately needed hemostatic clamps.

With no time for chitchat, Cass said to me during a rare pause, "This makes 'hitting the ground running' seem like a stroll down a shady lane."

Even Lottie, Kitty, and Eve, with no ambulance to drive yet, worked in the hospital and assisted as something like nurses' aides. They grew up overnight. Already we had to designate an area on the grass outside in the courtyard for bodies. We had yet to set up a morgue.

After I picked up the clamps and brought them back, I continued to transport the injured and those who died on the way or soon after arrival, and I felt the same way as I had during Papa's funeral, as though everything stood out in etched-line detail. Colors were too bright, and smells too overwhelming, but sounds were muffled as though my body had diminished one of my senses in some sort of protective means.

Now I not only knew death; I knew the shade and scent of human blood and the charred appearance and stench of burnt human bodies. I knew the look of what lay beneath our skin. By the end of the day, we had transported thirty injured and six who had died. That night, a leaden exhaustion came over me, and I fell into bed and a bottomless sleep before the villagers had a chance to bring us food.

The next day, it all began again. We brought in the less seriously injured from the bombed village and other sick refugees and locals. Before we left for the village, as we stuffed croissants in our mouths, we discovered that a new German offensive had reached Château-Thierry, only twenty miles from Paris. Due to a new round of nightly raids, Paris had been put back under military control. We also learned that the Spanish influenza had reared its ugly head all across France, including the front.

Dr. Logan gathered us together at the end of the third day and said we must prepare for things to get worse. Already I'd seen a lovely young lady die because a Hun pilot, not able to land with a bomb aboard, had decided to drop it on a sleepy village away from the front, probably just for sport. I'd seen women and men too old to fight pulverized by being in the wrong place at the wrong time. How much worse could it get?

Warned not to drive unfamiliar roads after dark because we couldn't use our headlights, we washed down the ambulances, inside and out, conducted maintenance checks, and procured gasoline in the village every night. No flirting required.

I'd received a letter from Maman while in Paris, but I'd sent back only postcards showing the beautiful sights of the city and offering short, cheerful notes. I hadn't written a letter yet. Now, as I finally readied for bed on that third night, I wondered what to write. What I'd experienced already felt like walking into a weird and awful underworld. I could tell Maman about our safe arrival in a village, but I couldn't imagine telling her about the suffering of soldiers and civilians alike, so I closed my eyes and willed some peace of mind to arrive. In some ways Maman and Luc stood right there with me and had been doing so every day since I'd left Paris, Kentucky; but in other ways we walked in different worlds now, and they felt so far out of reach, it was like trying to hold fog in my hands.

No one on our team had slept or eaten much for three days, and I wondered who, if anyone, would pack a bag and catch a ride away. It wouldn't have surprised me if some found this more than they had bargained for and decided they couldn't or didn't want to continue.

When I fell asleep at night, sheer exhaustion took over. Cass and I shared a bedroom on the second floor of the château, and during the night, at some strange hour, I heard her slip off the bed and almost silently dress. My nights of sound sleeping had forever ended; ever since the fire and Papa's death, a feather falling in my room could awaken me.

Although I wanted to ask what she was doing, it was obvious she didn't want to wake me and have to offer an explanation. So in the end, I didn't say a word.

About two hours had passed when Cass tiptoed back into the room, undressed, and slid under the covers. But even after her breathing fell into a heavy, regular rhythm, I stayed awake. I couldn't imagine that Cass had already fallen for one of the *poilus* in the village. So maybe she suffered from a delayed reaction to all we'd seen, perhaps nausea and vomiting, and wanted to go off to get past it alone. Maybe she sought solitude. But none of these possible explanations fit the Cass I knew.

In the morning the villagers brought us more food, and as we wolfed it down before heading out, I yearned for Cass to tell me where she'd gone. Perhaps she'd eased away silently only to avoid disturbing my sleep, but then why didn't she say something about it now? Something distant now roamed around in her eyes, and I had no idea how well I really knew Cass. Although I considered her the best friend I'd ever had, I knew almost nothing about her life before I met her. I thought hard about saying something or leaving it alone, and finally asked, "Are you tired?"

Focused away on what looked like nothing, she gazed back at me in a way that saw past me. In the next instant she focused. "Why would you ask?"

I shrugged.

She sighed and said, "Don't even think about getting *tired.*"

"Yes, we should probably remove that word from our vocabulary."

She nodded but said nothing more. Cass, the most capable person I'd ever known, could stand out in a group. She had potent opinions, and she had no reservations about sharing them. But when it came to anything related to family or former beaus, even her past or present hopes and dreams, she kept herself behind a closed door. Why? And what in the world had caused her to slip away like a sleuth in the middle of the night?

I didn't know, and Cass didn't say.

Chapter Eleven

MEAUX, FRANCE

JULY 1918

Later that morning, before we had a chance to head out in the ambulances toward other villages, Dr. Logan weaved among us and told us that our commanding officer in the French Sixth Army had ordered us to cut back on hospital operations in Neufmoutiers. The Allies had retaken the Aisne, and our refugees could return there to harvest wheat fields that had escaped ruin during the German retreat. We would relocate to a new village closer to recently devastated areas.

A new offensive, the Allied counterdrive for the Marne, had begun. The operation would most likely decide the fate of the war. All the khaki- and blue-clad uniformed men in our village vanished in the face of orders to take up new positions, and we received instructions to send two teams, each with a surgeon and a nurse, to Meaux to treat wounded French soldiers brought in by ambulances from the front.

Quickly Dr. Logan decided that Beryl Rayne and Nurse Helton would comprise one team, and Dr. Kitchens and Nurse Carpenter would make up the other. Cass and I would transport them and provide assistance with our ambulances as needed.

The six of us gathered our belongings, left Neufmoutiers in less than an hour, and drove away as a flock of starlings arced their wings against a golden-purple morning over the village rooftops.

It had happened so quickly. We would work at the front after all. The women surgeons had always wanted to use their skills in the war theater to help soldiers, but, turned away by the American military, they had eagerly accepted helping villagers instead. Now they would do both, and I was to be a part of it.

I found it a little surprising that our leader and the person who had made everything happen so far chose to let others go. But I'd seen Dr. Logan defer to Beryl before, and one always had the sense around Dr. Logan that she didn't seek personal glory, that instead, some kind of faith guided her. I often bore witness to her selflessness.

Dr. Logan had probably chosen Dr. Rayne because of Beryl's sense of mission and air of self-assurance tempered by kindness. Probably Dr. Logan also knew that Beryl could lead our little team as needed. I supposed Dr. Logan had chosen Dr. Kitchens because our shy young doctor could speak some French, or else Dr. Logan wanted to boost the confidence of the most modest doctor on our team.

In the lead today, I had the job because, if need be, I could ask for directions and gasoline in the language of the land. Beryl and Nurse Helton rode with me while the other team joined Cass in her ambulance behind us.

With utmost care, I proceeded, following the directions given to me in the village. I'd studied them quickly as best I could before we left, but road markers were often missing and landmarks didn't appear where I thought they would. Conveying precious cargo, I couldn't allow myself to make any mistakes.

Beryl sat in the front with me. She focused straight ahead, as though weighty thoughts had filled and stilled her.

Despite the rough living conditions in the château, Beryl appeared to have bathed and washed her hair. Her silver-blond waves were combed away from her face and still damp. Her uniform couldn't have been laundered yet, but it looked clean and pressed compared to mine. Her oval wire eyeglasses gleamed spotlessly. Maybe she'd always kept herself immaculate or maybe Dr. Logan had rubbed off on her. I'd put my hair up in a tucked bun and brushed my uniform, but it still looked dull due to the dust.

Sitting in the back, Nurse Helton, a trim-waisted, pale brunette who viewed the world through straightforward, intelligent eyes, rarely engaged in conversation. In silence she peered out of a determined face with wary anticipation but never opened up to or shared herself with others. She and Cass could've had a silent friendship.

After some time Beryl glanced my way. "I'm sure you're wondering why we want to do it, why we want to enter the theater of war under such grim circumstances. Perhaps you think we're bloodthirsty thrill-seekers."

Stunned, I said, "Not in the least!" But then I pondered what else to say, because no one had explained the doctors' determination and desires to us. "I suppose you want to prove yourselves."

"Yes," she said pensively. "But it's more than that. We want to do what most of us know we can do and what we think we were born to do. The old order"—she turned a bit in my direction—"and I mean the old order dominated by men, wants to contain us within certain situations and believes that war is too tough for us women to endure. When one's personal fortitude and skills are discounted, it can be so very discouraging. But we never faltered in our quest to help."

"I can see that."

She continued as though she really wanted me to understand: "The military almost kept us out of this. They came much too close to succeeding."

I'd noticed her grasping her hands together in her lap, then releasing them, only to grasp them again a few moments later.

"Are you ever nervous?" I asked.

"Of course. We're confident, but also still human." She raked her hair back and rubbed her neck.

Her openness, her willingness to share her fears, moved me. I found myself speechless, amazed that a woman of Beryl's stature would admit to doubts and fears. But everything about Dr. Rayne had surprised me. I saw her as crossing her own version of a no-man's-land; on one side, the limitations and expectations put on women, and on the other side, her drive to do what she knew she could and must do. I viewed her as charting a new course through a changed world.

She asked, "Are *you* nervous?"

"Without a doubt," I answered. "But I've already seen some terrible things."

"I expect it will get worse. More death, more suffering . . ."

At least Beryl didn't mince words.

As we made progress toward our destination, we had to cross an area of razed earth that looked as if a meteor shower had scarred and pitted it, and I had the feeling this place could swallow us without anyone noticing. Dust covered the ambulance as though it had sprouted gray mold. Streams had become muddy channels. Allied air squadrons heading to the front flew overhead in grand V-shaped formations consisting of twenty-five to thirty planes.

War felt closer. I could sense it like the electricity that remains in the air after a lightning strike. In the midst of this brutally altered landscape, something tightly wound within me started to unravel. Beryl continued: "I suppose I'm afraid of what I can't even imagine. I'm not religious like my husband was, thus I gather little strength from faith."

After a moment's hesitation, I asked, "When did you . . . lose him?"

"Interesting you put it that way. He died seven years ago, and then my daughter died two years later. She was like him, artistic and spiritual. I was too scientific for her. I believe I lost both of them before they died. I tried to change, but I didn't."

I had no idea why she'd chosen me as a confidante. I wanted to know more, but then thought better of asking her. "I'm so sorry—"

She said, "Don't worry, Arlene. You'll do well here, I know it."

I wanted to believe her, but a shudder moved through me then. "How did you meet Dr. Logan?"

Although she kept her gaze ahead, she answered me without hesitation, "At a conference of the American Medical Women's Association. We shared the belief that women shouldn't be excluded from the war zone, or anything else for that matter, and I joined her force trying to make it over here. Otherwise we probably would have never met. She's from a wealthy, prominent eastern family. Very conservative and resistant to change, although I did hear that they supported her medical career. Still, she probably had to fight her way into medical school. I grew up in California with very little."

"That makes your journey even more impressive."

"Not so. I was raised with very little of anything, including restrictions."

"But with more difficulties."

"Oh, I doubt that. Herberta hasn't had an easy life. She lost her husband and only child, too. Her parents lived long lives, and she had no one else. She once told me they praised her accomplishments, but they would've forbidden her to come over here during the war."

"Would that have kept her away?"

"Oh yes; had her parents not eventually succumbed to old age, she wouldn't have come to France. She would've been too torn. I'm sure of it."

Had this war made everyone cross over into someone else?

I asked, "And it's clearer for you?"

She half laughed. "Despite my inner resolve, everything seems to be getting *less* clear. But here we are."

We approached an area of forest that stood alongside ancient villages, charming châteaux, and country farms still trying to feed Paris.

Every mile or so a small copse of woods stood between wheat fields dotted by occasional large stone farm buildings with courtyards.

As sunset turned the grit in the air to pink and gold, we arrived in Meaux, a pleasant old market town of ancient mills along the Marne. We entered the town center with its Gothic cathedral that dated from the twelfth century, having passed the Pont du Marché—the Market Bridge, which the British blew up in 1914 along with Meaux's famous floating baths during the First Battle of the Marne.

Now again, the large town had become a concentration area for the military forces, having fought another battle for the Marne here. Several German bombardments had left craters in the town square and near the railroad station, and a cathedral in the center of town was lined on one side by headless statues—this damage had not been done by the Germans but by the French during the Revolution. It seemed a warning or a prediction.

I navigated the ambulance along streets clogged with uniformed troops marching toward the front. Mobs of mostly silent refugees, their faces folded and sagging, moved in the opposite direction. Many of them pushed farm carts piled high with their most prized possessions—mattresses, pots and pans, tools, clothing, and chickens in crates. Some pushed baby carriages and wheelbarrows and drove sheep and hogs.

We pulled up to the French Evacuation Hospital No. 18. Around a large tree-bordered courtyard stood various buildings converted for medical use from their former occupations as cavalry barracks. The entire area teemed with the comings and goings of ambulances and military jeeps, with nurses and volunteers giving aid to some patients outside on the spot or shuttling others inside. Ambulance drivers unloaded stretchers, supply trucks backed in for unloading, and village women bustled about offering help.

A steady stream of ambulances kept flowing even as dusk settled in. A nurse said to me, "We hoped you were the supply wagon. All the booze is gone," and I quickly came to see that balancing the horrors of war with humor could help one survive. Laughter, at the very least, let you know you were alive.

The drivers efficiently delivered white-bandaged and blue-clad French *blessés*—the wounded—to the compound. Bloodied men, some with missing limbs, cried out in pain. If any morphine had been administered at the front, it had apparently worn off. Some soldiers looked to have hemorrhaged during the long haul to Meaux. Some wore dressings over their eyes. Some smelled of sulfur; others of death. The injured men had received their treatment at one of the frontline dressing stations or advance field hospitals, where they'd also received anti-tetanic serum and had been tagged with a card stating the nature of their wounds, tied to a buttonhole on their uniforms.

One of the English-speaking nurses gave us a fast tour to show us how things worked. Upon arrival, the wounded went from the ambulance into the swarming *grand triage*, where many received emergency treatment or, if likely to die soon, were made as comfortable as possible. The more severely injured but still hopeful cases were carried into one of the hospital buildings for surgery. The largest contingency went to the *petit triage*, where less serious wounds could be speedily diagnosed and redressed before the men embarked on the long journey to Paris.

Between 1,000 and 1,800 patients passed through the triage daily, and the French medical officers had worked themselves to exhaustion. We watched many drained-looking French nurses running to and fro in blue chiffon veils, and through windows we could see doctors in blood-splattered white surgical aprons leaning over tables to tend to wounded soldiers. The French doctors gratefully welcomed our female doctors' arrival but ordered them to get some rest and report for duty at six the next morning.

My eyes latched on to the ambulances and their drivers. Both American and French male drivers worked with an air of calm efficiency, as if they'd seen it all and nothing could shock them now. With wan faces, they moved the dead, dying, and injured. Their movements smooth, they seemed unpanicked and expedient. Blood, gore, and suf-fering had become a natural backdrop. None of them acknowledged our arrival.

Cass had already adopted the rather blasé sense of gallows humor here and whispered, "Perhaps if we shot a gun in the air . . . ?"

And I followed with "Maybe if we stripped naked . . . ?"

Of course we didn't really want to distract them from their work. But despite our attempts to make light of it, we were lost, like pieces of dust blown about, then landed on this one small spot of earth by happenstance. It became clear that if Cass and I wanted to help, we'd have to find our own way.

Chapter Twelve

In the morning, as soon as dawn broke, Cass and I stood outside ready to drive to the advance field hospitals, where surgeons and nurses sorted the dead and dying, administered the most urgent care, washed gas burns, retained those soldiers who couldn't survive transportation, and sent the savable and movable away in ambulances. Under some circumstances, drivers might also journey closer to the front to retrieve the wounded from the advance dressing stations. The same nurse who'd given us a tour the day before informed us of all of this.

As she left us, she said over her shoulder, "Be careful. They all have cooties."

Cass and I stood and stared at each other in confusion until we figured out that by *cooties*, she probably meant lice. But when she said "they," had she referred to the other ambulance drivers or the men from the trenches we'd most likely transport that day?

We shrugged to each other. I supposed we'd soon find out.

A French driver gave us helmets and gas masks as casually as if handing out tablets and pencils to students in a classroom.

Cass looked apprehensive for the first time, and I mirrored her anxiety. Most likely nothing could have prepared us for the front lines, even after what we'd seen in the countryside around Neufmoutiers. Both of us had expected to transport civilian patients behind the lines, not military men at the front. But they needed us, and we couldn't back out now.

Attached to the French Army, we received orders to follow two of the French drivers. One of them shook his head before allowing Cass and me to join the convoy. I could sense doubt in the way he looked at us, this despite the fact that British women—most of them aristocrats, I'd heard—had driven ambulances in France almost since the war's beginning.

We shadowed the French drivers and troop trucks into a land scored by abandoned trenches, tangled by barbed wire, and strewn with blackened gravel and dirt. A rotten-egg odor permeated the air, and heavy dust dimmed the sun like a lighthouse blurred by a socked-in shore. The narrow road, pulverized by shell hits, thronged with fleeing refugees who seemed shocked that trucks carried troops to the front and not away from it.

A man called out, *"La guerre est finie!"* *The war is finished!* He gestured for us to turn around and go back.

The first driver in the line shouted, *"Non, c'est pas fini!"* *Not finished!*

The sounds of war roared in close, and fear twisted in my gut. The *rat-a-tat* of machine-gun fire, an eerie whistling of shells, and the rumbling, trembling earth reminded us that the front lay perhaps only a thousand yards away as we pulled into a pickup area adjacent to a makeshift field hospital.

The stretcher-bearers, *brancardiers*, with their clenched jaws and glassy eyes, brought in the wounded from the battlefield or frontline dressing stations. Within the tented hospital, one doctor performed a hasty emergency operation. The blood-splattered surgeon bent over a table, trimming and dumping things into some kind of bucket, and I began to feel sick. A nurse took the bloody instruments from his hands, and a stretcher-bearer offered the surgeon a quick draw on what was left of his cigarette. A line of men in various states of consciousness sat propped up against the side of a smaller tent, waiting for treatment, I supposed. One man cried while gripping a dressing on the stump of his leg. Another had fallen over to his side, his eyes open but devoid of any light.

I wondered if I should go to him, but then a few aides brought out more wounded soldiers from inside the surgical tent. The aides loaded three *couchés*, the nonambulatory, in the back and one *assis*, the ambulatory, in the cab beside me. Beneath a light dressing on my passenger's left arm, blood seeped from his shredded skin, and I couldn't imagine how he could sit and remain stoic as I drove away, following one of the French drivers.

A tall, thin man with a grizzled face, the driver had told me we would take another route back, as the latest reports indicated the road we'd taken to get here had been belted with new fire since we'd passed through. He also said that Germans had gassed the valley, which meant we best stay high. He explained quickly that he would lead me down a back road, a narrow, winding scar along a ridge that he hoped would take us high enough to avoid the gas but low enough to stay beneath the arc of artillery fire.

I'd lost track of Cass already. Her ambulance had left my sight. I looked about before I left but couldn't spot her in the surrounding commotion. Of course she couldn't understand directions given by French drivers, who rarely spoke any English, but I couldn't wait; my orders came, and I had to move.

My hands trembled as I grasped the steering wheel. I glanced back at the collapsed soldier beside the tent, his eyes still open, his chest not moving, flies beginning to circle.

As I followed the driver along the exposed ridge, the Boche artillery offense intensified, and shrapnel scuttled and thrashed on the ground around us in some kind of evil gravelly dance set to the sound of louder and closer booms. So the shells could reach us after all. Smoke and dust and heat and a gaseous odor everywhere. I heard a bloodcurdling shrill, and instinctively I ducked.

The French ambulance stopped dead in front of me. The engine hissing and steaming, it had to have suffered a hit. The driver helped his *assis* to my vehicle, telling me, "I took a whizz-bang in the radiator," and urging the soldier to cling to the right running board. Then he pushed his car aside and told me to keep driving. Calmly, as if we had met on a lovely road and had just pulled over for a chat.

"What about your *couchés*?" I asked in French in a voice that could not have been mine. It sounded almost composed.

He peered inside for a half second. "I'll flag down an ambulance on the way in and transfer them over. Now go," he said.

Something jagged lodged in my chest. "Will someone come along here?"

"That's my problem. Now leave."

Was I leaving them to die? I gripped the wheel and scarcely breathed as I squeezed past his ambulance and continued on my way, not sure how I would ever find Meaux again. It wouldn't matter, however, if we got hit. Somehow I blocked out the earth-shattering blasts and high-pitched screeches and concentrated only on the road ahead. I could hear shells whining in to make landfall, and I braced my body for the worst. Whenever I came to a fork in the road, I chose one path and hoped that an internal compass would lead me the right way.

Images of Maman and Luc flashed before my eyes. Now that I had come across an ocean and found myself in the midst of war, the rest of the world felt huge, and my life felt small. But to my mother and brother, my life meant everything. Maybe I shouldn't have come here. If I died, Maman and Luc would be left destitute. I couldn't imagine where they would go and what they would do.

At last I descended into a shallow valley away from the fighting, and it became apparent that I'd chosen correctly. The road, although heavily congested with service vehicles headed toward the front and more refugees escaping the area, looked familiar. My heart left my throat. When I encountered oncoming ambulances, I stopped and told one of the drivers about the man and his passengers I'd left behind. He nodded and waved me past. I didn't know if he went after his comrade or decided the rescue posed too big of a risk.

A terrible ache in my stomach convinced me I'd never eat again. I drove onward, and it seemed impossible that a flock of birds took flight over the road and soared above us, black wings against a blue sky, oblivious to the ugliness below. After a drive of almost thirty miles, I pulled into Meaux, where others unloaded my *couchés*, and the other two men could walk inside for assistance.

A French village woman shoved a cup of tea in my hands. I said *"Merci"* and gulped it down, but did not linger.

If I stopped for a moment's rest, I might not start again. Another French ambulance pulled out, so I followed it as it took a different route, which seemed quieter but took longer.

Reaching the front, we pulled up to an advance dressing station tucked into a cave. We found an ambulance driver and a stretcher-bearer standing nonchalantly under a tree outside the *poste* smoking cigarettes. I wondered what we were supposed to do. The French driver told us an artillery battle was raging in the valley below, and the *brancardiers* had probably crouched under cover trying to save their own necks. But they would come, he said, as soon as it quieted somewhat.

The men offered us a smoke, and I took one, but after a few puffs I began to feel dizzy and turned mine over to the stretcher-bearer, who had just ground his butt into the dirt at his feet.

Nearby, two military policemen tried to restrain a frenzied man who swung his arms in the air at nothing. One of the officers attempted to subdue him with handcuffs while the other offered soothing words. The French stretcher-bearer followed my gaze and flatly said, *"Commotionné."*

The doctors once told us about this condition; they called it war neurosis. I'd also heard it referred to as shell shock and fatigue of battle. I looked away from the scene, as it seemed disrespectful to watch. I glanced back only when it became quiet, and the tortured man had finally been restrained and maybe drugged, too. Now he lay passed out in something of a stupor on the ground and only jerked from time to time.

Finally there must have been some relief from the shelling below, because soon after that, a procession of stretcher-bearers brought in the worst of the wounded, many suffering from multiple bullet wounds—chest or abdominal hits—and others with pieces of shrapnel embedded in their skulls. The other driver told me those men wouldn't make it once the pieces were removed in an operating room.

Following yet another driver, I took a different route back, within sight of the German trenches. Another barrage launched, and the incoming shells erupted the earth with flying stones and shards as we took the road as fast as possible. We had to speed past a roadside battery of three thundering 75s.

Something exploded nearby, and my teeth vibrated as I airlifted from my seat for a moment. With everything silent after that, I feared my eardrums had shattered, but it turned out to be only a second's response to sound-shock, and my weight and hearing returned. Difficult to believe that only a week or so earlier in a Paris bar, I had casually sipped on a drink named for the French weapons at work that day.

Once out of firing range, we passed some former battlefields, the worst sights I endured during my time in France. Bodies lay along the road. Horses pulled the French supply wagons, and we passed over ground strewn with the stiffened bodies of horses. Covering my nose and fighting off a gag, I noticed that one horse still lived, although writhing in pain. Its legs likely broken, it would never stand again. Death would be slow and excruciating.

I had to turn away and gulp back bile. Some people would say we shouldn't care so much for an animal, but nothing could alleviate its suffering. We drivers had not been issued guns, so a coup de grâce wasn't possible.

After that, although I remembered everything later, a sense of numbness held me together, until finally by early evening we stopped driving, and relief *ambulanciers* took over. The upcoming moonless night meant that the front would probably get quiet, but the relief drivers would make careful rounds after nightfall anyway to look for those left behind.

My knees almost unhinged as I made my way among the released-from-duty French drivers, now quietly talking, leaning against their ambulances, smoking cigarettes, and drinking what was probably *pinard,* a low-quality red wine issued to French soldiers. Maybe they drank to bury all that we'd seen that day. Peace had left this place so entirely that I wondered if it could ever find its way back. But the other drivers seemed unmoved.

Time and again, I asked about the French driver I'd left behind on the ridge, but I didn't know his name or his ambulance number, my description of him wasn't specific enough, and the men couldn't help. They struck me as too weary to do more and wanted only to experience the relief of surviving another day.

Overwhelmed with loss for a moment, I searched the horizon. Despite the war dust in the air, the sinking sun left behind streaks of muted pinks and tangerine, and the coming night felt like a cool cloth on my skin.

But the nearness of so much death had transformed me. Never would anything look the same. I daren't think of Maman and Luc, of *home.* I was no longer the girl from Kentucky before Papa died, the girl who loved horses, who'd learned old-world manners from her mother, and whose worst days had occurred when it rained and she couldn't ride.

"Arlene?"

I spun around and saw a dirt-smudged American wearing a driver's uniform. With his face obscured by a thin layer of grime, it took me a moment or so to recognize him.

"Arlene?" he said again.

I blinked. Jimmy. Jimmy, the boy who'd worked at Favier Farm after he'd lost his family. Jimmy Tucker, a boy from Kentucky. A boy I'd grown up with. A boy who had known my father.

Breathing deeply as if he'd sprinted to catch up, he appeared tired yet happy. You might have thought he'd just hit a home run and had raced around the bases. Despite the dirt on his face, he looked much the same as the last time I'd seen him, back at our high school graduation. Of medium height and rangy build with an energy about him, he had an all-American face, unruly brown hair and eyebrows, and a level gaze as shiny and solid as a gemstone. "What are you doing here?"

"Papa," I said in a whisper, and then I raised my voice a notch to be sure he heard me. "My father died."

His expectant expression fell, but the light remained in his face. Jimmy had always radiated something warm. "Oh, Arlene. I'm so sorry. I didn't know."

"It was an accident."

He gently took my arm and steered me a bit away from the throng of other drivers. The sky had turned blood orange. We stopped and faced each other, and he hadn't dropped his hand from my arm yet. "What happened?"

"The house caught fire. Maman, Luc, and I got out, but Papa . . . went back . . . inside." I wanted to tell him everything, but my voice began to fail.

His charming face fell even farther, his eyes glimmering. "I'm so sorry to hear about this. Your father was a fine man. The best."

"Yes. Thank you."

"I want to hear all about it, but I'm so surprised to see you." I should've been a reminder of the days when he'd been weak and poor and had lost everything, including his parents, but Jimmy appeared genuinely pleased to see me. He asked, "Why are you in uniform? What are you doing here?"

"I'm here in service to the American Women's Hospital. I'm driving an ambulance."

He shook his head as though he couldn't believe it, and then a puzzled expression overtook his face. "Why are you doing such dangerous work?"

"It's a long story."

He shook his head just slightly this time. "You know the Hun has no scruples about bombing ambulances. In fact they seek out the roads we use."

"You won't talk me out of it," I said rather flatly and realized that I was almost too tired to talk. "What are *you* doing here?"

His dazed eyes never left mine as he answered, "I would've been drafted into the army but joined up voluntarily to drive an ambulance instead. It was my only way to stay out of the trenches. Your father taught me to drive your old Lizzie and even do some minor repairs on it. If I make it out of here, Arlene," he said, his eyes bright again, "it'll be because of your father. He saved my life."

A piece of grit landed in my eye. Even this far away from the front, the burnt wind blew dust and dirt coughed up by shells and mortars, and they fell in a grainy shower from the sky. My eye teared even as I tried to blink and then rub the grit away. Jimmy took his hand away from me and fished in his uniform pocket, then pulled out a handkerchief.

I wiped my eye and batted away the scratching sensation. Then I had to smile, weak as it was. Jimmy had always been so helpful. He had always loped his way into everyone's hearts. From the kids at school, to parents, to the usually grouchy old curmudgeons who sat on park benches in town and seemed to hold almost all others in contempt, everyone liked Jimmy.

I caught myself staring into his gemstone eyes. Never before had I noticed the surrounding fringe of such long black eyelashes. Something quaked in my heart, and I had to control the urge to touch him, instead focusing hard on staying composed. It felt as though Jimmy had simply dropped down from the stars, then flown here on a Kentucky breeze, and I had no idea why his presence moved me so profoundly.

It was probably just familiarity—a face from home. I didn't know. But our youth had ended, and now as adults, we'd come here from the same hometown and had landed in the same godforsaken place. It brought on a sharp sense of loss for our former naivete, and yet I would always be grateful for those days that now seemed so pure and innocent.

He glanced back toward the other drivers still congregating in the road outside the French hospital. Then he turned back to me and said in a smooth, low voice, "Can you meet me later?"

Then I remembered what I'd been doing. The man on the ridge who'd pushed me onward. He hadn't shown any fear; maybe he hid it well. My ears rang with the sound of the incoming shells I'd somehow passed through.

I stared at Jimmy. "I'm looking for someone."

"Who?"

I hoped the man I left had ultimately flagged someone down. I couldn't have left him to die up there. My lips felt salty-dry, but I still managed to wet them and talk. "It was this morning. I followed a French driver from a field hospital on a ridge. He broke down, but he insisted I go onward. I have to . . . I need to . . . make sure he got away."

"His name?" asked Jimmy.

I wrapped my arms around myself. "I never got any information. Everything was so chaotic . . ."

"Not even his last name?"

Ashamed, I shook my head. Why hadn't I thought ahead?

"I understand." Probably trying to hide the truth—that my search was hopeless—he shook his head. "There's so many of us here, but I know some of the French drivers who speak English. I'll ask around."

"Thank you."

"Tell you what, you should probably get something to eat. I will, too, but then I'll get on it, and we can meet again later. I bet you haven't walked the town or climbed Saint Stephen's tower yet."

"I also have to find Cass . . . my friend Cass." I hadn't seen her since our first stop.

His gaze flew over me—I must have looked filthy and disheveled—and then settled on my face again. "Was this your first day here?"

"At the front, yes."

His eyes reached out in a way that spoke of beckoning arms. *Come to me,* they said. He could've swept me up and taken me away, and I wouldn't have cared about anything else, not even my duty here. That wasn't, however, true. I muttered again, "I have to find her."

"I understand, but meet me later?"

I shook my head; it felt as if it would wobble off its base. But I could still think straight. Jimmy was an enlisted man, and I had promised not to fraternize. "I can't. We're not supposed to—"

"Oh, I forgot," he said, but I discerned no malice. He actually smiled but in a sorrowful way. "You've always done what you were told; you followed your mother's direction."

I came close to denying that, but could I truthfully do so? When my mother had discouraged friendship with Jimmy, I had obeyed her. Some of my mother's concern had probably come from fear of his bad luck, but some of it had likely come from her notions of class distinctions, too. Like my father, I had never considered those things much, and now I saw them as nothing. Less than hollow or empty, simply nothing.

I had always admired the way Jimmy never took himself too seriously. Long ago, a few times he'd winked at me when no one else was looking, and once after he'd saddled my horse, he left a little flower on the seat.

But even during our childhood, I perceived gravity beneath the surface. I came upon him once, and it seemed I had interrupted him in

108

silent prayer. And the way he sometimes looked at my father made me think he longed for his.

I could've so easily fallen for him and his charming combination of vitality and vulnerability, but during my teenage years I'd lacked the courage to go against my mother. How had Jimmy felt when I stopped going out to the stables to share jokes together, tease each other, and talk about horses, races, and jockeys? He probably knew it had at least something to do with our different stations in society.

And yet he treated me so nicely now. But that was Jimmy; he would never hold a grudge. And now I had to watch as his hopes for me caved.

I wanted to believe I'd flown away from the teenager who followed her mother's advice and preferences; I had to believe my wings, if I still had them when this war ended, would come away shaded differently. Before I left Kentucky, even Maman had told me to take my own journey. Now, both Jimmy and I had landed here, at this exact moment in time. He breathed in the same death-air I breathed.

Even so, his face held such sweetness and hope; he also looked a little dazed. Jimmy had loved my father. Jimmy was *home*. A place I hadn't seen for a long time and might never see again. Perhaps none of us would make it out of here. But standing before me now was a man who made me feel hope and happiness despite it all. How I admired him! I felt sure that at one time he had admired me, too. During all those years of school together and the time in our stables, had I ever touched him?

My hand went to his cheek, and he clasped it in his rough but firm grasp and held it there, closing his eyes for a moment and pressing my palm into his skin, then opening up slowly, his face a passage to another place. Together in that one touch and the look on his face, our youthful past caught up with the present moment.

I no longer cared about pleasing others. Jimmy had appeared as if by miracle, and my old feelings returned in a rush, like a wild burst of wind or a racehorse lunging from the gate. I wanted to talk to him; I wanted to be with him. But *Cass*. I had to pull away. Now that she had entered my mind, I couldn't let it go. I said to Jimmy, "I'll meet you later. Of course I will."

"Out here? An hour and a half?" He smiled. "Or should we hide from everyone down in some alley?"

I broke out into a real smile, the first one in a while. Jimmy had always had that effect on me. "Perhaps in the latrine?"

He laughed. "Here in an hour and a half, then," he said, and I nodded.

Inside the compound courtyard, I glanced around, longing to set my eyes on Cass, and when I spotted her along with Dr. Rayne and Dr. Kitchens sitting on the grass and heartily drinking tea, my strength started to return. She had made it back unharmed! I resisted the urge to collapse beside her and engage in gleeful hugging.

Like me, the others had just stopped working. The doctors had treated the wounded all day, and although they must have been exhausted, they also looked exhilarated. I could scarcely imagine what it felt like to save a life; they'd probably done that many times today. Shy Dr. Kitchens in particular seemed reborn. She rarely made eye contact and often faded into the background, but this evening she glowed, her eyes ablaze, her posture confident.

But Cass, why, her appearance shook me. Not only her soiled uniform and her face smudged with dirt, but her eyes, which stared out at me and gazed around as if they would never see the world the same way again. What had happened to her? Of course we'd seen horrendous things; of course it looked and felt worse than any of us could have imagined, but what else? Had someone mistreated her? Had she come close to her own mortality? I had to get her alone to find out.

We didn't talk about our experiences in any detail, and the doctors soon said they would grab a meal and then make rounds in the wards.

After they left, I said to Cass, "Go for a walk?"

She spoke as if from inside a hollow chamber. She wouldn't look at me. "I have to wash the ambulance. It's full of blood and . . ." She swallowed with great effort.

"I know what's there. The ambulances can wait. Please . . . go for a walk with me. I have to get away from here." That wasn't altogether true—since I'd seen Jimmy and my friends from the AWH, especially Cass, my strength had returned—but Cass would probably step away more readily if she thought it would help *me.*

Slowly she rose, and we walked out of the compound, through the village, and into some nearby woods, where dozens of makeshift huts and lean-tos housed refugees. Even in spots of natural beauty, human suffering had not abated. Those devastated, homeless souls were so kind as to offer us food. We thanked them but declined, of course.

After coming to a clearing, Cass turned to face me. Her face clouded, her eyes tormented, she said, "I don't think I can do this." Then she broke down.

Never had I imagined this. Cass, who could do anything. Cass, the most competent person I'd ever known, and here the situation had overwhelmed her, or worse. I took her by the shoulders and let her cry. She released pathetic sobs that racked her body, and she rubbed her eyes so fiercely I feared she would injure them.

"Did you have a close call? Did someone treat you unkindly?"

"No," she said and shook her head. "It's all of it. I felt sick from the beginning, and it only got worse. I had to get out and throw up, and my *assis* saw it. I don't think I'm cut out for this after all. I don't know if I can do this."

Stunned by her words, I slowly said, "Of course you can."

She stared into my eyes. "What are we doing here? It's not even our war. This has nothing to do with us."

I'd never heard Cass discuss the politics of war, but I knew enough to ascertain that she didn't really mean what she said. The Cass I knew would not say this. "Cass, you know why we're here. For a good reason."

"Are you sure? Have you found it?"

At a loss for words, I shifted my weight.

Just as I started to answer, she said, "Just as I thought. There's nothing you can say."

"Yes, there is."

"You haven't even launched a defense."

"I'm thinking about you, not about defending our position here."

Cass swiped at fresh tears. "Because there's no good reason, and I doubt you'll ever find one. But if by some rare chance you do, please let me know."

As expected, her breakdown didn't last long, and I hoped that perhaps the reaction to our experiences today would ease. What we'd seen would traumatize anyone. I hoped her mood would pass, but it looked as if something essential inside her had slipped away. Shell shock. Fatigue of battle. War neurosis. Apparently, it didn't take long to strike.

No one knew with certainty how he or she would react to horrors, but who would've guessed that bashful Dr. Margie Kitchens would blossom under such conditions and Cass Frank would wilt?

Afraid to leave her alone, I remained at her side for the rest of the evening. The time to meet Jimmy passed, but I told myself I would manage to get away later. I kept hoping Cass would go to sleep, but her wide-open, haunted eyes haunted me. If I left her, I worried what she would do. Jimmy would understand my tardiness once I explained about Cass. I owed it to her to stay until she got better.

Much later when Cass finally dozed off, I slipped outside and found the spot where I'd seen Jimmy before. Now hours past our meeting time, of course he was not there.

A chill rode up my arms and tightened my scalp. So tired and worried about Cass, I hadn't met Jimmy in time. And I had let it happen.

I had let minutes and then hours go by. I had put friendship and duty before my heart.

I pictured Jimmy's kind face and the disappointment he must have felt when I didn't show up, and I felt sick. Thinking it the right thing to do, I'd stayed with Cass too long. And now I thought of what I'd missed—more time with Jimmy, talking the way only those who grew up together can talk, looking into those gemstone eyes—and it devastated me.

Back in the sleeping quarters, I crawled into bed and stared at the water-stained ceiling overhead. Exhausted, I nevertheless could not close my eyes. So much had changed in just one day.

Sleep evaded me for hours. The old Arlene had died and returned to life, once after the fire and here again in the war zone. So far from friends and family, I recalled moonless nights on the farm, the sky strewn with a ridiculous number of stars, and I, as a young girl, reaching up, hoping to grab just a few for me. Today Jimmy had come within reach, and I'd touched him, then let him go. I imagined him billeted somewhere nearby and I would see him in the morning. I had to believe that Jimmy and I would have another chance meeting soon. But a lonely and regretful reaction surfaced within me, needling me with the awful idea that he might not come within reach again.

Chapter Thirteen

In Meaux, we slept in barracks-like rooms lined with single beds occupied by other women in the medical service. I managed to get a bed next to Cass, and when not asleep—fatigue took me away for a while—I could hear her tangling with the sheets and sometimes jerkily moving her body. At one point she turned around and put her head at the foot of the bed. She probably slept but a few hours, or maybe not at all.

In the morning, at first her face appeared wan, as if all energy and emotion had drained from it. "Are you alright?" I asked her as we readied ourselves for the day ahead. We'd gotten coffee in the mess hall and sat for a moment before the sun rose.

She shrugged and gazed off, but her jaw trembled. Sorrow floated in her eyes when she faced me fully, but then she looked away again. What had happened to my Cass? Last night gripped by awful doubts and anger, now she exhibited a terrible sadness. The anger felt more appropriate and safer than the sadness.

Cass and Beryl, so far, had kept me on course, like those planes flying in lofty V wedges over our heads. Now I had to fortify myself and stay solid for Cass.

She glanced over at me. "You seem to be holding up pretty well." A muscle in her jaw shuddered as she spoke.

I said firmly, "It's an act."

She rubbed her arms and touched her face. "Then you're a better actress than I am."

I took the first sip of my coffee. "My mother once told me that if you act the part, sometimes you become the person you're playing."

Cass said nothing.

"You actually become who you're pretending to be." No reaction.

"So . . . you just fake it for a while until it becomes true."

Cass squeezed her eyes shut as if warding off memories and images she didn't want to recall. "I don't think that's going to work for me."

"Of course it will. And you can talk to me anytime. Furthermore, I want us to stay together today and from here on out, no matter what."

She nodded.

I went on: "So we're scared. We can form our own little club—let's call it the Chicken Feathers Club."

"Chicken feathers? You're such a farm girl."

"At your service."

She smiled. I'd made her smile, and so I allowed myself a moment of relief.

Outside, I looked about for Jimmy but saw no American ambulances. I wanted to explain why I'd failed to meet him the night before and see if we could try to meet up again. But he must have left already.

Just after dawn, Cass and I got our ambulances started and got ready to leave. Starting our engines always turned into an adventure. The trick was to crank the engine to life without wrapping your thumb around the crank handle, or else you could really hurt yourself.

The others told us there might be less fighting today, and when we set out, I followed Cass. As we pulled up to the field hospital, a lone man in a bloodied uniform sitting outside flagged me over, and when he realized I spoke French, he said in a raspy, almost whining voice, "I've waited for an hour." He tried to pull in air, but it looked as if breathing took enormous effort. He nodded toward the hospital tent. "What's keeping them?"

"I'll find out," I reassured him. "Don't worry."

Inside I inquired of a French nurse on behalf of the man outside, and she said resignedly, "We can't help him. We're working on the ones we can save. He has a hole in both lungs. He's going to die."

I failed to swallow for a long time after that.

I could tell the nurse was impressed by my French, but not by the reaction on my face.

"Come now," she said and added the French equivalent of "Grow some skin."

With my ambulance almost loaded, I approached the man again. He had lapsed into unconsciousness, his breathing a barely discernible whistle. I stood quiet for a moment, little pieces of my heart falling away. Then even the breathing stopped.

On the ride back, Cass and I took our own way. My *assis*, a soldier whose hand was gone, sat still and stared forward and never said a word until we'd traveled about halfway to Meaux. Then he muttered in French, "God must have saved me." Maybe in some way, the soldier was grateful for the wound, in that he couldn't go back into battle again. Maybe the loss of his hand would save his life.

One of my other riders, a German soldier, had received the same treatment as that of a French or Allied patient. Later some mumbling came from the back that sounded German.

One of the French soldiers in back shouted to me, "Stop! He's full of bullets, and he is dying. He wants something."

I parked and walked around to the back so I could listen closer to the German. He tried to tell me to stop driving. I supposed he wanted some silence and peace before he died.

I quickly consulted with Cass. We decided to stop in the next village. For that moment, no hatred, no war existed—just human tragedy. But by the time we pulled up to a small Catholic church in the village, the man had died.

"So much for that," Cass said as we prepared to keep moving. Her eyes held a haunted shadow.

Pushing onward, only a stone's throw outside the village now, I spotted movement at the side of the road. I waved to Cass to stop. And then a group of men materialized out of the dust and smoke, like ghosts emerging from a fog. About ten of them, all wounded. They explained that their village had taken a barrage of shelling, and although injured themselves, they had set off on foot to find help, but now they couldn't go on. When they spotted our ambulances, they thought rescue had arrived.

When I explained that our ambulances could hold no more, several begged us to try to fit them in in any possible way.

Since the German soldier was dead, I drove back to the church we'd passed, and with a villager's help I unloaded the body. A priest appeared and said he would take care of it.

By the time I returned to the scene on the road, Cass had been forced to choose between the French men and determine which one would catch the ride on my now-empty stretcher. Together we loaded a man who held on to his abdomen as if for life. He said he'd taken several bullets there. The others protested, saying their injuries were worse, and we decided to let a couple of the more able-bodied men hang on to our floorboards. We reassured the ones left behind we or someone else would come back for them.

On the road again toward Meaux, I got to wondering how, if the men's village had undergone shelling, my passenger had received bullet wounds. Had Cass been duped into taking a man less hurt than some of the others? I hadn't seen a lot of blood. Even worse, they might have fooled us into transporting deserters, but then again, how had they obtained the civilian clothing? I didn't know, but something seemed amiss.

In Meaux I spoke to a French driver who said he would go by the village and find the men we'd encountered on the road as he was experienced and could spot deserters in his sleep. He promised that he would try to talk with the man we'd brought in, too, so I turned it over. Then I remembered the German I'd left at the church and hoped the priest would make sure he'd get a proper burial.

During our next run, we both carried full loads back to Meaux. The man in my cab, a French officer wounded in the thigh, wanted to talk. His injury didn't appear very serious or painful, and he liked that we could converse in French.

He had such a nice way about him when he told me, "We French are so grateful for you Americans here." My father would've been proud. The officer told me about his wife and son at home in Paris and his best friend, who had perished in the war during its first year.

Just past a tiny hamlet on the way to Meaux, I must have picked up a nail, and the rear right tire went flat. Cass pulled over, and we intended to replace the inner tube together, but two rangy, eager boys from the hamlet showed up and insisted we let them do it for us. We acquiesced and found a cool spot beneath a linden tree on the side of the road. The French officer hobbled over to sit with us.

Cass said, "I should probably go on."

"No," I responded quickly. I didn't want her to go alone. Our passengers didn't seem as seriously injured as the ones earlier in the day, and the boys would fix the tire in no time. "Just wait a few minutes."

She sat down with the French officer and me, but she gazed away and simply listened to the conversation the man and I carried on in French. I would've switched, but the officer couldn't speak any English.

Even in the midst of this awful war, surrounded by conflict, I found a moment of peace simply sitting beneath a tree and feeling the breeze on my face. Cass would get through this, I told myself. We would both get through this.

The tire soon fixed, we rose to go onward. But Cass whispered rather urgently to me and in a strangled voice, "You belong here." As I drove away, I tried to figure out what Cass had meant. Did she mean I belonged here because I could speak French? Or did she mean I was doing well here and implying again that she wasn't doing as well?

Ordered to stay put for a while in Meaux, we searched out some bread, cheese, and coffee and waited. It gave me another opportunity to search for Jimmy, but I didn't see American ambulances anywhere.

I sat on the trampled but dry grass in the courtyard with Cass for a few moments' rest. There was no such thing as an easy day in France. But it had somehow turned into a lovely afternoon.

Cass, however, wasn't eating her bread, and she stared away with an absent look on her face I'd seen before. I had no idea where she went or what filled her head.

I scooted closer. "Why won't you eat?"

"I can't," she said, still staring away at nothing. "I can't stop seeing it."

"Seeing what?"

"What one of those men on the road told me. He could speak some English, and he pantomimed the rest of it."

"What did he say?"

She faced me, and her pained expression hit me with a bit of a shock. Her brow furrowed with deep lines, she answered, "He said that in no-man's-land, hundreds of contorted human beings lie in different states of rot. Headless bodies, arms and legs, hands and feet, all in piles being picked over by big black birds."

I pulled in a long breath. "Don't think about it."

"I see it in my head."

"Well, I wish the man hadn't told you about that. We don't even know if it's true."

"It's true," she said and then looked off again.

"We can't be certain that everything people say is true." I found it maddening that this soldier had described the gruesome scene to Cass for no apparent reason. I wished he had told me instead. Somehow, someway, I *was* taking it all better than Cass was.

Later one of the volunteers who served coffee and food searched me out and passed over a folded sheet of paper, which I opened immediately.

> *Dear Arlene,*
> *Our company has been ordered to another site in Charly-sur-Marne, closer to the front. Before we left I talked to several of the French drivers, and they didn't know anything about the man you drove with on the ridge yesterday. Rest assured that if someone had gone missing, they would've heard about it by now. Please don't worry yourself any more.*
> *I'm sorry I didn't see you again last night.*
> *Keep safe,*
> *Jimmy*

The letter drifted down into my lap. Even though I'd stood him up, Jimmy had tried to find out about the French driver, and he'd sought to reassure me. He hadn't berated me or even asked why I hadn't met him as promised.

I would've expected no less. Always the gentleman. I had to see him again; I just had to. But we'd met by happenstance, and ambulance companies had spread all over. Reassignments happened very often and quickly.

I'd probably lost any chance to grasp that star in my hand again. Most likely he thought I'd stood him up because I didn't want to see him, or because I was too scared to disobey orders. My eyes stung, and I damned myself yet again. Now I had no way to explain why I hadn't shown up and to ask for forgiveness. No way to atone.

And yet I'd seen him and touched him, such special gifts; he'd brought back memories of my father and my former life. At least I had those to comfort me.

I blinked and pictured a cold Saturday, a warm, sweet boy in our stables. He and I were about fifteen at the time, and he was working early, despite deep snow having fallen overnight. I bundled up as I made my way from the house, my feet sinking through the frozen waves before me, leaving perfect figure-eight tracks in my wake.

When I entered the open doors at one end, I heard Jimmy working in the stalls down near the other. The shovel made a scraping sound as he mucked out manure and soiled straw, and I could also hear some humming.

Jimmy, unaware of my presence, hummed.

The horses stood warm in their stalls, and each of their breaths released a frosty brew into the air that lifted and then vanished. The sun poured inside from the open door at the stables' other end, and an odd sense of peace and reverence came over me. Something there . . . caught in a perfect moment, held in the open palm of that perfect winter day, and I became lost in it, aware that for the rest of my life a morning would never again look this lovely.

Still unaware of my presence, Jimmy set aside his bucket and shovel and moved to the open doorway opposite me and then just stood there, hitching himself with one arm against the door frame, his silhouette all I could see. He didn't move and I didn't move, as though the same silence that had overcome me had overcome him, too. He gazed out over the blanketed land as though he imagined himself a part of it. He'd always treated our horses as if he were a part of them, too.

This was more than just a job for him; he felt at ease here, and he loved both this land and the animals. His involvement had always impressed me.

He turned and caught sight of me. He didn't jump, but his eyes widened. "Hello to you, too," he said with a smile that he crafted to appear as casual as possible.

Backlit, he made a perfect figure. When had he become so striking? I said, "I'm sorry."

"Sorry for what?"

I shrugged. "I suppose for startling you."

"Well, darn it all," he said and smiled. "I thought I'd hidden that."

I smiled back, and heat rose in my cheeks. "No need."

"May I help you with anything?"

"No," I answered. "I wanted to see the horses." I gazed around. "And I find the snow so beautiful."

He glanced down and then looked curiously at me. "Well, let me know if you need anything."

At a loss, I shrugged again, my way of appearing unfazed. "Again, I'm sorry if I startled you."

Jimmy held still for some long moments; he seemed to think very hard on a matter. Then abruptly he found the very center of my eyes. "The truth is, Arlene, you startle me every time I see you."

At that tender age and so unsure of myself, I wondered if he had complimented me or not. One could be startled in a good way, or one could be startled in a bad way. And so I said nothing. I said nothing and avoided anything I didn't understand and instead walked away and ducked back outside into the waiting cold, alone.

The memory came back to me powerfully, and now old enough, I could look back and see that of course Jimmy had meant startled in a good way. And I'd managed to hide the memory for years and years as though it had never happened.

I slipped Jimmy's note inside my pocket. I would place it next to Papa's wrinkled photo inside my bag. I had no place to set out any personal belongings in our present living quarters, but I could visit them occasionally and draw strength.

Cass had taken notice; I must have looked stunned or spellbound. "What?" she asked.

Now I stared off, but I swiftly pulled myself back. "It doesn't matter anymore."

Cass had perked up somewhat, even though her tone still rang flat. "Come on, Arlene. Don't keep me dangling in suspense."

I sighed heavily and then hated myself for it. It shouldn't have been possible for me to think of myself at such a moment, after all I'd seen the past two days. But I answered Cass truthfully. "I bumped into a boy from home. From Paris, Kentucky, home. Now he's an American ambulance driver, and I wanted to see him again, but his company was reassigned today." I'd never tell Cass I'd failed to meet him the night before because of concerns for her.

"That's unfortunate," said Cass.

"Yes," I answered softly. "But maybe it's just as well." I flashed her a smile. "He might have played havoc with my concentration and made it harder for me to keep my promises . . ."

For only a moment I glimpsed the old Cass again. "That good?" she asked.

And I nodded.

After our last run of the day, the same volunteer who'd brought me Jimmy's letter searched me out again. We ate in the mess hall, although Cass looked pensive and strange and only picked at her food. The volunteer said that someone had come and now waited for me outside.

Jimmy! Somehow, he'd come back.

"Pay me no notice," Cass said and made a shooing motion with her hand. A classic Cass move, but I saw no heart in it, as if it had become mechanical. It seemed to me that she relied on ingrained responses to hide what went on inside her now.

I said, "Please eat."

She shooed me again.

I'd only had a chance to wash my face and hands since we'd stopped driving. So I pinched my cheeks for color and strode away with the volunteer. Despite my concerns about Cass, I smiled.

Night had fallen completely, and a light wind had temporarily blown the smoke and ash of war away. In an impeccable uniform with his back to me as I approached, he suddenly turned around and projected a dashing smile.

I almost fell as I realized . . .

It was Captain Felix Brohammer.

Chapter Fourteen

I stopped.

"There's my girl," he said, the dazzling smile even more dazzling, if that was possible. Apparently I was the only person who saw something sinister in that grin.

My girl? He'd said it loud enough that some people in the courtyard had heard. A few glances landed on us. And my fear began to swell.

Still the same incredibly handsome man that women swooned over, tonight he looked strangely ill-at-ease. I stayed paralyzed by his presence the way a fox freezes when it senses some other creature has caught its scent. What was he doing here, and how had he found me, and why? Obviously he saw something appealing about me and had ignored what I'd said before.

But I rapidly told myself I had nothing to fear. Felix Brohammer, although an unlikable narcissist, didn't pose a danger. He was an American officer, an educated man, a man who'd come very far already in his life. Besides, others talked and walked and smoked nearby, and he'd never given me any reason to think he could turn violent.

I swallowed back the fear and calmly walked up to him. If I could handle all the horrific scenes and suffering at the front, I could certainly handle Felix Brohammer. "Good evening, Captain," I said. "What brings you here?"

His smile faded, but he laughed in a way that sounded forced. "You know what brings me here. I can't stop thinking about you. I can't stop missing you." He opened his arms and beamed again. "How are you, darling?"

I made no move.

His arms fell back to his sides, and then his eyes roved over my uniform. He looked back at my face with another grim smile. "I see. You need to get yourself cleaned up so I can take you out."

I didn't move. I already knew how I looked, and of course my appearance had suffered. I'd driven for hours on end, transporting the injured and sometimes the dead. He must have not done any work that day. His uniform looked perfect. Most of the other officers I'd seen appeared as haggard and worn out as the rest of us did. Felix Brohammer was a mystery, but one I had no desire to solve.

"I'm sorry, but I don't have time to go out," I said as firmly as I could while also trying not to project any fear or anger.

His expression fell flat, and his face tightened. "Do you know how difficult it's been to track you down, my dear? I thought you were in Neufmoutiers, so I wasted a trip there only to find out you'd moved here. Do you know how long I've been driving around to find you?"

Not far from him sat a Cadillac open touring car like the ones officers used. An enlisted man lounged behind the wheel, smoking cigarettes and puffing out perfect smoke rings that slowly rose in the air.

"Is that your driver?" I asked while making a small gesture that way.

He glanced over quickly, and just as quickly dismissed the fact that he himself hadn't driven. "Of course I have a driver. And of course I'll get rid of him so you can take a drive with me. I know a place—"

"I can't go. I just got in a little while ago, and I have too much to do."

As if I hadn't spoken, he went on: "It's a ridge overlooking a valley that's still untouched. It's clear tonight; we'll see stars. You'll love it."

"I can't. I can't go off like that; I still have things to finish tonight."

Standing very tall, he said, "I'll wait. I went to a lot of trouble getting here, so what's it to me if I have to wait for you to get dolled up?"

Dolled up? So many things this man said made me incredulous. How could he possibly have assumed that we ambulance drivers had any clean clothing left with which to get dolled up? But I let that go.

"Come on, sweetheart. Come out with me."

Genuinely dumbfounded, I asked, "Why?"

He grinned. "I have selfish reasons."

"Well, that's a surprise."

He threw his head back and laughed, a touch on the hysterical side, I thought. Then he stopped and looked at me with arrogance like I'd never seen before. "You're so adorable; you know that, don't you? And your resistance is rather fetching, too. But even you can't mask the obvious desire you have for me."

I shouldn't have made him laugh. "Captain Brohammer, I'm flattered by your attention, but I don't understand what you're looking for. I went out with you once, and as I recall, the evening didn't end well."

His face turned crimson, and his posture lowered for just a half second. Then his back jolted upright again. "The evening was perfect. You were the perfect blend of naivete and sophistication, of defiance and longing."

I wondered if the captain suffered from a different form of the shell shock plaguing so many soldiers. Maybe this was another manifestation of that illness, and maybe he needed help. Those considerations kept my heart leaning toward kindness.

But I had to remain firm and put any sarcasm aside, couldn't act in any way playful. In fact something about him felt even more off-kilter tonight. A little bit ominous, not just odd. "I'm sorry, but it wasn't that way."

"Of course it was. You mesmerized me. And look at all I've done to track you down."

His assertion hit me as a bit desperate. "As I said before, I'm flattered, but that doesn't mean we're a couple. We weren't a couple in Paris, and we aren't one now, either. I apologize if that's not what you want, but . . . it's the truth. I'm genuinely sorry if I gave you the wrong impression."

"It's not just an impression. It's something I know."

"But I don't see it the same way."

He took a few breaths while studying me, his eyes now darker with anger. A line etched between his brows, marring his silky face. "No one ever turns me away."

Reason wasn't working, and now I saw him as rather wretched. "Look, I'm sorry. I really am," I said. "Any other girl would find your interest most flattering. You can date any American woman, British woman, French woman you want. You're very eye-catching, as you know. It's just bad luck that you set your sights on me; I didn't come here for romance."

An image of Jimmy's face jumped into my mind. I *had* planned to meet him that night, and who knew where that might have led us? But Jimmy's presence had moved me and pulled me in, whereas Brohammer frightened me and made me want to run away.

I pushed those thoughts aside, however, and said, "There simply is no time for it, and my team leaders forbade us to fraternize with men while over here anyway."

His pupils went huge. "But you went out with me in Paris."

I said simply, "I did. But I shouldn't have done so."

How I wished I hadn't done it. I should've followed my instincts. I could've avoided all of this unpleasant business.

He interrupted my reflections. "At Neufmoutiers, I spoke with the lady in charge . . . it's Dr. Logan, isn't it?" Hair lifting on my arms, I slowly nodded. "She told me straightaway where I could find you. And she smiled as if you were her daughter. She was more than a little charmed, if I must say so myself. She knows a prize when she sees it."

"Did you see Kitty, Lottie, and Eve? The other ambulance drivers? They're all adorable." I stopped myself. I couldn't send someone ailing from a strange delusional state to those sweet girls. Any one of them would jump at the chance to be his girl, and I couldn't imagine anything good resulting from that.

"I saw them," he said matter-of-factly. "Do you think you're going to convince me to turn away and find someone else?" As if I'd answered yes, he went on. "You don't know me very well, then. When I go after something, I usually get it."

"All I can offer you is my friendship."

He stood still for several long moments, blinking every few seconds. As if soaking it in, trying to make himself believe it. Then his shoulders lowered. "Friendship it is," he finally said with another forced smile. "For now."

I nodded. "Thank you."

"So now that that's settled, will you go for a ride with me?"

This man was relentless, and I then knew that I didn't have the knowledge to deal with this. I'd convinced myself I wouldn't have to see him again, but now it seemed I'd created a personal mess, one I could've avoided had I not gone out with Brohammer in the first place. "I really can't. It's hectic here from the crack of dawn until nightfall. This isn't a party. I can't just . . . just . . . go off on a drive . . ."

"A stroll, then?"

I had no idea what to do. Would I make it better or worse if I went for a stroll? Would he see it as encouragement, or would he finally see that my mind was made up?

"Come on, say yes," he said, and then his smile gleamed again. How could someone who looked so well in fact be so troubled? "I don't bite."

Breathing out a big release of held-in air, I answered, "Very well."

We made plans to meet again in an hour's time.

When I returned to the mess hall table, Cass sat and played with her food. She perked up when she saw me.

"And . . . ?" she asked.

I shook my head. "It was Brohammer."

She openly gaped and dropped her fork. "Brohammer? You don't mean—"

"Yes, I thought I'd gotten rid of him, but he has found me."

She stared hard at me now as I slipped down beside her on the bench. At least I'd taken her focus off the war for a few minutes. She said, "This is getting kind of odd now, isn't it?"

"I agree. He thinks we're a couple. It's odd, yes, but I also wonder if it's some weird effect from the war."

"I doubt that. Everything has hit me hard here, but I'm not having any delusions. Bad memories, yes, but really, Arlene, I don't think fooling oneself about love is a symptom of shell shock."

Relief washed over me. Cass had brightened. Maybe some focus on my problems *had* helped her. "I said I'd take a stroll with him later."

"What?"

"At first he insisted we take a drive. I turned him down and offered my friendship."

"He's disturbing, isn't he?" She paused as something dark seemed to cloud her thoughts. "Everything about this place is disturbing. I'd never imagined . . ." Tears gathered in Cass's eyes. "I haven't slept a full hour."

Cass took turns so quickly.

I shifted my weight to face her. My problem couldn't compare to hers. "We won't stay here forever. The front will move, Cass; believe me, the needs will change, and at some point, we'll move back from the front lines. All we have to do is get through it a little longer."

She shook her head. "I hated it back in Neufmoutiers, too."

"But you seemed fine."

"I wasn't fine."

I had to watch as she moved even farther away. Somehow I'd used sheer determination to get through it all, but the same ability loomed just beyond Cass's reach. She disappeared again, back into the nightmare.

I touched her arm. "We'll stay together. That helped today, didn't it?"

Her brows knitted. "Not much," she eventually answered, and the way she spoke told me it came from within some gory scene in her mind.

I sighed and said, "Well, it sure helped me."

"You're different. I never saw it before."

"Yes, we're different. You've always had more strength, much more than me."

She shook her head and then whispered, "Nothing . . . nothing . . ."

"Cass." I scooted closer. "What do you mean by *nothing*?"

"Nothing can help me."

After Cass told me she wanted to rest and left the table, I returned to the spot outside where I'd talked to Felix Brohammer. An hour hadn't yet passed, but he stood there already, or perhaps he'd never stepped away. His car, however, was no longer parked in the same place, and the area seemed deserted.

"Captain," I said as I walked up. There it came again, that dazzling smile so bright that few people would ever see beneath the shine. "I can't go for a stroll with you after all. I'm worried about a friend of mine and don't want to leave her alone. I'm sorry."

His smile soured. With his eyes trained on me, he laughed without mirth. "Sure you are."

I gave a half shrug. "Believe what you will, but someone else needs me tonight."

He shifted his weight. "So, who is he?"

"He?" I spurted out. This was getting even crazier. "It's a woman, a dear friend of mine. She's not dealing with all the awfulness over here as well as she thought she would. And I've pledged to myself that I'll remain as close as possible to her until she gets better."

"Very noble of you," he said.

I prepared to turn away and leave. "As I said, believe what you will."

"What's her name?"

I halted and turned back. Why would he want her name? Perhaps he was trying to make me stumble and somehow reveal that my cause for refusing him *was* another man. But I'd never give him Cass's name. I couldn't imagine what he might do with it.

"I'm not giving you her name." I took a step backward. "Good night, Captain."

He said nothing as I turned and strode away.

Another voice, however, caught my attention. I hadn't noticed them before, but a couple of French soldiers sat in the grass over in the shadows, their elbows resting lazily on their knees as they smoked cigarettes. Their eyes glued to me. How long had they watched? I witnessed them glance back at Brohammer, too.

The conversation was muffled and in French. Still, I distinctly heard one of the soldiers say in a disgusted manner, *"Il se fait du beurre sur le dos de ses propres hommes,"* a French saying that essentially translates to "He makes money off his own men."

Someone was making money off his own men? Brohammer?

At the door, I glanced behind me. Brohammer still stood there, but I never met his eyes. No one else stood or sat close to the two men sitting in the grass. They must have been talking about the captain.

I waited a while inside, giving Brohammer time to leave, while my thoughts turned into a maze. Then I went back outside to search for the French soldiers I'd overheard. I needed to ask them what they had meant.

Makes money off his own men . . .

Instead I saw that Brohammer had left, but so had the French soldiers.

I returned to the mess hall, where on many evenings small groups of medical staff stayed up late, often drinking, playing cards, and gambling. They told trench jokes, and one doctor who could speak English translated the *Wipers Times*, a British trench magazine full of tongue-in-cheek humor, and read it out loud to the others.

Knowing I probably wouldn't sleep, I joined them for a while and found myself admiring how people so close to the battlefield could laugh and play and talk, completely absorbed in the moment, as if no war existed and certainly not just outside their door.

I didn't stay long. I couldn't stop hearing those soldiers' words in my head.

Makes money off his own men . . .

That night as I lay in bed, sleepless as I'd predicted, I turned that phrase over and over in my mind. Why had they said that, and did they really say it about Brohammer? How had I let them slip away? I would have to search for them in the morning to find out more.

Makes money off his own men . . .

Chapter Fifteen

When I looked back on France later in my life, I would remember it as a series of contrasts. We stepped from quiet scenes of beauty and tranquility into the urgency and thunder of war, like stepping from one foot to the other. One call, one sight in the distance, one message received, and everything changed.

I would remember lounging amid flowers in a Meaux garden, eating cake and listening to the sounds of a softly tinkling fountain; I might see a burst of artillery fire in the distance, but all else around me made no sound, no movement. At the start of the day, we could gaze at a field coming into daylight and teeming with life. I might look up into a cloudless sky and spot a single star or an airplane looping lazily overhead.

Then orders would come to leave, and we would immediately enter a world of horrors. We drove past stiff bodies and partially decayed bodies, crumbled villages, weary *poilus* on the road, and charred and cratered fields, while nearby, men in barbed-wire-protected trenches waged war with machine guns. A world of ruin—gray skies, gray roads, gray fields, empty gray villages—a place decaying before its time. What a mess man had made of it.

Even looking back on it years later, the two sets of memories seemed completely unrelated to each other.

Every day as the sun set, we felt lucky to have made it through another day. Overhead the enemy Gothas searched us out. They had no qualms about striking ambulances and hospitals. Several French drivers had perished since we'd arrived at the front. On top of it all, I never saw those soldiers who'd gossiped about Brohammer again, and I never heard anything else from Jimmy, either.

And still I found comfort in the twilight, as we were safe for now, and it made me think of Papa. Often he had smoked a cigar on the porch; other times he drank bourbon. But more than anything, he loved to simply sit and watch the sunset in something of a hypnotic state. He seemed even more awestruck as the fireflies came out. I closed my eyes and saw him there.

But his features had begun to blur in my mind, and, horrified, I willed them to clarify. And yet the harder I tried to conjure them up, the faster they faded. Each day the sights and sounds of the world in chaos drowned my memories, burying them farther and farther beneath the surface.

One day Cass and I teamed up with a French driver named Emile, a small, dark-eyed man who, despite his obvious war-weariness and grimy uniform, had me imagining him wearing a beret and making brushstrokes on a canvas. Emile turned out to know the land by heart, and he was an excellent driver with good instincts.

Near the front lines, we detoured toward smoke we could see from a distance. Most of the towns close to the front had been abandoned, but some villagers remained in their homes no matter what.

We moved onward to an unadorned hamlet of simple stone-and-plaster houses built along a low ridgeline that led to a church and what I could only assume was the village center. Germans bombarded the village with shells and mortar as a fire raged, making sure no townspeople could douse the flames. The sounds of hits ricocheted and echoed off the walls, making us experience everything two- and three-fold. No one tried to get into the homes, and no one brought out the injured and burned.

Emile hand-signaled out of his window to indicate that we should head in, so we crossed a small bridge and headed up a narrow road with a high village wall on one side that I prayed would hold.

My chest wracked with coughing and my eyes burning, I took up the rear as we sped on toward the central square, where we parked under some bedraggled trees in an attempt to hide from the German planes. Although not at the front, our position terrified me more than any other. Sitting ducks, we couldn't hide, and my forehead started bleeding sweat.

The fire hadn't reached the village's heart, but the walls of the church standing in the middle were pitted, the steeple cocked and mutilated, every window broken. To the side of the door lay a dead man on his back. Someone had thrown a blanket over his body, but his head rested in a perfect circle of blood like some macabre death halo.

I glanced over at Cass. She had laid her head against her steering wheel. I started to jump out and go talk with her, but a few stunned-looking village men began bringing us their wounded and burned. With all three ambulances loaded full, we promised to return for more of the injured. I followed Cass, who had picked herself up and now trailed Emile. We crossed the small bridge again and turned back toward Meaux.

Mere yards past the bridge, a loud hissing screech chilled my blood, and I braced for impact. The Germans had found us. I turned in terror as the bridge exploded into pieces. The water rose as if in slow motion while bits of sharp wood and pointed mortar pieces fell all around. Luckily the debris didn't puncture a tire or penetrate the body of my ambulance.

So we had survived, but for how long? Emile signaled for us to leave the area at once.

As I drove away, I asked myself if the bridge was the only way in and out. Two of my passengers in the back screamed in agony from severe burns, however, and I had to get them to the hospital as quickly as possible. Horrible to admit, but I had grown more accustomed to hearing the sounds of human suffering. I smelled burnt flesh, even up front in the cab, and my *assis*, her head wrapped in a bloodstained shawl, covered her nose with a handkerchief.

We delivered our villagers and then turned back immediately. Emile said perhaps we could get back in via a road on the other side of the village. But we found it riddled with craters, so battered one had to peer closely to make out a road at all. Emile told Cass and me to stay put, and he slowly started driving it, picking a course over the remains of the road, but only a hundred feet in, his ambulance got stuck in a shell hole—he called it a crump-hole—and I had to help him pull the ambulance out.

Failing to find any other route, we drove to the ruined bridge and stopped. The Germans had ceased shelling, probably because the village was obviously doomed. Flames rose like columns amid churning clouds of black smoke, and the floating ash filled the air so thickly it made our eyes water. We stood outside our ambulances waiting to see if anyone could make their way across the creek, which looked shallow but passable, even strewn with sizzling debris.

Standing next to Cass, I said, "How are you doing?"

"Dandy," she answered, not meeting my eyes. But she stood solidly. By then I was beginning to see that Cass could get through the work at hand and only fell into despair later.

A hobbling village man appeared, assisting an older man with an arm injury across the water. After we'd loaded the elder man into my ambulance, the villager explained that he didn't think any of the other injured could make it to our side.

He said, *"C'est inutile." It's no use.* Emile offered to go back in with him and take a stretcher, but the man shook his head. Then he bravely headed back into the inferno of his village. Emile told Cass and me we needed to move on. Dispassionately, he led the way.

Later, Cass went to bed right after we'd cleaned and serviced our ambulances, and I took the opportunity to find Beryl Rayne. I found her in the mess hall sitting with Dr. Kitchens and a French doctor as Dr. Kitchens attempted to translate. Engaged in an animated pantomime and discussion about how best to remove a bloodied and stiffened uniform from a wounded man, they didn't notice me. Initially I hesitated to interrupt. But then I gathered myself and asked Beryl if I could have a moment of her time.

We moved to an empty mess table and sat across from each other. I hadn't spent any time with Beryl since we'd arrived in Meaux. The doctors worked in the hospital, and we worked in the field of battle. It was nice to look into her face, which appeared a little drawn and tired. Her pupils, however, were sharp points of energy, and I sensed her satisfaction with what she did here.

After I described Cass's condition and relayed some of the things she'd said to me, Beryl clasped her hands together on the tabletop. She gazed at me with concerned eyes now. "This happens to soldiers, but I've not heard of it in a civilian. That said, I'm sure Cass and plenty of other civilians have seen horrors that would upset many a soul."

I gazed away, where I could see the sun sending its last beams of daylight tripping across rooftops, fields, and gardens. Then I lifted my eyes to meet Beryl's. "Is there a cure for the condition?"

Beryl shook her head. "Sometimes a soldier has to get away for some rest and peace. But that's frowned upon, as you can imagine, by the military. Some men are reluctant to talk about it, as it could reflect a lack of courage."

"Cass won't usually talk about it unless I make her."

Beryl pursed her lips and appeared to think hard on the matter, then said, "Has she ever mentioned . . . doing harm to herself?"

Momentarily taken aback, I said, "No, never. She just seems sad and withdrawn."

"But she *does* talk to you?"

"Yes."

"Good, that's good. Try to get her to talk about how she's feeling. Encourage her to confide her fears. And if she ever mentions anything about her life being over or wanting to die, let me know right away."

This talk had taken a completely unexpected turn. I had hoped for some reassurance from the doctor. I had hoped she would tell me Cass would most likely rally. "Are you saying . . . ?"

Her eyes level and unblinking, she said, "Yes, the biggest risk is suicide. I'm told it happens."

I let out a long breath. "I can't imagine Cass doing that, but then again, I never imagined she would be so affected . . ."

"These things are difficult to predict."

I looked at Beryl's hands, which hadn't moved. And then I glanced up. "What happens if she doesn't get better or does talk about suicide?"

Beryl appeared as though a weight had fallen over her. Her jaw slackened, and her eyes had misted. "Then she would have to go home. As I said before, the only thing found helpful to soldiers was leaving here and returning to a place that felt familiar and safe."

I tried to imagine Cass being forced to leave. Would she welcome some time away, or would she see herself as a failure? "If worse comes to worst, could she recover somewhere nearby . . . perhaps in Paris? And then maybe she would get better and come back?"

Beryl shook her head sorrowfully. "We don't have any means for sending people to Paris for recovery from shell shock. Besides, I think you can either cut the mustard or you can't. If it turns out she can't . . ." Beryl shrugged in a way that seemed sad and heartfelt. "Then I think she should go back home."

I gazed outside, where the sun had disappeared and stars had begun to prick little white holes in the sky. I looked at the doctor again. "Do you think it could be a temporary condition? We've only been in the field for two weeks or so, although it feels much longer . . ."

Beryl nodded in agreement, but I could tell she had doubts. "It *is* still early; you're right about that. Perhaps her melancholy will lift as other illnesses sometimes do. At the very least, we can hope for that."

Somewhat relieved, I said, "I'll keep an eye on her."

"I'm glad you two are close."

But were we? When our conversation ended, I turned another corner and started to berate myself. Beryl saw me as a good friend to Cass, but perhaps my openness toward the doctor would backfire. Maybe I should've kept my worries to myself. If they forced Cass to go home, it would devastate her. On the other hand, how could I live with myself if something happened to her and I'd told no one of my concerns?

Cass still on my mind, I remained sitting in the same spot. Later a letter arrived for me from Maman, forwarded from Neufmoutiers. I tore open the envelope; I couldn't wait to read the first mail I'd received since leaving Paris.

Maman wrote that she now lived with a friend and that Luc came by often and sometimes they took a drive out to the farm in the old Lizzie. With regard to money, she gave me only a little bit of vague information. Before we left the US, Beryl had loaned me an advance on my salary, which I'd sent home. Maman wrote nothing about how much remained, simply stating all was well enough, that Luc had received some stud service contracts. Then she told me something I didn't know. Back in April, after I left for Cincinnati, Luc had dropped out of school as he couldn't keep up with both the work on the farm and schoolwork.

I had to stop reading and bite my knuckles. Only one year left! Why had they kept this from me all this time? Stunned that my brother hadn't graduated from high school, I determined then and there that I would make sure he went back for his diploma after I made my way home.

More upsetting was Maman telling me about it now, clearly revealing her distress. I could read between the lines. The absence of financial details told me things weren't going all that well, and the revelation about Luc provided a glimpse into Maman's state of mind. As soon as I received my first paycheck, which Beryl had told me would be drawn on an American bank, I would have to figure out how to send the money to Kentucky. Part of my pay would also come in francs, which I hoped to use here. But many establishments wouldn't take paper money, only gold and silver coin.

I slumped down and put my head on the table. No progress back in Paris, Kentucky. I had to stay until the end of the war and receive my bonus. Of course I would have worked until the war's conclusion anyway. I could never abandon a post for which so much need existed. But I also had to stay for the money. The pot of gold at the end of the rainbow held the only hope for the Faviers to recover even a smidgen of what we'd lost.

But if Cass had to return to the US, I couldn't see myself letting her go alone. If she remained in a diminished state here, at least I could look after her. But if she worsened enough to need to go home, she might not have the strength to care for herself during the long crossing. And who would she have to help her back in Cincinnati? If the worst happened, what would I do?

Chapter Sixteen

As the Allies made progress, the front moved farther away, and the wounded started getting routed to us through Marolles. Other injured came by barge from Charly.

In his note to me, Jimmy had mentioned Charly, so when an occasional ambulance arrived from that place, I looked for him. When we picked up patients closer to the front, I always tried to search him out before I had to leave. I could never find him, nor did any but a few drivers look familiar to me. Once, I thought I recognized an American driver from back in Meaux, but when I asked him if he knew Jimmy Tucker, he said no.

On one of our runs from Meaux, Cass and I had to detour through an early battlefield area. Helmets, old bayonets, and cart wheels lay abandoned on the ground, which was snake-lined with old trenches and tangled with shredded barbed-wire barriers and snarls.

Some days we traversed the rocky roads under a heavy rain, and other times we pressed on beneath a blistering sun. Sometimes we drove in muggy and wet air, and other times in dry, scorching wind as if we crossed a desert. We had to deal with overheated engines, increasing motor oil needs, punctured tires, gasoline shortages, and the occasional inexplicable stalling. Cass could usually get the ambulance running again, even if she couldn't determine the cause of the breakdown in the first place.

Even though the Allies had gained ground, we witnessed no excitement or bravado among the military. Though still willing to fight when needed, everyone struck me as war-weary and eager to save his or her own skin. The French looked tattered, and the American soldiers no longer looked spick-and-span.

At times, we drove through shell attacks, under circling bombers, and through lingering gas. It felt like running the gauntlet. We learned to respect our helmets and gas masks and used them often. Shell holes in the road gaped as big as houses. We also learned the value of utilizing camouflage along the sides of the roads, and when we stopped for water anywhere, we cased the area for deadly gifts left behind by the Germans—hand grenades and unexploded shells.

Other drives felt like tourist trips to the old France, taking us through small, untouched villages and impossibly green fields, or past the occasional old man grazing a goat herd on a stony hill patched with grass. Those scenes seemed as far away from the war as the damp green earth was from the blazing hot sun.

Once, we learned that a dressing station had been targeted in a gas attack, and we transported two medical officers and a nurse suffering from burns. One of the doctors begged to die quickly, and the nurse called out a man's name, her husband's perhaps. Safety existed for no one, and it shocked me that I could sleep at night. Exhaustion always swept me away, but Cass still barely slept at all.

One evening, I received a letter, and I didn't recognize the handwriting on the envelope. I tore into it and unfolded the pages; it came from Captain Brohammer. My throat constricted. I'd tried to put him out of my mind. I'd tried to put everything about that night in Meaux out of my mind. But the soldiers' comment about the captain making money off his own men kept creeping back into my consciousness. I could suppress it while working, but it always came back. Just as my father could sense a horse's spirit, I sensed something very wrong with Felix Brohammer. Those words uttered by the soldiers held court in my head every day as soon as it got quiet.

The letter read surprisingly chipper, informative, and . . . almost normal. He wrote about his engineers having to erect a field hospital very near the front, and how upon their arrival they'd found no local help and had to do the hasty construction on their own. He also relayed a story from his days in officer training. When competing against his peers, he had earned the highest scores in both physical stamina and mental capacity. Then he inquired of my health and finished by wishing me well and saying he hoped to catch up to me sooner rather than later. He signed off: *With love, your Felix.*

Your Felix? I crumpled the letter in my fist. Would I ever get rid of Captain Brohammer?

When I spoke to Cass about my problems, it always seemed to lift her spirits and free her from her demons, at least for a little while, so I told her about the letter while we stood outside our barracks in the courtyard that night. She had gleaned a cigarette, which we shared while standing in the fresh night air under a splattering of stars.

I also told her about my last meeting with the captain outside the compound at Meaux, when he'd accused me of having another beau. "This place is making him crazy," I said.

"That's the best thing you've said about him. At least he's human."

"I mean it. He won't listen to what I say. He won't let it go. Don't you think that's a little crazy?"

Cass smirked. "I think it's the way of love. Love makes people do crazy things."

Surprised, I recoiled just a bit. "You don't mean to insinuate that he truly loves me, do you?"

"It's impossible for me to say."

I shook my head, puzzled at her reaction. "It's impossible to fall in love over the course of one short evening." Even as I said this, I recalled the few moments I'd had with Jimmy, the way nothing else had mattered and how I'd been willing to push all rules aside. I couldn't shake the image of him and that touch and that smile and the warm, welcoming shine in his eyes.

Cass wore her faraway face again, but this time it felt as though her thoughts mirrored mine. I had to believe she had slipped away to somewhere pleasant. It took a long time for her to respond, and her voice came surprisingly soft, her eyes, too, as she gazed back at me. "Are you sure about that?"

I remembered when she'd gone out in the middle of the night back in Neufmoutiers. Perhaps she really had met someone during the short time we'd been there, and perhaps it had made a powerful impact on her, and she remembered it now as I remembered Jimmy. Again and again, I wondered why she'd never told me.

This conversation had started with Brohammer, and he came back to mind like a shell hole I'd just fallen into. "Most of the time, I think love at first sight makes a travesty of real love," I slowly answered.

The pleasant expression vanished from Cass's face then, and she shoved her hair behind her ears. "This war is a travesty."

Just that day, the field hospital in Marolles had become so crowded, the staff had to put many of the stretcher cases, in addition to ambulatory patients, out in the rain before arranging transportation to Meaux. Those battered men lay outside, drenched and shivering, and when finally loaded in our ambulances, they still could not keep their teeth from chattering.

We drove them away in complete silence soon interrupted by a man in Cass's ambulance whose leg had been amputated. He'd probably received some morphine after surgery, but it wore off during the drive to Meaux. He screamed, prayed, cursed, and wept so loudly I could hear it in my ambulance. Maybe he had just realized that most of his leg was gone. Still, Cass and I continued on helplessly with nothing else to do but keep driving.

Not a single good thing had happened all day.

Recalling all of it as I stood with Cass, I pressed my hands into my cheeks, then said, "I suppose we could always leave. We came here voluntarily, after all."

Cass looked astonished. "Never" was all she said.

A night breeze had made its way into the courtyard, and I rubbed my arms. "But if you don't believe in it any longer . . ."

Her face showed offense. "When did I say that?"

"Our first day here, when you were upset."

"Precisely. I was upset."

"I was only thinking of you."

"My God, Arlene," she said, waving me off with dismay. "I would never leave. You should know that. My God," she said again. "You don't know me at all."

Stung, I tried to figure out how to respond to Cass, then a sound behind me broke my train of thought. I turned around and looked up and into Jimmy's face. A face I had never needed as much as I did in that moment. Jimmy, finally, as if the strength of my desire had summoned him here. He was so shiny clean that night, his eyes open and sweet.

"You found me," I blurted out, and my eyes started to sting. Yes, being startled could be good, very good. I could've floated out of my shoes and into the heavens above, only I'd pause to grab hold of Jimmy and take him with me. "I thought I'd never see you again."

He smiled in the kindest, most lopsided way. "Now, you ought to know I'd never let that happen."

Suddenly remembering Cass, I turned and took her arm and brought her beside me. "This is my dear friend Cass, another ambulance driver."

"Hello, dear friend Cass, another ambulance driver," Jimmy said and took her hand lightly.

She said, "Hello to you as well, and never fear, I'm leaving you two alone. This is definitely a case of 'three's a crowd.'" Her anger with me had apparently abated as fast as it had arrived, and she looked pleased. Of course Jimmy had already charmed her without even trying. "Just don't get lost." She gave me a half-smile then, and I knew she meant *Don't get lost in the moment.* But then she cocked her head and said, "You're one lucky girl, aren't you?"

I nodded. Sometimes Cass was opaque to me, and this was one of those moments. I watched her leave.

As soon as I turned back to Jimmy, my heart beating faster, I grasped the sides of my skirt. "I didn't meet you that night because of worry about Cass. She hasn't fared as well as I'd expected, and that night I realized how much she had broken under the pressure. I couldn't leave her alone."

Jimmy stood still, soaking it in, his eyes planted on mine, but I perceived only empathy and nothing more. "Hello to you, too," he said with a wry little smile. I think he had said those very words to me on that snowy day in the stables.

"I'm sorry; I just have so much to say. Have you been in Charly?"

"Most of the time, yes."

He simply studied me then, and I caved under his gaze and gave in to every impulse that surged through me. "I've felt sick about not showing up that night. I expected to find you the next morning and explain myself. I've worried so much about what you might think, and I've looked for you everywhere. Someway, somehow, I knew I'd find you."

His smile widened and added to the pull he exerted on me. "I assumed you'd forgotten, that I hadn't made much of an impression."

"You did. Of course you did," I said and then quickly continued: "I wanted to see you that night. I wanted it badly. I'm so sorry, Jimmy. What you must have thought of me . . ."

He blinked, and his eyes landed on me like a gentle caress. I put my hand on his cheek, just as I'd done on that first night, and again he held it there and closed his eyes, and it was exactly as before—it was everything, and the world and life came down to only this. Now the future unfurled before me as clearly as a path that led only one way. When he opened his eyes, he didn't speak. Then he slowly lowered my hand and gave it back to me.

I didn't know how to take that. "Oh, Jimmy, do you forgive me? I do hope you understand and can put it behind us. Now you're here, and it feels like an answered prayer. I can't believe it. This is the best thing that has happened in . . . forever."

He nodded.

Glancing about first, I asked, "Do you want to get away from here for a while? I still haven't walked the streets of Meaux or climbed that tower."

He looked down and seemed to study his feet, then gazed back at me. "Did you really plan to meet me that night? Like I said, I assumed you'd forgotten or maybe . . . come to your senses."

"Of course I did. I mean, I did plan to meet you, that is." I'd become too flustered and excited; I needed to calm down. "I'm no longer that girl who always obeys. I'm not letting anyone else make decisions for me now, and I never will again."

He looked toward his feet once more, his eyes remaining downcast for a while. He murmured, "'Never' is a strong word."

Fear climbed up my body. Maybe he wouldn't or couldn't forgive me after all. But then why the sweet touch?

By then he appeared as if he got a grip on something, and he faced me again, his expression ever the sweeter. But he said, "I shouldn't have asked you. You're in a susceptible way, and I was being selfish."

I shifted my weight. "What do you mean?"

"When I asked you to meet me later that night, I was being selfish. You said you'd agreed not to get involved with any soldiers, and I shouldn't have asked you to break your promises and take chances. Of course I forgive you, Arlene. You were right not to come, even if you *had* intended to come. Perhaps the distraction Cass provided did you a favor. I shouldn't have asked, and I won't ask you again."

I rocked back on my heels as if I'd been slapped, and the warmth in my cheeks drained away in the time it took me to blink. Had he really said he wouldn't ask me again? "I-I don't understand."

In the softest voice he said, "We have to finish our work here . . . first and foremost, we need to do that . . . and maybe I need to prove some things to myself."

Duty first—that didn't sound like the Jimmy I knew. I took a step back, even though I wanted to sink into his arms. And what did he have to prove to himself? Maybe that he was more than just a stable boy? I didn't know. "I'm sorry . . . again . . . so sorry."

I could barely hear him whisper, "I'm sorry, too."

Fighting to swallow, I wrapped my arms about myself. "When I saw you the first time in this place . . . it really did feel like the answer to a prayer, and everything suddenly came together inside me so clearly. I was sure of it; I still am." I paused and searched his eyes. Even though they remained full of compassion, I couldn't read anything else there. Blindsided and also blind, even so, I glimpsed Dr. Kitchens walking nearby, across the courtyard. Maybe she saw us, and obviously my conversation with Jimmy was not a casual one, but I no longer cared. "And now seeing you again tonight, it's all back. I've never felt so strongly about anything."

Jimmy said, "I'm the one who should apologize. I'm not going to ask you to take a drive or a walk in the town. I understand now how it might look. You're probably supposed to stay away, especially from us lowly recruits—we come from different worlds—and if I convinced you to do something that ended up hurting you, I'd regret it too much."

His caution could not be real. Jimmy had always struck me as a bit of a daredevil, a risk-taker. "It's my decision, what I do."

"Of course, Arlene, but you're in a weakened state. You've just arrived at the front, you're worried about your friend, and you've only recently . . . buried your father."

His words true, of course, but I'd never felt so sure of myself. Perhaps I had, as they say, risen to the occasion. I did my job and, according to others, I did it well. No longer a pampered daughter, I had left that girl back in Kentucky.

I took a step closer to Jimmy, and the distance between us closed to mere inches. I could feel the heat from his breath, see the pores in his tanned skin. I worked to sound convincing; after all, I spoke the truth. "I can see clearly. I can make decisions."

He didn't respond, just kept looking at me with the strangest but most beautiful combination of adoration and concern.

I continued: "I *do* want to see you away from here. I want to see you alone."

He raked his hands through his hair, and I saw surprise on his face along with some torment. "I'm sorry," he whispered as his hands came to a rest again at his sides. "I just don't think it's a good idea."

His words like a punch, my muscles nearly gave way. I spun around, too injured to face him now. I swiped away a stray tear. Surely Jimmy hadn't meant what he said. Surely he would hold on to me and tell me everything was alright. But he didn't, and the moments passed as if endless.

Finally he put his hands on my shoulders and gently turned me around. "I didn't know you felt this way, Arlene. Especially since you didn't show up that night. For a moment I had kind of a wild dream, but it wasn't a real dream."

I drew in a ragged breath. "But it was; it still is, a real dream."

"No," he said softly, his voice rich with conviction, cutting me to the core. "It can't be."

I wanted to scream, *But it can!* Somehow I held myself in check; I had no right to demand him to profess feelings for me. "Why, then, did you come into the courtyard tonight? Why did you come over when you saw me? You could've kept away."

"Arlene," he said, looking ever so regretful. "It doesn't mean I can't check on you. I still want to see you. I'm more experienced here, and maybe I can help you get through it. The most important thing is for you to survive this, get back to the living, and return to your life back home."

"That life is over."

He closed his eyes. "No, it isn't."

I swallowed twice against a thick sensation in my throat. "I'm working to get at least some of it back, but without Papa, nothing . . ."

Studying me softly again, he said, "Dear, sweet Arlene, you'll succeed; it runs in your blood. I knew it the first time I saw you riding a horse way too big for you, and yet you handled that animal like a queen."

I nodded repeatedly until I realized what I was doing and stopped. I must have looked like a madwoman, one whose heart continued to beat despite the hole ripped all the way through it.

Jimmy went on: "I'll always be your friend. If I can ever help you with anything—I mean anything at all—just say the word."

I stared up into the blackest sky I'd ever seen. Even the starlight had dimmed. How ironic that the man who didn't interest me pursued me, but the man who could have so easily held my heart in his hand had chosen to let me go. Jimmy didn't share my feelings, or else he'd opted not to act on them. Either way, he had just pushed me away.

A moment later I gathered myself together, even though I could make no sense of his decision. The way he'd held my hand pressed to his cheek, twice now, had seemed the most loving and hopeful and intimate thing. It had meant everything to me, but perhaps to Jimmy, it amounted to nothing more than friendly affection.

Of course I would take his friendship—at least I would remain in his life in some way. I would take whatever he offered, even if I wanted more. The feeling of refusal was new to me; I'd almost always received what I wanted. Perhaps yes, Papa had spoiled me.

Then, to my horror, an image of Brohammer swept across my pupils like the flash of light from an exploding bomb. Maybe I had more in common with the captain than I realized. Maybe I didn't know how to accept a rebuff, either.

"What is it?" Jimmy asked me as I dropped my gaze from the sky and shuffled my feet in the dirt below. He said, "Something else is bothering you."

He had no clue how much damage he'd done. Would his offer of friendship hold true? I hated that Brohammer had crossed my mind. "It's the strangest thing . . ."

"What?" Jimmy said.

I shook my head.

He insisted: "Tell me."

Shaking my head again, I replied, "It's probably nothing."

"Let me be the judge of that."

"A captain I know. A very strange and vain man. I don't like him, but for some inexplicable reason, he keeps after me. The other night when he found me here, after I'd said *again* I wouldn't go out with him, I walked past a couple of French soldiers lounging about and watching us. I heard them say in a disgusted manner something about making money off his own men." I paused. "Do you have any idea what that means?"

Jimmy listened, then looked focused on an internal deliberation, as though his mind spun with new and unexpected thoughts, but he held his eyes wide open. They shined brightly with awareness of this moment, sharply, as if something very important had dawned on him. "They said that? That he made money off his own men?"

"Yes, they spoke in French, and they didn't think I could understand."

He rubbed his forehead. Then he touched my arm. "Are you sure, Arlene?"

"Yes," I answered. "What are you thinking about? What does it mean?"

He rubbed his forehead again and then scratched his head. Almost sheepishly he answered, "You'll probably have a hard time believing this, but I've heard rumors that some big-shot American officer is making a tidy profit by selling high-quality barbed-wire gloves and wire cutters at a hefty price to the men on the line and in the trenches. The other day a dying soldier in my ambulance pulled a pair of wire cutters out of his pocket and asked me to pass them along to a man in the infantry. Any man. Before I honored his request and gave them away, I took a closer look. They weren't army issue." I made myself concentrate as he continued: "The army doesn't have enough of those tools, and the ones they had in the beginning were of poor quality. Many have been lost or destroyed and never replaced. But here this officer and a few of his trusted comrades come along and offer the tools that might very well save soldiers' lives—but only if they pay up big-time. I hear he's making a small fortune off the men."

I tensed as he spoke.

"He uses intermediaries who won't talk—yes, how convenient—so no one knows for sure who's behind it, except now maybe . . . you."

Now *I* rubbed my forehead, trying to take it all in and imagine the ramifications if this proved true. "If people know someone is doing this, why don't you all report it to your superior officers?"

He half laughed. "First of all, the men in the trenches aren't going to report someone who's supplying them with things that might keep them alive, and those of us who would report it haven't had a name or any proof. Imagine a lowly driver like me accusing an officer of a crime, based on a rumor."

"Do you really think an American officer is doing this?"

He said, "I have no reason not to believe the men who mentioned it to me."

"Do you think it could be the man I know?"

Ann Howard Creel

"It sure sounds like it."

I made myself wrap my mind around this new information. Brohammer still considered me his girlfriend. "Maybe I can find out."

"Oh no," Jimmy said, leaning just slightly backward. "Don't you dare try to get any information from him. In fact, steer clear of that man. He has to be the most self-serving man on the planet if he's doing what we think he's doing."

My heart raced, and I had to bat my eyes and glance away. So perhaps Brohammer didn't suffer from shell shock after all, but instead had an evil nature that could commit a crime against his own, taking advantage of people even during these most desperate of days.

"So, who is he?" Jimmy asked.

And now I had involved Jimmy. I turned back to him. "What would you do if I told you?"

I watched him try to temper his reaction. "Don't worry, I'm not going to seek him out and walk up and accuse him of anything. It's not my place. But I'm near the lines and around the infantry enough to do some digging around. I could probably find out if he's the culprit."

I hesitated, afraid that knowing Brohammer's name might bring trouble to Jimmy.

"Come on. You can't just tell me what you heard and then not give me his name."

"Yes, I can."

He almost smiled. "But you won't, will you? Tell me and only me. Please don't mention it to anyone else. How can we know who to trust? And believe me, I'll keep the name to myself and conduct the most careful and quiet of investigations. If he's really the one, we can stop him."

Incredulous, I asked, "Stop him from providing life-saving tools?"

"*Selling* life-saving tools at a high price *for profit*. There's a big difference. The men in the trenches don't have much, if any, money. If the tools have somehow made it here, they should be *given* to the soldiers."

"I understand."

"In many ways he's determining who lives and dies. The men in the trenches have a much better chance of survival if they have those tools. Whoever this man is—he's giving some men a better shot at making it out of here in one piece and denying others the same chance because they don't have the money. Arlene, don't you see? He's playing God."

I made a quick decision; I found it too difficult to refuse Jimmy anything, despite the fact that he'd just split my heart from front to back. He was more interested in what I knew than in me. "Felix Brohammer, a captain with the engineers."

Jimmy listened, pondered hard for a moment, and then har-rumphed. "That's perfect. He can move around more than other officers, and he has strong connections to the infantry."

"But as you've said, there's no proof."

"I'll work on that."

I would work on it, too.

Jimmy must have read my mind. "I'm saying it again. Don't do anything. Concentrate on yourself and forget about this. I beg of you: don't do anything, and tell no one."

After a long moment I nodded. But I didn't mean it. Now that I knew what Brohammer might be up to, I would do everything in my power to make sure he didn't get away with it. I couldn't change anything about the daily horrors of this brutal war, but this—exposing a conscienceless profiteer—this I could do.

Chapter Seventeen

MEAUX, FRANCE, TO NEUFMOUTIERS-EN-BRIE, FRANCE

AUGUST 1918

The front advanced even farther into lands formerly occupied by the Germans, and our wounded arrived from Château-Thierry by train. Despite military and tactical success, the suffering never ceased. The endless river of wounded and maimed kept flowing and swelling and almost drowning us.

But I had to stay afloat. Work was paramount. The hospital was so overcrowded, now only the most gravely injured were operated on in Meaux, and it became necessary to transfer any other wounded soldiers on to other locations. The ambulance drivers' work became that of transferring seriously wounded soldiers whose surgeries couldn't be completed in Meaux.

It sounded easier, but it wasn't. Those men deserved the best of care on the spot, but they had to be shuttled away. I tried to make the men I ferried faceless so I wouldn't remember them, but it never worked.

One of my passengers once awakened screaming and started beating on the side of the ambulance. I pulled over and scurried around to the back door. Sitting up and blinking wildly, he cried, *"J'y vois rien! J'y vois rien!" I can't see! I can't see!* His face looked burned, but no bandages covered his eyes. Had his eyes suffered burns and no one noticed? The doctors and nurses might have focused on his more obvious abdominal wound.

I grabbed his outstretched hand and held it for a few moments. "Dear sir," I said in French, voice cracking. "I'll get you to help as fast as I can."

I relived the faces and expressions of the men I ferried as I lay awake trying to relax. By then I struggled to sleep each night, just as Cass did. I couldn't think of the eighteen-year-old double amputee crying for his mother, or the man whose face was so badly burned he appeared almost inhuman.

And now some new awful images haunted me—a man belly-crawling, picking his way through barbed wire, his hands shredded and bleeding, his grip so slippery he can't fire the gun he holds when a German soldier runs up on him; and a man whose foot is caught in barbed wire in no-man's-land, struggling but unable to release himself, as there's nothing to cut the wire, while German bullets fly in. All because they couldn't buy what they needed.

Other times I dreamed about Jimmy to push the harrowing memories away. But Jimmy had squeezed all the blood from my heart. I hadn't seen him or heard from him since that night in the courtyard.

When Cass and I both lay in bed, sometimes I tried to engage her in conversation. Turning to face her bed right next to mine, I whispered her name, but she pretended to be asleep, even though I felt pretty sure she was awake.

Eventually I'd succumb to exhaustion but often awaken when Cass gave off a little shout or a deep moan. I awakened her to stop the nightmare, but as time went by, I became more and more concerned that those outbursts came from Cass not while she slept, but while she lay awake.

In mid-August, Beryl heard from Dr. Logan that the American Women's Hospital had found a new location and would move to Château-Thierry. Apparently, however, Dr. Logan had left the decision about whether to go or stay here in Meaux in Beryl's hands.

She stopped me early the next morning as I leaned over the engine, readying my ambulance for the day ahead. "Prepare to leave tomorrow. We'll rejoin our team in Neufmoutiers before proceeding to Château-Thierry."

I couldn't help but smile. At that point I felt strongly that Cass needed to go back. I straightened up and said to Beryl, "That must have been a tough decision."

"We're needed everywhere, but we came here because of the AWH. It's time to go home."

Of course by *home* she meant back to our original team and our original mission. I couldn't have agreed more, but it didn't take long for me to think about myself. Once we left, Jimmy would probably have no way to find me. On the other hand, Brohammer knew I'd come to Meaux by way of Neufmoutiers; he had looked for me there before.

After our last ambulance transfer of the day, I took a walk through the town and headed toward the flamboyant Gothic edifice that was Saint Stephen's Cathedral. I had to climb its one finished tower, even though I should've done it with Jimmy.

Trudging up the steps, I tried to imagine Jimmy, where he'd moved on to and what he was doing. Most of all, I wanted him safe.

At the top, the tower windows afforded a magnificent view of where the 1914 Battle of the Ourcq took place, and beyond. In the rarefied air, I stood still, soaking it all in, stunned that I was here and grateful for my life after so many endless days of death.

Following the loop of the Marne with my eyes, I imagined the days before men had settled here and cleared the land, when nomadic clans roamed it but didn't disturb it very much, the loamy soil not yet tilled. Someday it might revert to that wild state. The land would always remain, but what of us? What would happen to us?

That night, I stayed up late composing a letter to Jimmy. I stuck to using a pencil because I kept changing my mind and starting over. He had split me into two pieces, part desire for him and part shame and pain. The pain of being pushed away. Of somehow, someway . . . losing him.

Never would I forget seeing him, talking to him here. Maybe I was the selfish one now. Jimmy wanted friendship—he'd made that pretty clear—but I had seen more than that in his eyes. I glanced through the window to the stars outside. Jimmy and I had touched the near-impossible in this place, we had touched love among such loss, and I couldn't bring myself to give up yet.

In the end, I wrote very little, only that we would return to Neufmoutiers for a short stay but would soon move on to somewhere near Château-Thierry. I left the letter with a French volunteer who had helped us so often in Meaux. She assured me that when American ambulances came, she would ask about Jimmy and do her best to deliver my letter.

If Jimmy ever wanted to see me again, he would have a map.

After almost seven weeks in Meaux, we took our leave at the end of August, driving away early in the morning. Beryl rode with me, in the lead. Cass and Dr. Kitchens followed behind us, with the nurses in the back of their ambulance. We kept silent. None of us would go back the same person.

I took one last look over my shoulder back at the compound, and the lump in my throat slid down into my stomach, where it expanded and hurt so much it brought on tears. Meaux would never leave me. I would never forget it. Despite all the horrors I'd witnessed in that place,

I'd seen Jimmy for the first time in years there, too. Now I knew what it felt like to want someone. My soul had opened in that place and also emptied.

I hadn't spent much time with the doctors during all those days in Meaux. After fighting with myself whether or not to tell Beryl the rumor about the captain selling tools and gloves, I eventually opted to say nothing. What could one of the medical doctors do? Especially those not in the army? And I hadn't forgotten the last thing Jimmy had said, so urgently: *Tell no one.*

After riding in silence for about twenty minutes, Beryl asked, "Are you happy to leave?"

"In some ways, yes, especially for Cass," I answered.

Beryl glanced in my direction. "How is she?"

"About the same."

Leaning forward, she made some adjustments to her collar, then sat back in her seat. She didn't speak, and all I heard was "Hmmm."

Explaining my thoughts further, I said, "She wasn't in this condition back in Neufmoutiers, so I'm hoping she'll improve once we return."

"We'll probably see more of what we saw in Meaux when we work in Château-Thierry."

"I know," I said. "But at least we should have a reprieve while we move."

"I see your point," Beryl said. "But do keep a close eye on her, please."

"I will," I said. "What about you? Are you happy to leave?"

She shrugged. "Exhilarating as it was, we need to get back to our team. Tough decision, though. I also wanted to stay."

"How wonderful it must have felt to operate on those soldiers and save their lives."

She turned a bit in her seat toward me. "Oh, we didn't operate."

My eyes flew wide open. "What?"

"Yes, we didn't operate. We did many other things."

Puzzled, I shook my head.

"We gave emergency, life-saving care. We washed wounds and removed fragments from them. We splinted broken bones and applied sterile dressings, and all of it had to be perfectly executed. No contamination. And bandaged in a way that reduced pain. Without enough surgical tables and operating room equipment, we had to postpone many operations and sent many, many men along to hospitals farther down the line for surgery. You must have driven some of them."

"I don't understand. You were so excited. And all they allowed you to do was splint and bandage?"

"Don't discount it. We had to quickly diagnose correctly. Believe me, we might not have operated, but we saved lives."

I remembered the conversation with Beryl on the way here and her excitement about finally getting to utilize her skills in the operating room.

"Besides, what were we to do? Become insulted, turn around, and leave?" She faced forward again. "Not when we could apply our skills in another way, and they'd asked for our help."

I simply sat with that for a while. "You must never think of yourself."

"Of course I do." She laughed. "Please don't sanctify me; otherwise I'll have to start avoiding you."

I smiled. "I'll admire you in silence, then."

She reached over and squeezed my arm. "It's nice to have a fan, though."

How wonderful to talk to Beryl again.

A few moments later she said, "Once we arrive, be sure to get some rest."

"I hope you do as well."

Beryl gave off a skeptical look and scoffed. "I'd feel like the devil if I ever rested now."

When we pulled up in front of the château in Neufmoutiers, I noticed two new ambulances parked in front of the building. Then Eve—sweet, freckled, girlish Eve—ran out to greet us. You might have thought we'd just returned from a journey around the world. After we stepped out of the ambulances, Eve made rounds to all six of us and gave us hugs, saying, "Welcome back."

Eve sported a sunburn over her masses of freckles, and I imagined calmer days here, so much so that she'd had time to sit out in the sun. Her fingernails appeared freshly painted, too.

Looking elated, she told Cass and me that three new ambulances had arrived from Paris, but one was out in the field. Lottie had gone to pick up the sick in Château-Thierry. Every day, two ambulances, each holding a driver and a doctor, made the trip there.

Inside the château we found most of the hospital equipment disassembled and prepared for shipment. We kept what we would need for emergency treatments, along with one extra hospital bed. Only a few hospital patients remained. During our absence, dysentery had struck, and the last recovering patients still convalesced. Besides these was a young village boy who'd fallen while playing on a roof and had broken his leg. Soon he would go home.

During our time away, most of the refugees had returned to the Aisne to harvest the grain not destroyed during the German retreat, and no shells or bombs had landed near the hospital; therefore, the work centered on taking care of sick villagers. The doctors opened dispensaries and a dental office. The pace had slowed in our absence, and I filled with gratitude that I'd helped out during the desperate days, horrific as they had been, in Meaux.

Cass and I sat down across from Eve and then also Kitty, who emerged from the second floor, rubbing the sleep out of her eyes.

"Sorry for how I look," Kitty said as she fluffed her pillow-flattened hair with her fingers and slid onto the seat. Compared to Cass and me, her hair looked beautiful, her fingernails, too. I imagined her, Lottie, and Eve styling each other's hair and painting each other's nails. Such sweet girls, they deserved it, and I couldn't envy them. "I'm on rest today."

Eve added, "Two of us work all day, picking up patients or taking the doctors to administer care, the third one resting during the day and doing maintenance on the ambulances, or going out if necessary in the evenings. We rotate positions every three days."

Their organization impressed me, and even Cass lifted her eyebrows in surprise. Apparently Eve had taken charge and had done a good job of it. I could see satisfaction on Cass's face. A bit of color had risen in her cheeks, and she smiled at the girls as if she really meant it. Maybe back here, she could say goodbye to her demons.

Other people came by and welcomed us back, too. Some clapped us on the shoulder or patted us on the head as if we'd just performed well on a school examination. Thankfully, no one asked us what we'd seen and done. We couldn't have put those memories into words, and Cass certainly didn't need to relive them, either.

Hearing a noise behind me, I discovered the boy with the broken leg had swung his way up to us using his crutches. He looked about eight years old.

Kitty said, "Hello, Poppy."

"*Bonjour,*" the boy replied. He reminded me of a younger Jimmy— all boy, all smiles, and full of life. Some mischief probably mixed in there, too.

"Are you bored?" Eve asked and patted the bench seat beside her, indicating that he could sit there.

He shook his head. He must have learned the meaning of the word *bored.*

To us, she said, "He's going out of his mind here. We call him Poppy because he makes us happy, like seeing a field of poppies. We have to keep him occupied—"

"Or he'll get into the kitchen or try to escape," finished Kitty.

"Haid-hand-seik?" Poppy asked Eve.

She replied, "A few minutes?"

He nodded enthusiastically, his eyes now alight with that mischief I'd sensed earlier.

Facing us, Kitty said, "We've taught him some English."

Eve added, "But he prefers to play games, especially hide-and-seek. We hide a small ball in places he can reach, but it's getting harder and harder to find good hidey-holes. Everything's gotten so bare here. By the way, may we utilize your shoes?"

I glanced to my side and discerned a tiny bit of pleasure on Cass's face. Thank God. Far removed from the front lines, this place almost felt like a vacation.

Sunset arrived soon after we pulled up, and we dived into the cook's fine dinner, then Dr. Logan surprised me by coming to our table and addressing me.

"Did Captain Brohammer find you in Meaux?"

The mention of his name sent a shock up my spine. Her face looked open and expectant. I tried to appear unaffected as I reminded myself that he told me he'd come to Neufmoutiers looking for me and had spoken to Dr. Logan.

"He did," I answered.

She looked even more pleased. "What a charming man," she said before smiling and then turning to leave.

As she left earshot, Cass said, "What'd I tell you?"

I shook my head.

Despite the mention of Brohammer, I prepared myself for the first good night's sleep in what felt like a very long time. My eyelids glued themselves together as soon as my head sank into the pillow.

To my surprise, however, in the middle of the night, a sound awakened me. In our absence the other drivers had taken turns sleeping in our room for a night alone, but they'd cleaned it and turned it over to us upon our return. Cass and I shared the same bed just as before.

My body froze as she rose off the mattress and slid from the bed, then I barely heard her dress. The air moved as she opened the door and slipped out of the room . . . again! Going out in the middle of the night again.

I wondered if she went out alone, and if so, why did she never do it in Meaux? Back there, maybe the strain of it all had left her too shattered and upset to seek solitude. Maybe the horror had sapped her energy. I convinced myself that just now, she'd headed out to meet someone, perhaps a villager from Neufmoutiers or nearby.

If true, however, how had she let him know she had come back? I'd stayed near to Cass ever since we'd arrived. I supposed she could've slipped away for a few moments while we washed up separately, but I doubted it. And then the obvious. All anyone had to do was see our ambulances back in front of the château to know we had returned.

Minutes later I sat up in bed and hugged my knees to my chest, trying to tell myself to leave Cass's affairs to her. She didn't owe me an explanation, and I'd be feigning sleep or actually sleeping by the time she slipped back into the room anyway. I could let it go and allow Cass to keep her secret.

As I sat longer, Cass's escape acts brought to mind an idea, however, not about Cass but about Brohammer. Although I dreaded having to deal with him again, most likely he'd find me here or at our next location, and when he did, I knew exactly what I would do.

Chapter Eighteen

As I lay there waiting for Cass, sleep eluded me. The wind had settled down, whereas an hour earlier it had rattled the windows and wailed down the road outside.

The lumber that held this old château together shifted and made strange cracking sounds, and Brohammer invaded my thoughts. I relived what Jimmy had told me, and I wished to talk it over with someone and get a second opinion. I had come up with a plan, but I would've benefited from some advice and help enacting it. Already, I'd considered telling Cass and Beryl, but then Jimmy's words of caution came back to me. *Tell no one.*

Brohammer made me examine my beliefs about the human soul. I closed my eyes and talked to whatever supreme being might drift out there in the inky depths of the mysterious unknown. Perhaps I'd never know who or what really guided us.

The war tested our humanity, and I wondered if people could really contain the far reaches of the extremes—heroism juxtaposed with greed. For some, perhaps there was no middle ground. Brohammer, so handsome, successful, and admired, seemed to have a much darker side to him, one capable of betraying his own men, our honorable soldiers who deserved nothing but praise, prayers, and help.

And if he did, what would that cost him? What would it cost me to find out?

After Cass came back stealthily but safely into the room, finally I slept.

The next day, the sky was half-clear and half-dark. The sun glared down in the west, while from the east, a vast, turbulent storm churned its way in. An older gentleman in a nearby village had taken ill and needed transportation, so Lottie went for him, insisting that Cass and I rest for a few days. We loaned our extra pairs of shoes to Eve so she could use them as hiding places during her games with Poppy, and then we helped her search for new hiding spots.

No wonder everyone had fallen in love with the boy. Told he could start his first search that day, he took off on his crutches with the enthusiasm of a kid who's seen presents under the tree on Christmas morning. Joy on his face and his eyes dancing, he'd come back to Cass, Eve, and me within twenty minutes, presenting the ball, which he pulled out of his pocket.

"You do have a problem, don't you?" Cass said to Eve.

Eve took the ball and rolled it in her hand, then answered, "Yes, he's getting faster and faster, and he needs entertainment all day long. I'm running out of ideas. Lottie and Kitty are, too."

Poppy said, *"Encore, encore!"* Again, again!

Eve sighed, a happy sigh.

Cass said, "You need some new games."

"You think?" Eve shrugged. "Try finding toys or even some jacks or marbles in this village."

"I have a deck of cards," Cass said.

Eve straightened up and visibly brightened. "You're not teasing me? My goodness, a deck of cards would be great."

"We can teach him all sorts of table games and even solitaire," Cass mused.

"Poker!" Eve insisted. "Will you play with us?"

She nodded. Here in Neufmoutiers, Cass was returning more to her former self. I glanced outside and into the courtyard. Birds sang and flitted through the limbs and little trees—such a peaceful sight, but I don't think I'd ever felt so alone.

That evening Cass and I took a walk through the village and sat on the stoop of a house that looked unoccupied, and although we had several hours of each other's uninterrupted company, she never said anything about the night before. It seemed she would never confide in me, and I told myself I had to accept that.

The thunderstorm had passed over quickly in the late afternoon, leaving air so still we could hear sounds of life from the village nearby—dishes clanking and buckets being filled with water at the pump, snippets of distant conversations that floated out of open windows, children's laughter as they scampered across the stone streets, and the building song of crickets and grasshoppers. I welcomed those sounds of ordinary living: they kept me company, my friends for the evening.

Two days later, on the way back from a stroll with Cass, I spotted a familiar staff car in front of our château-turned-hospital-now-clinic, and lo and behold, Brohammer had come with it. He leaned against his vehicle, smoking. He called out, "You made it back to paradise," then spread his arms open wide as if he expected me to run into them.

I'd hoped he would come soon, but I hadn't imagined it this soon. And still I recoiled from the sight of him. I made myself keep walking.

Cass murmured under her breath, "Not this again," left my side, walked past Brohammer, and stepped under the arched entry to the château.

The moment had come, the moment I had to make a decision. *Don't hesitate,* I told myself. *Do as you've planned.*

I made myself smile at the captain as I walked up to him. "It is paradise compared to Meaux."

Dressed impeccably as always, he seemed to register my tone of voice as friendlier than before, and he smiled in a genuine way. For a moment he looked almost human, not a beast at all. I found myself faltering. It felt impossible that someone who could smile so beautifully could also take such advantage of others.

"A little rest suits you. Although you're still my beautiful girl, you were looking rather rumpled back there," he said. How did he do it? Brohammer had perfected the art of pairing a compliment and an insult in the same breath.

"It's not as busy here now."

"Then you have no excuse. Go out for a drive with me."

Perfect. The last time he'd visited, I'd seen crates in the back seat of the car. Crates perhaps filled with contraband in the form of wire cutters and barbed-wire gloves. I had to find a way to look inside them without Brohammer knowing.

He grasped my hand. Surprisingly his hand was soft like a woman's, and not only that, almost cold to the touch, even though the outside air was warm. "Say you'll go," he said.

I tried not to appear overly eager. "Maybe . . ."

"No maybes," he insisted.

I shrugged. "I have to service my ambulance tonight, but perhaps I can go for a short ride now."

His eyebrows flew upward. "Good for you, sweetheart," he said and then turned to the car and opened the passenger door. Before I stepped in, I stole a glance into the back seat. Crates. Several closed crates.

As I slid in, it hit me what a vulnerable position I had put myself in. If Brohammer could profit from his own soldiers' desire to stay alive, maybe he could do something even worse. But I told myself not to worry. Cass would figure out that I'd left with him and would let someone know if I didn't come back shortly.

"Where's your driver?" I asked.

Brohammer cranked the engine. "In the village somewhere, probably trying to find himself a stiff drink." He jumped into the driver's seat and got the engine rumbling.

I had no idea what to say to Felix Brohammer as he drove us down the village lane and out into the countryside. But he had no problem filling periods of silence with stories about himself. He told me his family had ties that went back to aristocratic forebears in Sweden who lost almost everything in some kind of dispute. He claimed that his grandparents had immigrated to the USA with almost nothing but had ended up wealthy and influential. I could've told him that my grandparents had immigrated, too, but I wanted to share as little as possible. *Reveal only what you have to,* I told myself.

As he chatted on, I couldn't believe what I planned to do. I told myself it was justified and important, but my head started pounding, and I had to rub my temples. The pressure inside my skull had started to build from the first moment I saw Brohammer.

"Are you alright?" he asked as he glanced over at me with cold eyes, so in contrast to his smile.

"It's just a headache."

"That's what they all try to say." He almost hummed with a sly smile. "Until I convince them otherwise." I wouldn't look at him, but I could feel the smug, overly confident expression on his face.

Suddenly I laughed ridiculously and let my hands fall; nothing would ease this explosion in my brain.

Then he surprised me by finally asking me a question. Where had I come from?

"Kentucky," I answered.

"Hmmm," he murmured. "And what does your family do back in Kentucky?"

I watched the land glide past me as he drove onward. I couldn't remember the last time I'd sat in the passenger seat in an autocar and not the driver's seat. I closed my eyes, letting the end of summer lie on my skin and smelling the freshly shorn grass, both sweet sensations in such contrast to riding beside Brohammer. Along with Jimmy, I'd kept Maman and Luc close to my chest. Together, like hope and dreams. I would tell Brohammer nothing about them.

I said through a long sigh, "They're farmers."

He laughed and then launched into a litany of negative comments about farmers. Something about pigs and hoes, chicken shacks, and straw mattresses. He'd assumed we were poor crop farmers, which made his interest in me even more confounding. Felix Brohammer was a snob. I wasn't about to give him anything he might want to hear; I would say nothing about our horses. This man had a way of getting under my skin, and I began to regret my decision. I had to change the subject.

I couldn't appear as if rushing this, but a few moments later I said, "Could we pull over somewhere?"

He looked surprised. "Of course, baby."

After he parked on a high spot along the road that afforded a bit of a view, I realized my mistake. I'd hoped for something to take him away for a moment—relieving himself, picking flowers for me, something—but I quickly realized he had nowhere to go. I had no reason to ask him to leave me alone with the car, and I couldn't dig around in the back seat with him sitting beside me. My plan had come up utterly short.

Instead of stepping outside the car, he pulled me closer; he wanted to kiss me. I had to keep my eyes closed, but I turned my face up to his. And let him kiss me with lips that felt soft but also chilling, like his hands.

Everything about it felt wrong, the press of his lips like a sudden illness. For the rest of my days, the memory of that kiss would haunt me. I remembered it as one of the worst things I'd ever done.

And yet I let him do it again, and again, until I could stand it no longer. I shifted my weight so my face pulled back a few inches away.

He perused me. "I knew you'd come around," he said. "But you resisted longer than most girls do."

What to say to that? Thank you?

Perhaps by making him believe I'd become interested, he'd leave me alone. All along, he'd wanted more than anything to conquer me and win me over. Now that he believed he'd succeeded, maybe he'd lose interest and move on to new prospects.

"What made you change your mind?" He cocked his head, his once-handsome face now wan and flat to me. "My good looks, my many charms, my chivalry?" He was only partially joking.

"You were persistent."

"I see," he said and smiled. "You're still not going to shower me with compliments—I will allow you that. I'll let you play coy for a while longer."

"I have to go back now. Remember I said a short drive?"

"You just made my point!" he exclaimed.

"I have to service my am—"

"Your ambulance," he interrupted. "Yes, I remember."

He seemed a bit peeved, but he released me and prepared to drive away.

Pretending was squeezing the soul out of me. And yet it didn't keep me from telling him, upon our return to the château, that I would like to take another drive the next day for a picnic, if only he could stay over. With enthusiasm, he told me that of course he could stay overnight. He assured me that he and his driver would find a place in the village to billet, and tomorrow he would procure all we needed for a special day away.

I wondered how he could so easily abandon his duty. Where were his men? Where was he supposed to be?

The only thing—Cass could ruin my plans if she went out tonight as well. If she interrupted me, it could put her at risk, too. So I decided to slip away earlier than she usually did and return before she woke up.

That night the moon hung almost full against the black sky, sending silver beams of light through the tall windows of the château like the long trains of wedding gowns. Bouncing back and forth between determination and doubt was driving me mad, but tonight I had a chance to get answers. And yet this waiting—it was worse than the actual doing of something.

When the time felt right, I rose from the bed, dressed, and eased away just as Cass had done every night since our return. Beyond the château walls, the colossal moon shone even brighter, almost as bright as the sun at dawn. My eyes accustomed to the moonlight, I could see like an owl. That meant anyone else outside or looking outside could see like an owl, too.

But I could not let another opportunity slip away. I had to find out about Brohammer. I had to, at the very least, try.

My shadow made a distinct black figure against a broad glade of silver. I couldn't hide in this light; if seen, I'd have to come up with an excuse. I'd have to say I had gone for a walk to clear my mind or some such.

The air cool on that night, the breath in my lungs felt as brittle as ice. I didn't allow myself to hesitate. I walked on the balls of my feet as I crossed the road. Once on the other side, I realized I hadn't even drawn a breath. I had become the stuff of this still night air.

As I searched along the road for Brohammer's car, I tipped a few small stones and stirred some dust in the dry spots, but still I made no sound. The village sat in eerie silence, and I didn't know if that was a good thing or not. Few others would venture out at this very late hour, so any noise I made would reverberate.

Then I spotted the car, in the heart of the village, parked next to the church.

My feet hitting the ground silently, I had the sensation of flying as each step rapidly took me closer to an answer.

Then I was leaning into the side of the church. Panting. But I had done it. I had found what I'd come for, and so far, I saw no indication that anyone had heard or seen me.

I peeked into the car. The crates still there. Nailed shut. Nailed shut! I hadn't thought of this. I hadn't thought to bring tools with me. Obviously I had no calling as a sleuth. The crates were made of tightly slatted wood, and I couldn't see or feel for sure what lay inside. I would have to pry one of them open. Therefore I had no choice but to retrace my steps back to the château, fetch a hammer, some oil cloths, and a screwdriver from my ambulance, and tuck them into my pockets.

A rush of potent adrenaline surged through me as I started to make my way back to the car. Again I saw no indication anyone was awake and about. No lights in windows. No smoke from chimneys. My luck holding, maybe I could do this.

Back at the car, I leaned over and shifted one crate closer to me. Then I wedged the flat end of my screwdriver in the seam between the lid and the body of the crate. I used an oil cloth to muffle the sound of tapping the hammer against the handle of the screwdriver. It would take a while. The lid barely budged, so I kept on hammering, over and over. My hands began to sweat, and my heart raced as time ticked away.

After what seemed like forever, one corner of the lid lifted off an inch or so. The nail was still in place connecting the two pieces, but I thought I could reach inside . . . I tried and could get a few fingers into the interior, but they landed on nothing. I would have to either loosen another corner or keep lifting this one, perhaps removing a nail.

Even though the night remained cool, my forehead started sweating, too. It took all my concentration to tap powerfully enough to cause a little movement, but quietly enough to make no sound. After about a half hour of more muted hammering, I'd made no progress. My shoulders ached. I had to remove the nail.

Using the hammer, I hooked the nail head with the claw and pulled to lever it out. At first it didn't move, but when I tugged with just a bit more strength, it gave way quickly and made a high-pitched *screech* that rang shrilly through the air. It shuddered through my bones and teeth. Then it echoed back.

I dropped to my knees. How had this happened? I'd had no idea it would lift out so abruptly and make such an awful noise.

Surely someone had heard that screech and would soon peer out of a window, so I shimmied flat on my stomach to get under the car. My heart pounding so hard, my entire body shook, and my breath came out in short, silent puffs. Time stopped ticking forward, and only my breathing and heartbeats let me know the minutes continued to pass. I still held the hammer in my fist, the nail still caught in the claw. But I'd left my oil cloths and screwdriver in plain sight.

Then the low rumble of voices broke the silence and the scrape of boots as someone—or was it two people?—walked closer. They would probably notice the oil cloths and screwdriver. They would probably see that a crate had been shifted, and the corner had been lifted off.

I bit my lip until I tasted blood. If whoever came toward me noticed anything amiss, they would probably think to look under the car and catch me red-handed, my purpose obvious. No stories came to mind. I would have to admit to my plan.

A man said in English, "I'm telling you I heard something."

"Heard what?" said a different voice. Brohammer! The other man had to be his driver. "Be quiet, damn you. All I can hear is your fucking feet clacking on this fucking street. I can't hear anything else."

It shouldn't have surprised me that Brohammer spoke so crassly. My body screamed internally. *Please, please don't let them notice anything.*

The driver said, "It sounded like a . . . baby, a baby's wail."

A long moment of silence. I remained motionless and flat on the ground, and I could see only a line of moonlight between the bottom of the car and the street. Then four boots broke the line. They stood just inches away.

Laughter and then, "Haven't you heard coyotes sound like babies? Maybe there's some coyotes in the woods. That's probably all you heard, a coyote." Brohammer laughed again.

"No," the driver said slowly. "There ain't no coyotes here. Besides, it was more like a . . . cat."

Brohammer hissed and laughed again. "*Me-owww.* Mountain lion."

"Hey, don't joke about mountain lions. No, sir. I'm from Colorado, and I know me a bit about mountain lions. They can kill you like that"—I heard the snapping of his fingers—"but I don't think none of them's here, neither." What sounded like genuine fear and nerves cracked his voice.

"Maybe there are. And oooh, I'm so scared. Here, kitty, kitty, kitty . . ." Laughter. "Kitty, kitty, come get some fresh meat."

The driver, sounding resigned, finally said, "I guess it ain't nothing. Ain't nothing here."

"Let's go."

One set of feet turned and scraped away, and then after long minutes the second set went away, too.

My body wouldn't move at first. True, I was no sleuth, but I had escaped discovery. I had to congratulate myself. Right under Brohammer's nose, I'd found proof of his treachery, and he didn't even know it.

I couldn't imagine why Brohammer and his driver had stayed awake so late at night. It had taken but a few minutes for them to arrive. Where had they billeted, and did it sit close by, where they'd see me before I could slip away? Common sense told me to leave as soon as possible. *Flee.* Forget this mission and disappear before I could be discovered. But I had a job to finish. My body returned to my control along with my determination.

Hearing no other sounds, I shimmied out from under the car and quickly reached into the crate. And pulled something out. A cutter. About six inches long with rubber handles and very sharp blades. So Jimmy's suspicions were correct. Tools, not issued by the army, in unmarked crates in an engineering officer's motorcar. The cutters and gloves couldn't be intended for Brohammer's men. Engineers didn't need them; the infantry did. And as Jimmy had pointed out, an officer of the engineers had the freedom to move around when others didn't.

I slid the cutter back inside the crate and took almost an hour getting the lid nailed shut again silently, and then I shifted the crate back to where I'd found it. Afterwards I crept back along the same route. Some guiding and benevolent spirit must have looked down on me fondly. I'd made it; I had done it. Once back inside the château, I breathed a huge sigh of relief. But all I'd done had left me too wound up to sleep.

I found our room empty. Cass had gone out again, so she had to know I'd gone outside, too. But our missions had nothing in common.

The exhilaration of succeeding left my heart still racing, and now as far as I knew, I was the only one outside Brohammer's ring that had laid eyes on evidence, evidence that could prove his crime.

The thrill quickly dissolved. Should I have felt proud that I'd discovered something important? Flooded with feelings, none of which was pride, I let thoughts run around in my mind. I hoped that all of a person's actions and choices meant something, and Brohammer's crime would catch up to him. I wanted to believe that one day everyone would have to stand face-to-face with themselves.

How would I face my own dishonesty? My scheming? The things I had done—leading on a man, kissing him when I hated doing it, and sneaking around in the middle of the night to uncover his secrets. What of me?

In the morning, on the first day of September, a cool rain pounded the ground and sluiced down the steep sides of the château's roof. Falling like little pellets, rainwater had already gathered in shallow puddles that reflected the dull-gray sky above. Perhaps I truly lived under a lucky star. The weather would ruin my picnic plans. I wouldn't have to go out with Brohammer again after all.

Chapter Nineteen

When I left my room that same morning, I heard the news. Poppy, the sweet, adorable boy who'd stolen all of our hearts, had developed a mysterious fever, and so far, it showed no signs of breaking. A silent gloom had settled over the hospital in Neufmoutiers. Poppy was bedridden and groggily refusing to ingest anything other than a few sips of water offered by his mother.

The nurses sponged him to reduce the fever, and although all the doctors looked in on him, Dr. Logan took charge of Poppy's care. Wearing my street dress in preparation for the day ahead, I translated for the mother while she talked to Dr. Logan. Of course the woman wanted to know how her son's health had so rapidly taken a turn for the worse.

Dr. Logan explained that sometimes an infection could set in, even in a bone that appeared to be healing well, and no one knew why. When the mother asked about treatment, Dr. Logan said that other than trying to keep him cool and hydrated, we could do little else. Her hope, she said, was that Poppy's own healing capabilities would soon turn the tide.

Poppy's mother never asked if her son could lose his life to the infection, but I saw it in her eyes—a question she would not ask. She knew the possibility existed but didn't want to put it into words.

After the meeting ended and Poppy's mother left for home for some rest, I joined the other ambulance drivers at the table for some morning sustenance, but no one ate much except for Eve. Eve, who by all appearances loved the boy the most, kept insisting that all was well and Poppy would be up and about again in no time.

"He's too ornery to let anything get the best of him," she said as she finished eating. Her voice sounded determined, but she wouldn't meet my eyes, and I doubted she allowed anyone else to see inside her, either. Sweet Eve, who still looked like a child herself, couldn't face even the possibility . . .

The nurses who weren't working with Poppy prayed their rosaries, and I saw Beryl, holding an umbrella high over her head, escape down the road in the direction of the church. Beryl, who'd once told me she had no faith. Whenever Dr. Logan appeared, we all studied her expectantly, but she did nothing more than sadly shake her head.

And soon I would have to face Brohammer. As Cass and Lottie prepared to drive two of the doctors to one of the dispensaries nearby, I decided to go for a walk down the road toward the village center. I located an umbrella and took it, although for a moment I considered walking in the rain and letting it drench me. Maybe it could wash away the awfulness around me now.

Halfway to the village center, in the hammering rain, the purr of an engine made me halt. I turned to see Brohammer in his car, smiling hugely at me from the driver-side window. Gleaming and gorgeous in his uniform. His scrubbed and shaven skin radiant as if the sun were out, and his hair looked freshly pomaded, as usual. "Too anxious to wait for me, I see," he said. His smile reminded me of the cat that had swallowed the canary.

I shook my head. "That's not it."

"Get in," he said. "I've completed my search mission and have found everything we need for today."

"But the rain . . ."

"Phooey on the rain," he said. Then again, "Get in."

After walking around to the other side of the car, I collapsed my umbrella and slid into the seat beside him. It didn't escape me that now I sat just inches away from wartime contraband that represented just how depraved this man was.

I forced a tight smile and said, "You couldn't possibly think about a picnic now."

His smile fell a notch, but he kept his poise. He also didn't drive away; therefore we sat in the middle of the quiet street by ourselves, the engine running, steam rising off the hood in the pouring rain. "This is no way to start our day together, my dear. How are you today?"

I pushed drooping hair off my forehead. "To tell you the truth, dreadful. A boy we've all become quite attached to has been recovering from a broken leg, doing well. Then out of the blue, overnight, he developed a fever, an infection in the bone, and I'm not sure now"—I had to pause—"if he'll even make it out of there."

"Hmmm," said Brohammer. "All the more reason to get away and have a wonderful day together."

I turned to face him. "I shouldn't go now. I'm about to jump out of my skin waiting for news, and I might need to translate for his mother."

The smile left altogether. "They can find someone else, and let me tell you something—waiting around isn't going to make something happen any faster."

"I know that . . . but I don't want to leave the others while this is still going on. Please understand."

He turned away from me then and stared through the windshield. "I have wine, bread, some good cheese, berries . . ."

"I'm so sorry."

"Don't be sorry. Do what you promised. The picnic was your idea."

I smoothed my skirt across my lap. "I'm aware of that, but circumstances have changed. Look at the weather."

"We can have a picnic inside the car, sweetheart, or we'll find some-place under cover. Trust me. I'll find the perfect spot. I always do."

I stared down at my muddied boots. "It's a slick mess out there."

He remained silent, and I dared a glance at him. His jaw clenched, released, and then clenched again. Apparently noting my attention, he shifted his gaze over to me, and I found his eyes such a cold, hard, and utterly clear blue they reminded me of ice, so smooth and slick they reflected me like mirrors.

Keeping his voice under control, he asked, "So which is it? You can't go because of the boy, or you can't go because of the weather?"

The small amount of food in my stomach froze. "In truth, it's both. I'm sorry, but I just can't go today."

"I stayed over for you. You asked me to. And I went to a lot of trouble."

"Again, I know, and again, you have my apologies. But no one expected this horrible development, and no one realized the weather was going to change, either."

He turned back to face the windshield and said, "Do you enjoy making a fool of me?"

"I haven't made a fool of you. Plans change all the time, don't they? We're in a country at war. Besides, who would see you as a fool? Who knew of this planned outing?"

"My driver, for one."

"So share all that good food and wine with him. That's sure to make him happy."

A snorting sound escaped him. Then silence. Still staring out beyond the windshield, he said in a rather seething manner, "If I ever find out there's someone else . . ."

I sat up straight. "Are you threatening me?"

Finally he looked at me again, and the rage on his face answered my question. No longer trying to hide his fury, he said smoothly, chillingly, "You think this is threatening? Girl, you have no idea. When I pose a threat, you'll have no doubt about it. You don't have any clue what I'm capable of."

It sat on the tip of my tongue—*I do know what you're capable of. Profiting off our deserving soldiers, giving some men and not others life-saving advantages, and the evidence is just behind me.* But thankfully I kept silent. If he knew, no doubt he'd probably get rid of the evidence quickly, and who knew what else.

I grabbed the door handle.

"Oh no, you don't," he said. "You're staying put."

"No, I'm not."

"Think better of it."

"I already have." Then I proceeded to open the door and step out.

"Don't walk away from me, Arlene," he said as I slammed the door.

But I did walk away from him and never once looked back. To my surprise, however, he gunned his engine, and the tires spat a fine spray of mud and a few larger clods of gunk on my dress as he turned around and drove past me. I didn't look up then, either, just stared down at my now-soiled dress. After his engine noise died away, I stumbled upon a bouquet of fresh flowers lying in the mud beside his tire tracks.

I'd clearly made an enemy, and I'd never known the feeling before. The weight of knowing someone out there in the world—and so close by—might wish me harm felt new, unsettling, and frightening as it sank in.

Back at the hospital I learned that Dr. Logan had called a meeting of all AWH staff in an hour, and it made me nervous. All of us wondered what she had to tell us. Maybe something about our next assignment. Or an update on Poppy. That hour passed like molasses, and everyone stood silent, stoic, as we waited in the parlor, where Dr. Logan usually made announcements.

She soon appeared and told us that the morning after next, we would relocate to a hospital in Luzancy near Château-Thierry. We would occupy a lovely old château that had served as a hospital for most of the war, first by the Germans, then the French, and finally the Americans, who had made it an evacuation hospital for the Château-Thierry and Belleau Wood fronts. Large and with abundant hot water, it would support our cause very well.

The Germans had abandoned Château-Thierry and left it in shambles, she also told us. The retreating and defeated Boche had made sure to destroy the interior of every home and every piece of personal property in the town as they fled. Now, French refugees were returning to the area en masse and finding everything they'd owned in ruins. Many of them sick, hungry, and defeated. We would probably take care of some men of the French Sixth as well.

We would leave two doctors, one driver, and three nurses behind in Neufmoutiers to run the dispensaries. Once in Luzancy, however, we would soon welcome the second, larger wave of arriving AWH personnel, along with another ambulance that had been brought over and adapted, too. A second unit, AWH Hospital No. 2, would soon open in La Ferté-Milon, and the Red Cross had asked for six more units. Our operation was growing.

My first thought: Cass should stay behind. She seemed so much better in this place, but I didn't know who would make that decision. On the other hand, despite our friendship feeling broken at the moment, I still needed to look after her.

Dr. Logan told us we had only one full day to ready everything for moving. She made no mention of Poppy. She acknowledged what we were going through, however, by ending her announcement with a simple statement: "It's best to stay busy."

That night I wrote a letter to Maman and Luc, telling them we would move again to another location and asking how they were. So far, I'd received only one letter from Maman, and I didn't know why.

Perhaps our unit was difficult to find, or the mail service had worsened. Or maybe Maman simply hadn't written. I didn't feel that no news was good news; instead, the absence of news made me think that for some reason, they wanted me left in the dark.

The next day, with still no news on Poppy, everyone went to work disassembling hospital beds, beating mattresses under the eaves to avoid the rain, packing medical equipment of all sorts, and gathering up our meager possessions.

In the early afternoon, one of the nurses appeared and tearfully told Cass and me that the infection in Poppy's leg had entered the bloodstream, and yes, it had killed him. As she told other waiting groups, who paused in their packing to hear the news, we could hear gasps, some sobbing, and also periods of utter silence. But when the nurse reached Eve, a scream full of anguish pierced the air, and then Eve tore out of the château into the rain.

"Someone should go after her," I said to Cass, whose eyes looked muddled by a combination of disbelief and shock. "Kitty or Lottie? Do you know which one she's closest to?"

Cass shook her head. "I'll go."

"How kind of you—" I began to say, but Cass had already started walking briskly toward the exit, grabbing an umbrella on her way out.

An hour later she returned and told me she'd never found Eve.

Burying my concern, I continued to work on moving preparations while Cass stared into the empty courtyard, now battered by rain that fell even harder than the day before. My heart went out to Eve. Perhaps she hadn't suffered a personal loss before this one. How would she fare from here on out?

Soon Dr. Logan called a meeting and told us she had spoken to the family, and in her own words she relayed what had happened. She said she knew how sorry we must have all felt to have witnessed this tragedy.

As she finished, Eve, dripping from head to toe and wiping her face, which was so wet it was impossible to tell where the raindrops ended and the teardrops began, appeared in the back of the room.

She called out in a voice I didn't recognize, "When is the funeral?"

I had to steal a glance over my shoulder. One of the nurses put a jacket around Eve's quivering shoulders.

Dr. Logan answered as I faced forward again, "Tomorrow afternoon."

Eve cried out, "We all must go to the funeral!"

Dr. Logan's shoulders fell. "My dear, it's imperative that we leave in the morning. We won't have time—"

"We must go!" Eve shouted, looking around the room for support. But no one else would openly defy Dr. Logan.

"We shall not delay. Hundreds and maybe thousands of people await us," Dr. Logan replied calmly.

"We cannot wait another day?" Eve exclaimed, and I glanced over my shoulder again. The nurse who'd wrapped the jacket around Eve now held her close to her side. I perused the group for Beryl. Why wasn't our Dr. Rayne intervening, at least defusing the situation?

Finally I spotted her, staring ahead and unmoving.

After a long pause, Dr. Logan, looking ever so serene and untouchable, said, "We shall not wait another day. I'm sorry to have to say this, and I do know how most of you probably feel. But another most difficult truth to face is that we shouldn't attend villagers' funerals. If we attend one, then we have to attend them all, or else we show favoritism. Other villagers have perished, and we—"

"He was just a boy!" Eve said, and, turning around again, I couldn't tear my eyes away from her trembling, rage-filled face.

"Yes," Dr. Logan replied calmly. "And many sick boys and girls await us in Château-Thierry."

Eve's voice cracked as she squeaked out disbelievingly, "And you can't make one exception? One day?"

"No," Dr. Logan eventually answered. "I won't."

Eve stood there fiercely, her chin lifted, her arms crossed, then two fresh tears ran down her cheeks and she folded over, burying her face in the jacket.

I turned back to Dr. Logan, whose composure hadn't fractured, not even in the slimmest of slivers.

In that moment I hated her so.

Chapter Twenty

LUZANCY, FRANCE

SEPTEMBER 1918

Château-Thierry lay snug in a valley along the meandering Marne, closed in by woods and overlooked by its ruined castle's crumbling towers. Only a few months earlier, it had been a charming town of stone buildings, walled gardens, and roads that ran parallel to the river in a series of steep terraces lined with poplars. Famous for its beauty, it featured cathedrals, a fountain, and at the top, a panorama of the valley. The town was also the birthplace of the poet and fable author Jean de la Fontaine, and its hotels were named for animals in his honor—the Giraffe, Deer, Elephant, and Swan.

The city, affectionately called Chatty Terry by American soldiers, had earlier that year suffered its second German occupation, when from late May through early June, it was the site of a great battle and a successful stand by the American machine gunners.

Because of Château-Thierry's railroad depot and vital bridges, almost all Americans engaged in the Marne battles had passed through the city. It had long been a center of action and a path to Paris.

As we passed by, we could see the once-sparkling Marne, now clogged with tree corpses, oily scum, and war debris—broken rifles and helmets, rusted shells and artillery. From outside the city we caught sight of heaped masonry, piles of rubble, and barricades, but the town hall still stood guard, minus one tower, and residents continued to return. This, despite all the sacking and destruction.

Before the Germans retreated, they stole and sent home whatever they could take and then destroyed everything they couldn't take. They entered every home, broke every piece of ornately carved furniture, smashed every set of china and pottery, tore down every swath of drapery and ancient tapestry, and ripped apart every handwoven rug. Surprisingly, they'd bypassed the rock cellars that were older than Napoleon and held millions of bottles under the houses of wealthy wine merchants.

Despite it all, we could see why the city had been considered so beautiful. The church of Saint-Crépin with its carved buttresses and rough-hewn tower still stood, and the sixteenth-century belfry of the Belhan Mansion remained intact, too.

Passing through, we learned the good news that the Allies had made remarkable progress against the Germans, and the US First Army had pushed back the Saint-Mihiel salient, or "bulge," as they called it, on September 12.

The city was bisected by the river, once crossed by three lovely bridges. But one of these, an old triple-arched stone one, lay in pieces, and my throat tightened when I noticed that American engineers were at work here, clearing the blockage in the river and rebuilding the bridge, and they had already constructed two new pontoon bridges.

Brohammer could be here with his engineers. That is, if he ever did his job instead of gallivanting around selling war contraband.

Lottie had stayed behind in Neufmoutiers, and so Cass drove the ambulance directly behind us, escorting Dr. Logan. Beryl and I had not spoken of Dr. Logan, her unpopular decision, and the funeral that perhaps transpired at that very moment. Before we left, it looked as though Eve had pasted on a stiff paper face and forced herself to do as ordered.

For Eve's sake, I had to say to Beryl, "I wonder if the funeral is over by now."

My eyes focused ahead as I drove beyond the city. I could hear Beryl sigh. "It's obvious you didn't support leaving today."

"I was surprised you did." I took a glance at her, nervous about her reaction, but I'd always spoken openly to Beryl. "At least you appeared supportive. You never said anything against her."

"No, I didn't." After a few heavy moments, she rubbed the back of her neck and said, "I do understand how many of you feel, but Herberta has to make difficult decisions every day."

I said nothing.

"I don't envy her," Beryl said.

I bit my lip, but then I responded: "I don't envy her, either, but I would've made a different choice. It seemed a simple thing to leave Eve behind; it would've given her a chance to at least recover for a bit."

Beryl's hair had grown longer, and she was trying to fashion it into some kind of bun. We'd had no time to seek haircuts, and most of us would've cringed if we'd done something that unnecessary and self-indulgent. "And why should Eve receive more consideration than the rest of us? Why would she receive special treatment?"

"Because she's the most devastated."

Beryl gave up on the bun and dropped her hands into her lap. "On the exterior. But we have no idea how others might suffer, too. Think of Cass and how you've worried about her. No one else knows besides you and me; is that correct?"

"Yes, I haven't told anyone else."

She sounded a bit bristly then. "That's my point. We don't know what others might be dealing with."

"Most of us would never tell."

"So, you've made my point again. With little information, Herberta has to make the best decisions she can for our group as a whole. Perhaps if Eve had come to her, however, Herberta might have left her behind."

"Eve was probably afraid to ask. Maybe she knew Dr. Logan wouldn't honor her request."

"Do you call what Eve did in the meeting yesterday a *request*?"

"Yes, a request from a distraught person holding herself together as best she could under the circumstances."

"Well . . . ," Beryl said. "It's done now, and now we enter a new area, a new phase." She shifted a little in my direction and fixed her gaze on me. "Will you forgive our Dr. Logan?"

"It's not my place to forgive." I paused. "But do I think as highly of her as I did before? I don't know." I coughed. "I understand she made some hard decisions, but as I said, I would've made different ones."

Beryl turned away and faced forward again. "Perhaps, then, that's why you're not a leader."

My heart staggered. Beryl had always treated me with kindness, we'd never disagreed, and she'd never said anything so full of disdain to me or anyone else, for all I knew. I had believed she valued my opinion, and her words bordered on cruel and sent a clear message: the doctors were in charge and didn't welcome any questioning of their decisions. Or perhaps the war was getting to everyone by then.

My mouth filled with retorts almost too ardent to contain. But contain them I did. I owed Beryl. I coughed again, and for a few moments feared I might have to pull over, halting our entire caravan, and we had already stopped for lunch. Instead I pushed on.

Her harsh words echoed inside me—*Perhaps, then, that's why you're not a leader.*

How hollow was my existence in that moment, the world empty and cold, far from human kindness, far from touch and love.

Now I'd lost everyone.

At last we arrived. Fifteen miles outside Château-Thierry stood our new facility, a stately old château located in the advanced frontline area of Luzancy, along a loop of the Marne and behind Belleau Wood. Palatial in size, this château sat back from a vast lawn and overgrown gardens that had probably flowered and flourished and looked lovely when tended to before the war. Inside we found enormous rooms with walls and floors that showed lots of wear and tear, but the chandeliers overhead still hung from unmarred ceilings decorated with murals, and remained intact. The facility held 150 beds and had a good water supply and a water-heating plant. While the doctors set up dispensaries to serve the vicinity's five thousand residents, the rest of us whitewashed the walls, scrubbed floors, and polished windows to ready the hospital for patients again. Designated as both a military and civilian hospital, it would house separate areas for each.

Luzancy turned out to be a woodsy place where fireflies filled the evening with dots of white light. Standing in the forest full of squirrels and birds, one might never guess that the surrounding area stood in ruin, heavily shelled and bombed. Most houses had suffered hits, and the first returning refugees scavenged what food they could, dealt with unsanitary conditions left behind by the military, and tried to take care of each other.

Although the front had moved on, the Marne remained in a state of destruction. More hungry, listless, and often sick refugees returned, only to find nothing but roofless remains amid the rubble, and despite warnings about the conditions, they came back to save their wheat and oat fields, tend to vineyards, harvest grapes, and weed the graves of their buried dead, even if it meant sleeping on the floor. Without medical care for three and a half years, they had survived three epidemics. No wonder they welcomed us with open arms.

After I'd spent only two days on the cleanup crew, Beryl summoned me, telling me we must leave for a nearby village, where a breakout of a potent typhoid strain had struck twelve souls. Beryl stood at the side of the ambulance as I cranked the engine to a start, and before we took our seats, she extended a hand and said, "No hard feelings?"

I took her hand and breathed out, "No hard feelings."

Despite the devastation and hardships the French had endured, still they greeted us with glee, especially the young, who with cheerfulness and bravery made light of their problems. It seemed everyone had taken up the cry *"Vive l'Amérique! Nos sauveurs sont arrivés!"* Long live America! Our saviors have arrived!

In the village, we started with the first ill family, who had holed up in one room of their house, two children to a bed, their windows closed and their courtyard reeking of garbage and manure buzzing with a horde of flies. The mother and father had nursed their children as best they could, helplessly watching as each of their two daughters worsened and died, then their infant son, who had succumbed just hours before our arrival. The villagers buried him while we treated the parents, then we transported those poor souls and their only remaining living child, a boy of about four, to the hospital. Even though our facility wasn't ready, it was a far better place than the one they'd come from.

On the way back to Luzancy, we had to pull over, give aid to our patients, and clean them. The smell so overwhelming, I had to keep myself from gagging. At the hospital we learned that several other Luzancy villagers, diagnosed with pneumonia and influenza, had been admitted, too.

Our primary work was serving the destitute and seriously ill civilians of France, and although the horrors didn't seem as dramatic as the injuries we'd seen in soldiers, now we bore witness to another kind of suffering—among families, the most seriously ill were often the children. Most of the villages had no drainage, and we had to move from filthy barnyards, to hovels where people tried to stay alive, to villages whose streets teemed with disease-breeding muck and debris.

During dinner after our first day of driving in the surrounding area, few people spoke. Even the newly arrived team members who had joined our group kept their thoughts to themselves. Perhaps all humbled by the generosity of people who looked near to starving, we'd gratefully accepted their gifts—fowl, rabbits, butter, eggs, and even some flowers for the table. Those of us from the original team braced ourselves for the deaths of more children we would come to care for as we had for Poppy. I feared for Eve.

But after witnessing what I'd seen that day in the typhoid area, I began to better understand Dr. Logan's decision to come to Luzancy as quickly as possible.

Instead of revealing her pain on that night, Eve talked more animatedly than anyone. She told jokes she'd heard from soldiers when we'd stopped for gasoline in Château-Thierry, and she pretended to be unaffected. In her eyes, however, I detected a sheen left behind from many shed tears, and the skin around her nose had turned red and raw. In contrast, Cass still seemed to improve every day.

Later that night Cass slipped out of bed and disappeared again for a few hours, and I found myself in a state of complete bafflement. I'd almost convinced myself that Cass had become involved with a man from Neufmoutiers, but here she was, creeping out again. Could the man have followed her to Luzancy?

A villager wouldn't have been able to—he wouldn't have had the means. Had a military man followed her and come to see her so often in the middle of the night? I doubted that. Brohammer had sought me out during the day, exhibiting more freedom than I'd ever imagined an officer would have, but even he hadn't come to see me as often as Cass had gone out on her nighttime forays. Only a high-ranking officer could have moved about so much, and if that were the case, why would Cass need to slip away and meet him in secret?

Cass had started going out in Neufmoutiers but never did so in Meaux, where only a few of us had worked. Her forays resumed in Neufmoutiers and continued here. Either Cass went outside alone, or she met someone who had not gone to Meaux but had moved with the team to Luzancy. One of the other women. And if one of the other women, why did they meet in secret?

A slow dawning came over me then. Once, I'd heard that some people fell in love with another person of the same gender. The comment had stuck with me: someone had described it as a rare condition. My mind spun a complex web while I imagined that perhaps Cass was one of those afflicted people and that perhaps her shell shock had triggered the illness.

But if she had fallen in love with another woman on our team, who was it? Cass had not gone out at night in Meaux, so it had to be someone who hadn't served there with us. Immediately Eve came to mind. But it was difficult to believe that two of our team members suffered from the same condition.

By the time Cass returned to our room, I'd convinced myself she went outside at night by herself and my earlier contemplations bordered on crazy.

For the next several weeks, Beryl and I drove to the typhoid area every day. She treated those she could and inoculated everyone else. In one tiny hamlet the children screamed when they saw us. The villagers explained that anyone dressed in uniform brought on such fear because earlier in the year, German soldiers forced children at gunpoint to march in front of them as a protective shield.

I helped move debris and dig drainage ditches in the village when Beryl didn't need me. I continued to transport people to the hospital, many of whom had fallen into delirium. We held meetings during which we told the hastily assembled villagers that the Germans weren't coming and typhoid was the thing to fear. Cut off from outside communications, we didn't yet know how rapidly the influenza had spread and killed.

After three weeks in Luzancy, we housed forty-nine patients in the hospital, among them our typhoid victims, those with pneumonia and influenza, and others with various infections and neglected surgical needs. Soon the influenza spread like a dense fog over our valley, and many children died. Infants died. Young adults and the elderly died.

One of the new nurses sat down at the table one night holding a canteen, swigged what was most likely *pinard*, then toasted another new nurse who sat across from her, and said, "Another day at the deadside."

The other nurse took the canteen and replied, "Hear, hear."

Gallows humor had spread, even here.

Our Dr. Kitchens became ill but made an almost miraculous recovery; two of the nurses became so ill we drove them to a hospital in Paris for care. We didn't know yet if they'd survived or not.

Once, Beryl and I were summoned to a village reduced to rubble, where we peeked into houses and found them empty. We finally walked in on a group of about twenty people living together in one room. They had no food or heat, and autumn winds whined through the open broken windows. The villagers slept on straw pallets.

We found a sick girl, eight years old, with auburn hair who could barely move but clutched a ragged and smudged doll to her chest. At first Beryl diagnosed pneumonia, so we took her to the hospital. Once rediagnosed as tubercular, however, she could no longer stay, as we had no provisions for those with such a contagious illness. We could find no other bed in any other facility, either. Therefore, with no other choice, we had to return her to the care of her family. We did the best we could to set her up with a bed, food, a stove, and instructions to the family on how to protect themselves, but it made me feel ill and awful to leave her there.

Diphtheria and scarlet fever cases kept increasing, as did more and more victims of the influenza epidemic. As we moved between the hospitals, dispensaries, and villages in need, officials of different districts often stopped us on the road and pleaded for our assistance, and similar letters asking for help began to arrive at the château daily. I hated having to translate to people in such need that we would do what we could but were already stretched to the limits of our abilities. No one on the AWH team had taken a full day off, and no relief appeared in sight as no leave could be granted. Our ambulances ran day and night, serving over a hundred villages.

Each day, we woke up hoping the war would end. In mid-October, after four weeks of doing what we could for the villages, we learned that the Allies had almost secured a victory to end this horrific war. US forces had broken through the Hindenburg Line at the end of September and had the enemy on the run in the Forest of Argonne. We knew the cease-fire would have little impact on what we did in Luzancy, but we nonetheless desperately hoped for an armistice.

Time slowed. Only then did it hit me that I'd heard nothing from either Jimmy or Brohammer. We had stepped off the map. The AWH had reached the end of the line, tucked away in one of the hundreds of Marne loops, but we didn't know our exact location along that famous river. And still it felt unfathomable that no one had taken care of these villagers for so long. I'd received no letters from home, either.

One day I had an hour to spare and took a short walk in the nearby woods, which seemed far away from everything and reminded me of the shimmering fall colors I would be enjoying this time of year in Kentucky. Autumn, my father's favorite season.

My feet came to a halt as I remembered. Six months had passed since Papa's death. I couldn't believe half a year had gone by, and it left me breathless. I had not seen him during the most remarkable period of my life, and never would I be able to tell him about it.

Chapter Twenty-One

The following morning, Beryl told me to take half the day off as she would be busy operating and enough of the other drivers were on duty. Thrilled to have a few hours to myself after working for four weeks straight, I decided to search out the gasoline I needed. I left Luzancy just as the eastern sky blazed amber and transformed the river into a silver-pink snake, and drove to Château-Thierry as I'd heard I could probably find fuel there and I wanted to see more of the city, which was slowly inching and crawling its way back to life. I had to bargain American cigarettes to get gasoline from a local man, but I managed to fill the tank and had several hours to spare.

I walked into the old city's narrow cobbled streets and witnessed the random damage from heavy machine-gun fighting and artillery fire. Bullet holes pockmarked walls, and most of the windows lay in shattered pieces on the ground, but here and there, one house would appear untouched while the next had disintegrated into heaps of stone, lumber, and tile.

Most of the wreckage from inside the houses, shops, and cafés had been carted off and discarded by then, but some piles of broken family belongings still huddled in the streets. I walked past one garden stacked with broken chairs, a crushed grandfather clock, and a few oil paintings with slash marks through them. Signs of life caught the eye in some of the homes, while others remained unnervingly still and silent. The sound of my footsteps echoing off the ancient stone walls rang lovely but also lonely.

As I climbed the winding streets toward the town hall, life in the village became more apparent on this, a Friday market day. In the old covered market area, some of the area's farmers again offered produce for sale from makeshift stands or baskets on the ground. An old woman offered me butter wrapped in grape leaves. Gladly I bought some, along with a few eggs she retrieved from deep inside a basket, where they had lain protected in a nest of lettuce.

Small groups of army men milled about, and a few of them wore the uniforms of ambulance drivers. My pace quickened as I approached two men taking up the rear of their pack, and I asked if they knew Jimmy Tucker.

They exchanged glances, and then the taller man said, "Sure, we know him. But you'd be wasting your time with that ole country boy." He bowed exaggeratedly, almost fell over, and then managed to straighten. "Corporal Peter C. Connor at your command, miss."

The other soldier beside him chuckled sloppily. Although it was still morning, the men had apparently started drinking, or maybe they'd been up all night.

"Are you in the same company as Jimmy?" I asked.

The tall man swayed on his feet and blinked against the light, as if fighting to stay conscious. "We could be," he slurred.

"Would you be able to give him a message?"

"A message?" the tall soldier asked. "Why would you want to do that?"

"I need to let him know where I am—Luzancy. I'm Arlene. Arlene Favier. Tell him I'm nearby, and I have some important information for him. Tell him 'Arlene is in Luzancy and needs to speak with you.'" I spoke every word slowly and clearly, praying one of them would understand me and could pass the information on to Jimmy. "Do you have that?"

The men seemed too drunk to remember anything I said. Instead of relying on their memories, I decided to write a note.

The tall man blinked hard again, and I turned to his companion, a shorter, gristlier man who badly needed a shave but appeared less intoxicated. "Would you happen to have any paper and a pencil on you?"

He stared into my eyes in a more comprehending way, but he said, "Pete here"—he slapped Pete on the back—"just asked you why you'd want to send Jimmy a message . . ."

I glanced about. The other men who'd walked ahead of these two were close to leaving my sight. Perhaps I should just abandon this attempt and go after them instead.

But then the gristly man said, "You don't need us to send him a message. He's right here in Chatty Terry."

Heat immediately flushed my neck and cheeks. I hadn't felt his presence. "He's here?" I touched my face and glanced about again. "Where?"

The gristly one rubbed his eyes. "Last I saw him, he was down near the quay."

"Thank you," I said and then walked briskly away. With one hand I raked the hair off my face and tried to smooth it down in back. How long since I'd taken a real bath or put on some makeup? Outside a tiny but intact house stood a tired-looking village woman holding a baby on her hip, and after I greeted her in French, I put the eggs and butter in her free hand. She stared down at the food.

I heard her call out *"Merci"* as I sprinted away.

At the quay, a crowd of townspeople had gathered, likely to watch for a supply boat slated to arrive. I tried to catch my breath and swept the area with my eyes.

Before I could find Jimmy, however, he found me. His hands on my shoulders, he spun me around to face him and pulled me into a quick hug. Then he held me back at arm's length. "I was hoping I might see you," he said joyfully—or did I imagine the joy?

"Jimmy . . ." It slipped out of me like a plea. He looked so tanned and robust you'd think he'd just returned from a vacation on the Riviera. Still winded from running, I managed to say, "I-I can't believe it. You're here. I'm working nearby. Do you know I'm now in Luzancy?"

"Yes," he said. "I received that message from Meaux, and as soon as I left here, that's where I was going. I hoped I might see you today, but I never expected to run into you in this town."

I stood before him as helpless and vulnerable as a chick fallen from its nest, whereas he seemed as pleasant and calm as always. "It's my first time here, other than passing through. I came for gasoline and then took a walk. I can't believe . . ."

He touched my upper arm. "Do you have time for a bite to eat?"

I didn't know the exact time, but the sun hadn't reached its apex in the sky, so I nodded.

"Just a little ways." He pointed toward a slanted street that ended where the ruined old stone bridge connected to the bank. "I know a place where we can sit down for a spell."

"Of course," I said.

A very short walk took us to a café with a battered exterior. The proprietor had somehow managed to get ahold of some tables and chairs, which he'd set out in the sunlight against a latticelike, vine-climbed wall. We sat across from each other on tiny round chairs at a tiny round table while the sun poured down perfection.

For a moment we sat in silence. Dazed by his presence, I didn't know what had come over him.

Then I started to ask "How are you—" while he said something similar at the same time. It had the effect of interrupting each other, and we both smiled.

I said, "You go first."

Jimmy gazed at me in that observant, unwavering way of his that left me longing, and he leaned forward with his elbows on the table and wove his hands loosely together. "We've been working in the Argonne and got here on leave late yesterday."

"Yes, I met some of your companions."

He straightened his back and scoffed in a humorous way. "No telling what they said . . . or did."

I shrugged. "It's no matter. They told me where to find you."

He dropped his hands and sat back, looking pleased, looking at me. "So here you are. Here we are."

As a waiter wound his way through the closely placed tables toward us, Jimmy turned his head, and I could see his profile—the olive skin of his neck, short stems of darker hair lying against it—and suddenly it hurt to breathe.

Jimmy turned to face me again and said, "We came here for dinner last night. You have a choice of an omelet or an omelet." He smiled as we waited, and I stared at him, tongue-tied and a little nervous, like someone who has just come upon a person they haven't seen in ages but who roams their dreams every night.

When the waiter approached, I said to him in French, "Two omelets, please."

The waiter nodded and asked, *"Vin blanc?"*

I nodded back, and Jimmy said to me, "To drink, they have white wine and white wine. They're making it easy on us. No decisions necessary."

I smiled. How wonderful to see him again! I should've held on to him a long time ago, and that truth had never hit me as hard as it did in that moment.

"No decisions," I said. "That sounds about right." My thoughts immediately flew to the decision Jimmy had made about ending us.

I saw a touch of sadness in his eyes; it seemed he'd had the same thought.

How I wished he would reconsider and let me into his life. But keeping his voice light, he said, "You might not believe it, but this was once the prettiest town in France."

It felt clear to me then; he meant to engage in nothing more than a friendly conversation. "I've heard."

"We came here before on leave, and we wanted to come back and see with our own eyes what the Germans had done to it."

"Terrible," I said.

"But enough of that," Jimmy said. "How are you?"

"I'm fine," I answered quickly. My pulse had quickened, and my breaths had shallowed—it seemed Jimmy took notice, but then I remembered why, other than feeding my heart, I had needed to see him. "I don't have a lot of time, and I must tell you about Brohammer." How ironic was it that Brohammer had provided me with a bridge to Jimmy.

His smile fell. "What about him?"

"He came to see me as I predicted he would, and I snooped in the crates he's been ferrying around in the back seat of his car. Jimmy, I found cutters, probably wire cutters, exactly as you said. They're new and probably not army issue. Besides, supplying things to the soldiers doesn't fall under the duties of an engineer, right? Those tools must be the ones he sells."

He sat breathing very quietly for a few moments, and each release of air touched me like the briefest of embraces. Here and then vanished. Now he'd turned completely serious. "I told you not to do any investigating, to leave it to me."

I shook my head. "An opportunity presented itself, and I couldn't pass it up. Anyway, what of you? You had a plan, as I remember."

Lowering his voice, he said, "I've done my share of snooping, too, and the only thing I've learned is that at least one of the men he uses for collecting the money and distributing his wares is an engineer."

I clutched my skirt underneath the table. "That puts a spotlight on Brohammer, doesn't it?"

Pensively, he answered, "I went to one of my COs, and I told him about the soldier's cutters, what you overheard, and also what I'd learned about the engineer delivery guy." He paused while the waiter brought our glasses of wine and set them on the table. "He told me it won't hold up. He can't take it up the chain of command based on such flimsy evidence. We need incriminating evidence. What did you do with the cutter?"

I gulped. "I put it back."

He stared down as his hands encircled the wine glass. Then he lifted it and smiled wryly as he gazed into the drink. On top floated a little drowned bug. He glanced up. "I suppose the waiter will expect a bigger tip for providing this charming little gift."

Lifting my own glass, I looked into it. "He didn't give me one."

Jimmy said, "I'm happy to share."

"Would you, please?"

"Anything your heart desires."

I held out my glass to Jimmy. "We'll drink this one."

When he reached to take it, his hand brushed mine, and it was an end-of-time moment, electricity as old as the ages in his touch. When I glanced up, I could see him holding his breath, but he quickly took the glass and then a long sip of the wine. Surely Jimmy felt something, but it looked as if he was trying hard not to show it.

After he set the glass back down, I gripped the edge of the table so fiercely and shakily that the table juddered, and both our drinks danced a little jig. Brohammer invaded my thoughts again. I had botched yet another opportunity.

Jimmy quickly flattened his hands on the tabletop to steady it. "Are you alright?"

I raked both hands through my hair. "Yes, but I messed up again; it's just so obvious, what I should have done. With the cutter. I should've taken it. I had it right in my hand. I can't explain why I didn't; it just never occurred to me."

"It's alright, Arlene. Do you know how many were in the crate?"

I shook my head. "It wasn't full, but I have no idea how many. It was dark. The middle of the night."

"The middle of the night?" Then, shaking his head and looking aside for a moment, he followed that up with "I have a feeling I don't want to know the rest of this story."

"It's so clear to me now. I should've taken it."

Gazing at me again, he replied, "No . . . you did the right thing. What if Brohammer keeps count and figured out one was missing? He'd know someone was onto him, and then he'd end up even harder to catch. He might have suspended his operation."

"But it's probably operating now, even as we speak. He's done this for how long?"

"I don't know."

"Maybe I'll have another chance . . ."

He leaned in very close. "Please don't say that."

"But we need that evidence. All signs point to an armistice soon. If we don't catch him now, he'll get away with it."

"I'll get the evidence another way . . . ," he said, his voice trailing off.

I focused on the ground, where the sunlight through the lattice made diamond-shaped shadows, so that I could hold still, and my heart could try to.

Gazing back into his face, I whispered, "Thank you, Jimmy, for your kindness. I'll never forget this . . ."

With a changed light in his eyes, he grasped my hand across the table with sudden firmness, then lifted it and pulled me to stand along with him. He fished out way too many coins from his pocket and left them on the table before he steered me out to the middle of the street. There he drew me in close. And then kissed me—his mouth of smoke and heat and hope and happiness—my shallow breaths completely lost, and my heart helpless to do anything other than fall even harder.

Until I pulled back and searched his eyes. "You said you didn't think it best for us . . ."

"I still don't." He then raised his hands as if in surrender, dropped them, and grabbed me again as he said through the most beautiful smile, "Oh, to hell with that."

He kissed me a second time, and then he anchored me at his side to walk me away.

"Mademoiselle, monsieur," we heard from behind. The waiter stood at our table holding two plates in his hands. Steam rose off the omelets.

"Don't worry," Jimmy said to me. "Someone will eat them."

Chapter Twenty-Two

That night just before midnight, I slipped out of bed, threw on the only street dress I'd had a chance to launder, and eased out the bedroom door.

As I tiptoed down the sweeping staircase of this grand old château-turned-hospital, I imagined how many ingenues might have gracefully taken these same steps down into a ballroom or into the waiting gaze of a young man intent to woo her. I imagined the sounds of the orchestra playing, but I heard the door to our room creaking open. Maybe I had awakened Cass, and now she was creeping out onto the balcony and looking down. Or maybe she was getting ready to take a midnight jaunt, too.

I never turned my head to check. It was my turn tonight to slip out and away from all this. It was my night for love.

Outside, the crisp night air seeped past my skin and rose into my chest. I felt like a girl again, creeping out in the middle of the night to curl up with a foal in the soft sawdust of its stable, or maybe to run my hands on the velvety muzzle of my favorite mare. I had loved those nights with only the horses and the hay and the stars and my love for those most elegant animals.

I had suggested the rendezvous. Tearing myself away from Jimmy in Château-Thierry had left me close to tears. When the time came and

I absolutely had to leave, I'd asked him, "When will we see each other again?"

He pulled in a profound breath as he held me, and the rise and fall of his chest synchronized with mine. I didn't know how I would manage this goodbye. I wanted to stay as close as humanly possible to him for the rest of my days.

He said, "We're on a short leave. We have to go back tomorrow."

I looked up into his face. "I have to drive this afternoon, probably into the late evening. But what about tonight?"

"Can you come back?"

I frowned and tried to think of an excuse I could invent, but nothing came. "I don't see how. I might offer to take another of the ambulances here for gasoline, but Cass or someone else might ask to come along. Can you get to Luzancy?"

"I had planned to come there today, just for a little chat in the middle of the day. I figured no one could frown on that. But all that's changed now." He kissed me again. "You know I want to come tonight. But wouldn't that put you in a precarious position?" Without waiting for my answer, he went on: "My feelings on that subject have not changed, Arlene. I don't want you to do anything that could bring disgrace on you here or result in you being reprimanded or even getting an unfavorable discharge from your service."

I breathed out heavily and laid my head back on his chest. "I understand what you're saying, and I'm trying to act sensibly as well."

"Is there a private place at the château?"

"No Juliet's balcony, I'm sorry to say. And we probably shouldn't meet near the hospital anyway. Luzancy is a small place." Then it hit me. How oblivious I'd been until that moment. I could do exactly what Cass had done ever since our arrival in Neufmoutiers.

I stepped back so I could read Jimmy's reaction. "I know. I'll slip out after everyone is asleep. Someone has done it and gotten away with it for a long time." I continued: "There's a wood near the hospital. You can't miss it. I'll meet you there at midnight."

First he appeared pleased, but his expression soon changed to hesitancy. "Are you sure?"

"No one will see me, I promise. The château is huge, and people sleep deeply. Well, at least most of them do."

I reached up and, barely touching him, brushed away strands of hair from his forehead, then I placed my hand on his cheek again. He grasped it and held it there, as he'd done before, but this time his hand trembled. Jimmy seemed nervous, afraid of something. Was it simply fear of the unknown, of plunging in and baring one's soul, the same fear as mine? Or was there more?

I relived those moments as I took silent steps away from the hospital and remembered Jimmy's last words to me that morning: *Don't get caught.*

The air felt as soft as a foal's breath; no wind blew, and the night waited for us, silently and calmly waited for us. The tart taste of autumn had arrived—the season of bounty and one in which we all hoped the war would finally come to an end. The leaves on the trees and ground made a moonlit canvas of color.

I spotted an army ambulance parked across the road from the woods, backed into what looked like an old cart trail surrounded by shade trees to hide it, at least partially.

Jimmy was already here.

I found him standing in a small clearing in a pool of moonlight. A beautiful man bathed in hazy, silvery light, holding still, waiting for me. His stance anticipatory, his hands at his sides, and his face a mixture of passion and fear, he watched me come toward him. I understood the fear, but I had no choice but to rush into his arms. And then into the brilliant perfection of it, kissing as though we had been starving, never enough of this, and it would never last long enough.

Jimmy respectfully pulled back and took my hand. He'd brought a tarp and some blankets, which he spread on the dewy grass, and he'd also come with bread—the yellow-brown loaves from Château-Thierry, the best to be had in those days—and a bottle of *vin blanc*. Under the luminous light of the nearly full moon, we sat on the tarp, me very close and facing him with my feet tucked beneath me, Jimmy sitting on the ground the way men do—one leg levered up and his elbow propped on his knee, his hand dangling loosely in front of him. He looked down into his wine glass. "Not a bug in sight."

We drank a bit but couldn't eat. I had a hard time doing anything other than believing I was sitting there with Jimmy and the moment was real, all of it really happening. I was the girl who had never looked for love, a daddy's girl forever, and now I knew how much I might have missed.

Any memory of my father brought on a spasm in the back of my throat. How I wished he could see me now. He would've approved; he'd wanted only my happiness.

"What is it?" Jimmy whispered as his eyes roved over me.

I shook my head. "Thinking of my father . . ." At that moment I felt the inscription of him in my every cell. He was half of me and always would be. He had led me to this moment; his spirit had shown me the way.

"Dearest," Jimmy said and took my hand. Then he half laughed as he glanced down. "He probably would've killed me. He would've wanted better for you."

"You're wrong about that. My father never ranked people. Maman did, although she didn't mean any harm. It's just the way of her generation . . ."

"No, Arlene," he said as he searched my face. "There's truth to the way your mother feels. I know I'm out of my league. You're a Thoroughbred, and I'm a workhorse."

Of course class separations still existed. How miserable that it should still affect any of us . . . after all that had happened in the world. "Now who's the person who believes in ranking people?"

He smiled. "Maybe it comes from following orders every day."

"Yes, we've all taken our share of orders."

He nodded. "I do what I'm told, and it has kept me alive so far."

"And yet you're here."

Half laughing again, he said, "Do you think I could've kept a clear head and turned you away again? I did it once, for your benefit. But not a second time. Nothing could've kept me away after what happened today." He stared and seemed to work up to saying, "Everything's changed. This war . . ." Then he looked off wistfully, painfully.

My voice came out sounding weak, although those old ways made no sense now. "Like France, all of us have changed. One can't see such suffering as we have and not come away with a different manner of looking at our lives. Our minds have changed. Our vision has changed. Now we can more clearly see what's most important."

Studying me, he appeared enthralled. Listening raptly to what I was saying, really hearing me. My words were important and heartfelt and came from the core of me, and they told the truth. Jimmy had to see. For him, for us.

"All that matters now . . . is finding what happiness we can in this world, because we have no idea, not really, of what's around the corner. I found that out when my father died, and I've learned it doubly and triply here."

His eyes full of admiration, he whispered, "I could never have said it so well. When did you become so wise?"

While we kissed, time did not exist, the night around us barely existed, and all losses and sorrows drifted away as though they'd never existed, either. A wave-swell of longing over a decade old swept away any words, and Jimmy, also too moved to talk, spoke with his hands, touching my face and neck, holding me as though he'd never let me go.

But time did exist, and ours was running out.

Before I said goodbye, Jimmy took hold of my arm. "Don't do anything about Brohammer," he said. "Forget about it. My only concern now is you and me."

We hadn't spoken of Brohammer all night, and it surprised me that Jimmy had brought him up. "But we—or someone—has to catch him."

"That would serve justice, I know. But it has nothing to do with you any longer. Please put it out of your mind. I don't want you caught up in this."

"Caught up? Jimmy, you don't understand."

"What don't I understand?"

A sick feeling always entered the pit of my stomach when I thought of Felix Brohammer. "I'm already caught up. I've seen the suffering our soldiers have had to endure, and you have, too. I have to expose him; he deserves punishment. I'm not fighting in the military—I can't—but maybe I can rectify a serious wrong."

"I don't want you to. Don't even try. He could be dangerous."

We couldn't disagree about it any longer, however, because our time had come to an end. Jimmy said he'd send a letter as soon as he received notice of his next leave. Then we would figure out a place to meet again.

Although thrilled that Jimmy and I would see each other another time, I couldn't escape thoughts of Brohammer. I clung to Jimmy as I became almost nauseous, and my vision dimmed for a moment as if a fog had rolled in.

He tilted my head up and stared into my eyes. "Arlene, pray tell: What is it?"

"He'll come see me again," I said, as I perused Jimmy's face and let out a pathetic breath. "I know it."

Chapter Twenty-Three

At long last, I received letters from home. The AWH mail had made the rounds of places we'd left and finally come in bulk. In my stack I found letters from Luc, Maman, and even my friend Olive.

The news in the US apparently full of reports that the war would end very soon, Luc wrote about our plans upon my return. He'd made enough money from the stud service to take care of our remaining horses and keep the stables in tip-top shape. But Chicory was getting old; he needed to retire. Our mare, Mary Blue, had foaled a colt, which he had sold for a more than fair price, and another of our mares was in foal and due next spring. He also wrote long descriptions of three stallions for sale in the area that could be excellent for stud service, but he didn't have enough money to purchase one, and he wanted me to help make the decision anyway.

Clearly Luc believed I'd come home with enough money to set Favier Farm's stud service back on track. And of course, I hoped to do just that. His faith in me made my faith in myself grow. The cease-fire should come soon, I would earn my bonus, I'd go home shortly after that, and now I had Jimmy, too. I dared to imagine a future that excited me.

I considered writing to Maman and Luc about Jimmy and me, to share my happiness, but I thought better of it. When Jimmy and I arrived back home, we'd have plenty of time to let everyone know, and Maman would probably take it better in person. After all the things that had changed our lives—we were no longer wealthy, after all—I found it difficult to imagine her unhappy with any man I loved. But I wanted her to hear about it from me, face-to-face.

Olive wrote about news and gossip in our corner of Kentucky and also informed me that she was pregnant, due in three months. She planned to hold off on the baby shower until I could be there to attend.

Maman's letters spoke in a mostly positive and forward-looking way. She expressed how much she missed me and living on our land and stopped just short of saying she hoped she wouldn't have to live with her friend much longer. In closing she sent stern warnings of caution that I should never find myself in the line of fire—obviously she didn't know anything about what I'd lived through—and she expressed frustration that the German chief of the general staff had contacted President Wilson to begin surrender negotiations, and yet the war raged on. If the end had been determined, why, she wanted to know, was any soldier on either side still risking his life?

As if I knew. Her little rant made me smile, however, as it showed that my mother had not lost her verve.

On the other hand, it fueled my anxiety over Jimmy and his safety. When we parted, he'd told me his unit had to head to the front again, and he had no idea when he'd get leave. All reports indicated that the Germans had run out of supplies and knew they had lost, and yet they fought just as fiercely, even as they fell farther and farther back.

In the meantime, children continued to get ill and die; mothers wept at their bedsides; fathers who'd miraculously survived the front succumbed to influenza, leaving families even more destitute; and the life drained from young women waiting for sweethearts to come home. Orphans spent time playing around the hospital, but we had to send them away for fear of exposure to a contagious disease; and one of our nurses, after a long illness, had finally passed away in a Paris hospital.

How easy it was to dwell on the awful. I had to think of something else. The sunlight pouring in through the windows in the morning and bathing the walls in a golden glow. The dew gleaming like little pearls on the grass. The butterfly that had landed on the hood of my ambulance, sunlight glinting on its wings.

Since Jimmy had left, time seemed to drag.

Once while driving back to the château, I passed by a bombed-out and abandoned farmhouse and spotted what looked like a flourishing kitchen garden. That evening after we stopped working, Cass and I drove back to see what we might harvest. In the long shafts of late-afternoon light with the warmth on our backs, breathing in pollen and life instead of dust and dirt, we picked some pumpkins and squash and then took them to the people who lived in the closest village.

Cass's recovery from her melancholia continued. Even after our difficult days handling the sick and dying, she maintained a regular schedule of going out at night. Each day, her spirit grew stronger. She had once again assumed leadership of the ambulance corps, and in addition to driving, she now trained the new recruits.

On the way back to the hospital after our harvesting jaunt, I said to her, "Cass, it seems you're faring so much better now. At one time I was so worried . . ."

Concentrating on her driving, she kept her eyes ahead. "Of course I'm better. The war is almost over. But thanks for worrying about me anyway."

"How did you do it? How did you recover so swiftly?"

"I gave myself a lecture."

Was that a joke, or maybe not?

"Seriously," she said. "I had little choice."

"I shouldn't have suggested leaving before our duty ended. I'm sorry."

She looked puzzled. It took her a second or so to say "I'd already forgotten about that."

For a moment I considered asking her about her nighttime expeditions, but then thought better of it. The day felt like a breakthrough, and I didn't want to ruin it.

At the end of October, every day brought rain. Dense clouds dropping cold downpours seemed never to dissipate, and everywhere we went, we had to step around ice-slushy puddles and avoid slick mud. On All Souls' Day, we led a procession to the graves of twelve American soldiers who'd died in the hospital during the battle for Belleau Wood, and there we placed the last of autumn's flowers.

My wish to stop worrying about Jimmy fell on my own deaf ears. The army engineers rebuilding the old stone bridge in Château-Thierry wouldn't leave my mind, either. Brohammer had worked in this area before; he'd been near enough to search me out in Meaux, so he could be in Château-Thierry now. And if he was, perhaps I might still make up for my mistake, this time grabbing some physical evidence to prove his criminal acts. Perhaps by taking only a fifteen-mile drive.

On the day we learned that the American doughboys had cleared the Argonne of all remaining German forces, it felt like time for a celebration, but the Germans still fought as they retreated. The rain stopped, and the sun peeked out from between clouds, as if inviting us to go outside and cheer anyway. Surely the end was in sight now.

We completed our village rounds early, and I had a few hours to myself before the sun went down. My fuel tank low, I took off for Château-Thierry in search of gasoline.

When I reached the city, the lowering sun was gold-washing the old stone walls of the city, the light so clear and clean and full of warmth, one could almost ignore the bullet holes. Nothing could mar the charms of that town in my mind; here Jimmy had opened his heart. I procured gasoline without having to barter for it, and then I parked and walked to the quay. Reaching the café Jimmy and I had visited, I had to stop.

I took the chair where Jimmy had sat, which afforded me a view of the river and the construction under way. Although a few engineers were gathering up tools and such, it appeared as if the work had ended for the day. I didn't know if the men worked for Brohammer, but perhaps by waiting and observing I would somehow find out.

I ordered a glass of wine from a different waiter who looked so much like the one Jimmy and I had run out on that I concluded they had to be brothers.

My plan was to watch where the engineers headed when they left the quay. If I could find out where they billeted, perhaps I could learn if they worked in Brohammer's unit and, if so, find his car. But the engineers stood around and chatted, making no moves to leave.

The waiter brought the wine. I sipped it and closed my eyes, face turned up toward the setting sun. This taste would always be Jimmy; it would always be ours. A little bit sweet, a little bit spicy, but also dry, which left the palate hungry and wanting more.

My back straightened when the men I watched began to move. Leaving the bridge, they turned up the very street where I sat. Maybe they would come to the same café. A tiny surge of panic. But why? His engineers didn't know me, and even if they did, they wouldn't know my purpose here.

Something big blocked my view and slipped into the chair facing me, cutting off the light.

My first thought: *Brohammer.* But instead I looked into the face of his driver. Unlike Brohammer's other men, he *did* know who I was; he'd seen me before, back in Meaux.

My hunches had paid off; I'd found Brohammer's unit. But where had the driver come from? It seemed as if he'd materialized from the air.

"Hello to ya, Arlene."

His words had the effect of dropping a loop of rope around me. Not tightening, but definitely there. His long face, off-center nose, and thin lips made him a plain man—not handsome but not ugly, either. One of those men you might never notice unless you knew him. He was slim and had a large Adam's apple, and his eyes were so black I couldn't distinguish the pupil from the iris.

I tried to smile. "I didn't realize you knew my name."

He shook his head as if surprised. "Don't take me for no fool, Miss Arlene. I been hearing your name ever since my captain met you back in Paris. I don't know what you done to him, but he ain't been the same for a good while now."

I didn't know what to say to that, and so I took another sip of wine and reminded myself that whatever this meeting was, it would soon end. The taste of Jimmy spread on my tongue. I relished it, as the driver's uniform was so dusty it forced me to inhale a musty odor.

"Whatcha doing here, Arlene?"

His eyes grew more sinister, and a tiny chill ran up my spine. "I came here for gasoline, for the ambulance . . ." He wore the insignia of a corporal. I leaned a notch closer and painted a pleasant question on my face. "Corporal . . . ?"

"Corporal Needles. Grady Needles."

"Nice to meet you," I said.

He shifted his weight. "As you was saying, you come here for gasoline?"

"Yes."

"Like you did a week or so ago?"

Now the rope around me did tighten. Being with Jimmy in this place on that glorious day must have made me oblivious to all others. "I didn't see you the last time I was here."

"Well, I seen you."

I shrugged.

"And I'm not the only one who seen you."

I wrapped my hands around the wine glass to keep them from trembling. "Oh, do tell me."

He laughed. "So proper looking on the outside, but we seen you. The captain and I seen you out there"—he pointed toward the street— "carrying on with that soldier."

After downing another sip and plunking the glass back on the table, I kept my voice pleasant but said, "And why is this any of your business?"

He shook his head. "You're taking this the wrong way, Miss Arlene. I seen what you done, what you are, but I don't mean you no harm. Tell you the truth, I don't care 'bout nothin' except getting out of this god-awful place. But my captain, why, he sure does care. I already knew he was a little crazy before, but I didn't know how bad it really was till that night after he seen you kissing another man."

Now the rope squeezed, and I feared it would cut off my air. "Is this a threat?"

He shook his head. "It's a warning. Believe you me, I'd rather stay out of this here business. After he seen you, it took three of us to talk him out of a fury the likes I never seen before, and we had to get him real drunk that night so he wouldn't take off searching you out."

"I see." I almost laughed. *Warning* was a bit of an understatement; I wasn't surprised by Brohammer's reaction, though I couldn't imagine what he would do now. And why hadn't I sensed that someone had observed Jimmy and me that day? Easy answer: I was lost in love.

I swallowed and asked, "Does he know where I'm working?"

"Not yet, but he'll find out." He sat back and rubbed two fingers along the line of his jaw, then leaned forward again. "Irony is, he'd just about gotten over you—he weren't even talking about you that much anymore. I think he'd purty much given up, but seeing you here was like letting an animal out of a cage. He's been asking around about where that girl-doctor gaggle has gone off to now, but even though one of the guys found out—it's Luzancy, right?—I told that fool kid to keep his mouth shut. So my captain knows you was here that day out of the blue, but he has no inkling you're staying so close by."

The sun had lowered enough by then that his eyes shone in a different way. Surrounding his pupils was a deep, soft brown, and I read no ill intent and no guile in his gaze. I studied my hands. "I'm sorry. I misjudged you."

"My captain, why . . ." He paused as if choosing his words. "He's got a screw loose, if you ask me."

An idea hit me at that moment, that perhaps I could ask Corporal Needles if he knew anything about the contraband. He didn't sound like a big fan of Brohammer's, and maybe he'd help me nail him.

"And yet you're going against his wishes by sitting here and giving me this warning?"

His face fell. "You could say that."

"He would expect you to tell him right away if you saw me?"

He looked sincerely befuddled by my line of questioning. "Right."

"So maybe we should cut this short. I wouldn't want anyone to think of you as disloyal . . ."

I was hoping the corporal would say something like *I'm not loyal to him.* But his eyes flew wide, and then I knew that Corporal Needles would never go against his captain. Needles was scared. "Thank you, miss." He stood and peered around, then gazed down at me. "If you be taking any advice right now, I'd say you should clear outta this town." His Adam's apple bobbed up and down. "Clear out of here fast before he sees ya."

Leveling my hand over my brow and squinting up at him, I said, "Thank you, Corporal. Thank you kindly."

Before he turned away, he said, "And don't never come back."

As he walked off, I wondered how much he knew. Was he a bad man, going along with making money off the frontline soldiers? At that moment, however, I had the awful feeling I would never know.

And that concerned me less than the question on my mind at that moment. How long could I count on Brohammer staying in the dark as to my location? If he found out where our team had moved, what would he do?

I had no answers to those questions, either.

Like a repeat of the first time I'd sat at this street café, I got up and fled. Putting too many coins down, just as Jimmy once had, I again left that lovely wine on the table.

Chapter Twenty-Four

A week later, when Cass went out in the wee hours of the night again, I lay there alone, then sat up in bed and hugged my knees to my chest. Ever since my conversation with Corporal Needles, I'd walked around on edge. Sudden sounds made me jump, and even when I drove, I perused my surroundings more carefully, as if something or someone might pop up on the road and bar my way. Needless to say, peaceful sleep was a place I sought for many hours but couldn't find.

I took the corporal's warning seriously, but the extra diligence made no sense, I told myself. If Brohammer found out about our operations in Luzancy, I could do nothing about it. So Brohammer was furious. But he'd been furious with me before, and maybe this time wasn't any different.

Even more concerning—Jimmy. Fear ran amok within me at the slightest thought of him driving near the front lines. Three weeks had passed since I'd seen him. This horrible war had to end. I'd sent him a letter but hadn't received one in return. How close to the front did he go and how often? How much fire reached the roads behind the front?

All of us hoped the cease-fire would come at any moment. Jimmy's luck had held for a long time, and what a cruel trick it would be to get hurt after staying safe almost until the end. Now that we'd rediscovered each other, I couldn't lose him. In my mind I could already imagine our lives back in Paris on the farm. But over the course of the war, many ambulance drivers had been injured and killed, and I had to push any thoughts like that out of my mind or else I'd fall apart.

The doorknob made a tiny screeching sound as Cass turned it from outside in the hall, and for some reason I made no move to lie down and feign sleep. Cass slipped past the door into the room and then stopped dead when she noticed me. Moonlight streaming in through the window allowed me to see enough of her dim face to ascertain that I had startled her—the bad sort of startled.

I asked her in a whisper loud enough to hear but not too loud to penetrate the walls, "You think I haven't noticed? All this time?"

Instead of answering, she treaded noiselessly across the floor and then sat on the edge of her bed, facing me. In a calm voice but one that held some dread, too, she said, "I was pretty sure you must have heard me once or twice."

Aware that Cass didn't have to tell me anything, I kept my voice steady and not accusatory. "I'm almost certain I've noticed each and every time you left this room, and I noticed it back in Neufmoutiers, too."

Likewise, her voice was soft and matter-of-fact. "And I've noticed both of the times you've done it."

"That doesn't surprise me."

"So, who is he?" Her tone remained moderate, and I detected a bit of a smile. For a moment she sounded like the old Cass.

I turned toward her and sat cross-legged. "The first time, I didn't go to meet someone. Back in Neufmoutiers, I went on a bit of a spy mission."

"Oh really? You've become a spy?"

I shrugged. "Not in any official capacity. I took something upon myself, but it had nothing to do with romance."

"Darn it all," she said, and I smiled. "I hope someday you'll tell me about it—that is, if it's not classified. I wouldn't want you to go to the gallows because of true confessions to me."

I inhaled deeply. I had no reason to tell Cass about Brohammer and his contraband at this point, and I guessed there never had been any point. As each day took us closer to an armistice, any chance of exposing him diminished. Most likely, he would get away with it all. "It's not important any longer. Someday I'll tell you, but for now . . ." I passed a hand through the air, as if I could swat away the awful response in my body when I thought of Brohammer. "The second time, here—"

"Surprise me and tell me you went out with someone."

"I did."

"The enlisted man from home?"

I nodded. I'd once told Cass everything, and I'd mentioned Jimmy even after she had closed herself off to me. It seemed like a long time since we'd grown apart, and such a waste. But tonight, the distance disappeared. I should've talked to her like this before. I should've given us both a chance to unburden our secrets.

"A lowly doughboy. Of course you had to meet him in secret."

I nodded.

"And because you were practically forced to meet him in secret, it could, in someone else's eyes, make it look . . . so very . . ."

"Tawdry," I said for her. "Yes, I'm aware I would appear to be a loose woman."

We both sat with that for a spell.

"So . . . remind me of his name?"

Clearly Cass intended to keep the conversation centered on me. "Jimmy. He resisted my charms for a while, but he succumbed."

Her eyebrows lifted. "You pursued him?"

"I guess I did."

"Well, I'll be . . ."

"Yes, I've broken the rules, but not as you have, Cass. I care almost nothing about rules now, but this has always perplexed me to no end. You've been sneaking out for months. Why have you kept it a secret from me? All this time . . . ? I thought you and I were—"

"Friends. Special friends," she answered.

"Yes."

She wrung her hands. "We were. We are, Arlene. But my situation is so much rifer with risk than yours is."

"Is it a woman?"

She sat rock-still then and looked as if she'd stopped breathing. She shook her head and then rubbed her temples, her eyebrows nearly reaching the ceiling. "I never expected that question."

Then we sat in silence for a while.

Finally I said, "Eve, I presume."

She still didn't move, but I could hear her breathing deeply and regularly. "I underestimated you. I never thought you'd figure it out."

"I've only recently arrived at it as a possibility. I figured you went out alone, or with someone within our team."

"I could've thought the same of you. You went out in Neufmoutiers and then here, too."

"Once in both places, and the first time had nothing to do with romance, as I've already said. Two times I went out, but you've gone out so many times I've lost count. I'm not accusing you of any wrongdoing; please don't misunderstand me. If it meant enough for you to take such chances, I knew something powerful must have propelled you." I stopped to assess how my words had affected her. She looked intent but not upset. "Besides, I've heard of your condition, Cass, and I want to help."

A long silence. Then after a long sigh, she spoke into her lap. "Condition? Is that what you call it?"

I shrugged helplessly. I couldn't even remember who had told me what little I knew. "That's how someone described it to me, as an illness of sorts."

She gazed off toward the window and said in a forlorn voice, "Now you understand the need for absolute secrecy." She continued to breathe deeply in and out. "Because if you think it's an illness, it rather confirms that even among our generation, things have not improved." She turned to stare flatly at me. "It's not a condition."

"Then what do you call it?"

"I call it love."

I swallowed back a bit of disbelief.

"You're repulsed. I can see it in your face."

"I'm not repulsed. I'm concerned."

Another long sigh. "People like Eve and me are made up in another way when it comes to love. There's nothing wrong with us. We simply love a woman and not a man. Some men love other men, too. The problem is exactly what you've shown me again tonight. People see us as mentally ill or deranged. I learned that a long time ago. I started off more transparent, but the few people I told during my youth shunned me, even threatened me."

"During your youth?"

"Yes, I've always felt this way."

"I imagined . . ." I clasped my hands and stared down at them. "That maybe it came on as a response to all the awful things going on here and seeing what we've seen."

"No. Not in the least. Eve has felt this way her entire life, too."

"Have you ever spoken to a doctor?"

I glanced up to see that her body had tensed, and then I resumed looking down, trying to put my mind around all she'd told me.

"There's no reason to speak to a doctor. There's nothing sick about it. It's the same thing I'm pretty sure you feel for Jimmy, but we feel it for a woman and not a man. That's all. Everything else about us is just like everyone else. We want the same things. We dream of the same things. We need the same things."

I believed her. I'd seen Cass at her best and her worst, and through-
out it all, she'd always impressed me as a vulnerable and imperfect but
sensible woman, and a fighter, too. Cass had suffered a short spell of
shell shock, but she'd pulled herself up by the bootstraps. Perhaps she
had found such inner strength because she'd had to utilize it before, out
of necessity. I couldn't imagine what she'd had to endure, and I hated
that the way she loved made her afraid.

Meeting her gaze, I said, "I'm sorry, Cass. I didn't know. I was
just repeating what someone—someone who probably knew very little
about it—told me quite a while ago."

After a few long moments, she responded, "So now, certainly, you
understand the need for our secrecy. Many people believe that women
and men like Eve and me should be locked up. In some places it's a
crime."

I simply listened.

"We have to be ever so careful about whom we trust. I wasn't sure
I knew you well enough."

"I understand."

After another thoughtful moment had passed, she said, "If you got
caught, it would be ugly, but can you imagine what they'd do if they
found out about us? If someone like Dr. Logan knew?"

I shook my head again.

Cass continued: "I don't ever want to find out."

Still soaking it in, I couldn't imagine . . . my love was a forbidden
love, too, but if Cass and Eve were ever discovered, the reaction would
be altogether more horrific. I looked at her again and hoped she felt my
sincerity. "I'm so sorry, Cass. I shouldn't have probed."

"I'm glad you did," Cass said. "In a way, it's a relief that someone
else knows."

"I promise to keep it secret."

"I know you will. You don't have to tell me."

In the morning, Cass and I went about our business as if nothing had happened. Nothing had changed, except I felt close to her again. I also felt sympathy and concern, but those feelings soon got buried beneath the surface when we received news that French forces were bearing down on Sedan and its critical railroad hub. If they took it, the Germans would have no recourse. They would have to surrender. Capturing Sedan would end the war, and it could happen any day now. Even in the hospital wards, a feeling of urgency, of hopeful energy, filled the air. When a boy on a bicycle arrived with some mail, we all rushed to the windows in hopes he brought news of a cease-fire.

He shook his head. Nothing yet.

In the stack of mail, I found a letter from Jimmy and tore it open. Jimmy wrote that he would have a short leave in five days and would meet me in the woods on the first night at midnight. I looked at the date on the letter. If I could get through this day and the next, the following night I would be in Jimmy's arms again.

Chapter Twenty-Five

I met Jimmy in the same moonlit glen hidden away in the woods. By that stage in the lunar cycle, the moon had peeled back into a crescent, a happy, lopsided smile that gave off barely enough light to see by.

We clung to one another greedily, searching each other's mouth and face, feeling our rib cages pressing together, our hands encircling waists and grasping onto backs, finding one another's spine, our hearts in our throats. He had become familiar to me—I craved the feel of him now, and the way he touched me showed me he felt the same way.

This time, Jimmy had brought the tarp and blankets but no bread or wine, explaining that he hadn't had time to pick anything up during the day. His ambulance had broken down on the way to Luzancy, and at one point he feared he might not get it fixed in time.

We sat on the tarp, and he swept his arm out and over it before he handed me a blanket. "I sure know how to woo a girl, don't I?"

I studied the empty tarp for a moment, then reached over and took his hand, finding his eyes. "You're the feast, Jimmy. You're all I want."

He looked so sincerely moved, I ached inside. "How did I ever get so lucky as to find you?"

"It was meant to be."

He smiled. "After the war ends, I'll lavish you with everything I have. I'm due quite a bit of back pay."

For a moment I simply basked in his presence. I turned Jimmy's hand over and studied his palm. The only thing I knew about palm reading was to follow the life line. I searched for his, hoping to find a long one, but the moon on that night didn't provide enough light for me to see it.

I glanced up. "Do you really think it's almost over? We hear reports every day, and even caught one false one proclaiming the end. But of course, that turned out to be a mistake. Now we don't know what to believe."

Jimmy answered, "It's almost over. Truly it is. And the miserable thing is that both sides know it. You can tell it by the Germans' moods. Sometimes they're defeated and going through the motions, then other times they fight with desperation. Our men are going into battle even though we've won, and there's no sense in fighting any longer. But they're under orders, and if they don't fight with all their might, they could die on the very eve of the armistice."

"It must be dreadful."

"Can you imagine being the last one injured and looking down at your body and knowing you weren't going to survive? Thinking, *Just one more day, and this wouldn't have happened . . .*"

"No, I can't." I reached around to the back of my neck, unclasped my baby locket, and handed it to Jimmy. "I want you to take this with you."

He stared at the locket and chain in my open palm. "Is this—"

"My baby locket, yes. I wore it on the night of . . . the fire. It's come a long way. I want you to take it with you for luck. It's a survivor."

"I can't take this, Arlene."

"Yes, you can." When he tried to launch another protest, I folded his fingers over it to hold the locket in place. "I insist."

He finally smiled and slipped the necklace into his chest pocket and buttoned it. "Enough talk of survival." He stretched out long on his side with his elbow levered on the ground and his hand supporting his head. "Before I tell you that you're the most beautiful and intelligent woman in the world, I have to ask you—"

"About Brohammer?"

He nodded.

"I haven't seen him."

That was the truth; I hadn't seen him, and I could ascertain no need to tell Jimmy what Corporal Needles had said. Jimmy didn't need to know that anyone had seen us together in Château-Thierry. I wanted him to go back to the front lines with a clear head, with only one aim in mind: stay alive. I didn't want him worrying about me.

"Good," Jimmy responded.

I picked at a nothing-something on the tarp. "So, I suppose he'll never get caught?"

He sighed. "It's possible, yes. If I'd had more time, maybe I could've set a trap using some infantrymen I know. But, as you're well aware, the work of an ambulance driver rarely lets up."

"You did your best, I'm sure."

"And so did you, Arlene. I have to believe that at some point in his life, a person like Felix Brohammer will get his just desserts. I have to believe that someday he'll pay for what he's done."

"I hope so."

His face brightened. "So now that I've taken you to despair, are you ready to hear everything that's remarkable and wonderful about you?"

And there again, that self-mocking smile I'd grown to love—or maybe I'd always loved it. "Of course."

The rest of the night passed as if in the blink of an eye. A rapid little bird's eye blinking so quickly that human sight almost couldn't register it.

We talked about Paris, France, and Paris, Kentucky. We talked about horses and Jimmy's days on Favier Farm, and with every tiny remembrance, a bit of the horror we'd seen here burrowed away a little deeper. We studied each other's faces. I memorized the little folds at the corners of his eyes, the shape and hue of his lips, and the black band around his brown irises streaked with gold. We kissed, and this feeling, this happiness, lay at the core of the world, deep in the center of all that had been and would ever be.

Back in the world around us, we had to admit our time had nearly run out.

Jimmy looked as though he was working to still a racing heart and finally asked, "When the war has ended, where do you think your team will go?"

I didn't want to think of such things, such facts and logistics, but I wanted to plan, to promise, and I felt Jimmy did, too. "I imagine we'll stay here. The French people and injured soldiers won't simply heal up all of a sudden because we've won the war. If only it could work that way!" I paused. "But it doesn't, and the doctors are so devoted, I wonder if they'll ever leave."

"But *you* can leave?"

I shrugged. "Yes, I suppose so. I promised to remain until the war's end, but I've always thought I'd stay as long as needed, within reason. What of you? How long before you're released?"

"Like your team, we'll still be needed for a while to get our men out of here to bigger and better hospitals."

He lifted my hand and kissed it, his breath on my skin so sweet. I started saving all of these moments with Jimmy in my mind so I could call them up after we parted.

He said, "I'm hoping we get it all done and then have a long stay in Paris. I'd like to learn more about the City of Light, maybe even stay on for a while after discharge."

"In Paris?"

"Paris or somewhere else. I like Europe so much better than I expected to. The war has shown me how big the world is, and there are many things on this earth to see and do."

I understood what Jimmy said, but the war had shown me that nothing was as important as family. Poor Jimmy had lost his family at such an early age, so how could he feel the same way? "Before you go home?"

He looked puzzled. "Do you mean Kentucky?"

"Yes, Kentucky."

He gazed up at the sky and stars above, blinking once, twice. "There's nothing left for me back there. Since high school I've worked on some horse farms, I took a job in Lexington for a while, and then I worked on the railroad until I enlisted. There's nothing that lures me back . . ."

I sat very still. I had to remind myself that I'd never explained to Jimmy what I planned to do with my money and how much it meant to me. How few opportunities we'd had to talk, to really talk! I softly said, "I do have family. And I've promised to return."

He stared at me.

Dreading a response I wouldn't like, I studied him closely, but I had to say it: "I've promised Luc and Maman that I'll come back and build a house and take over Papa's duties running the stud service."

He appeared crestfallen, and my feelings matched his. Never once had it occurred to me that Jimmy wouldn't wish to go back. In my mind I'd pictured that eventually all of us—every volunteer, every soldier, every journalist, every diplomat—would drag ourselves and our gear on board big ships and sail for home, all the while our spirits lifting, our hearts healing, our hopes revived.

He whispered, "You once told me your life back there was over."

Had I said that? Perhaps, on that night he pushed me away. "I must have meant that the way it had been *before* is over. We'll never regain what we had or how it felt now that Papa's gone, but I aim to get back what I can." I think I had said that, too.

Jimmy cocked his head a tiny notch. "But the world is so big, Arlene. Don't you want to see more of it? Now that you've seen France, don't you want to see other countries, too? We don't have important positions waiting for us back home. We don't have children. We can do anything we like. Wouldn't you like to explore for a while?"

He'd found a question I'd not expected and didn't know how to answer. The night air had turned cold. "Of course, someday . . ."

I picked at that invisible nothing-something on the tarp for a long time, feeling Jimmy's eyes on me.

Eventually he scooted over and pulled me close. "Now don't you worry, my little horsette, you. We have all the time in the world to figure this out." He lifted my chin with his fingers. "You hear me? We'll figure it all out, Arlene. When the war is over . . ."

I made myself nod. Of course we would work it all out together.

But Jimmy's path was flexible; mine wasn't.

After a gut-wrenching goodbye, I made my way back to the hospital across the stillness before dawn. The birds had yet to sing, and distant roosters had not yet crowed. The night held still around me, as silent as a crypt, and I could see no one out and about this time of earliest morning.

But an unpleasant feeling ran over me, something like premonition mixed with gut instinct.

A presence. Not Jimmy. Not a farmer up before dawn looking over his fields and thinking of his next planting season. Not a lost soldier finally finding his way to a place of safety.

Someone was out there, watching me.

Chapter Twenty-Six

My body shook. Someone was shaking me.

My eyes flew open and focused muddily on Cass. "Wake up, Arlene," she said with urgency. "Dr. Logan is asking for you."

I tried to sit up, but I was worn out, and I could tell by the light in the room that I'd overslept. I had stayed awake for most of the night with Jimmy. My head full of lead, my mouth dry, and my tongue thick, I asked, "What time—"

"Past duty time. I thought I'd let you catch up on some sleep after last night, but I lost track and forgot to come back for you. You must get up now and pull yourself together. Dr. Logan wants to see you."

I tossed aside the covers as I entered full awareness. "Dr. Logan? Why?"

"Beats me," Cass said and shrugged, but I could read worry in her face.

I splashed water from the porcelain basin onto my face, ran a brush through my hair, and quickly donned my uniform and shoes. On the first floor of the hospital building, Dr. Logan had made herself something of a private office, and I hurried there while still adjusting my belt.

After I knocked on the door, I heard, "Come in."

Dr. Logan sat facing me behind a table she used as a desk, and with her back to me sat Beryl, and then on the other side . . . Captain Brohammer!

I stumbled.

Brohammer wouldn't meet my gaze, just stared ahead at Dr. Logan. Beryl didn't turn to greet me, either.

"Please sit down," Dr. Logan said, and indicated the empty chair between Beryl and Brohammer.

I did as she asked, crossed my legs at the ankles, and waited for an explanation. My mind swam in a snarl of confusion.

"Miss Favier," Dr. Logan said while leaning forward and weaving her hands together on the tabletop. "It has been brought to my attention that you left this building last night in order to meet a man and put yourself in a compromising position."

My back straightened as though I'd been electrocuted. I shook my head and must have looked a bit crazy. I'd hardly slept; maybe I was imagining this. Only I wasn't.

How did she know? It had to be Brohammer. I'd felt the presence of someone, obviously Brohammer or perhaps Needles or someone else working for him.

"I won't deny it," I said, "but I have good reasons, and I never put myself in a compromising position."

"Miss Favier," Dr. Logan said again in a sterner voice. "You have put me and everyone associated with the AWH in a *compromising position*. We have been given passage, support, food, generosity, places to stay and work so that we can serve the people of France. We have been entrusted to behave with high moral character and unquestionable scruples, and you have taken that faith and betrayed it."

Beryl flinched beside me. I couldn't understand how I had hurt the people of France. How had my love for Jimmy hurt anyone? I thought better, however, of asking that question aloud.

Did Beryl agree that I'd done something so heinously wrong? I looked over at her, but she wouldn't return my gaze. Brohammer had come here to ruin my reputation, and it appeared he had succeeded.

"No harm was ever intended . . . ," I barely managed to say to Dr. Logan. I fought the urge to clutch the jacket over my chest. Inside, a pain in my heart exploded.

"Not only have you broken our rules, which I understand were explained fully to you by Dr. Rayne here, but you have conducted yourself in a way that brings shame on our organization. Going out and carousing with a soldier while leading on a man of Captain Brohammer's status and reputation, well . . . I have to say I'm stunned . . . and very disturbed about it."

My face stung; surely someone had slapped me. "I never led the captain to believe I was interested . . ." And then I remembered when I'd asked to go for a drive and then a picnic back in Neufmoutiers, all to look in the back of his car.

"That's not the story I hear from our dear captain here."

Brohammer had charmed Dr. Logan back when he'd come in search of me in Neufmoutiers. He had crafted his veneer so carefully and impermeably so that even a woman of Dr. Logan's experience and intellect hadn't detected the cracks.

"As I said, I'm disturbed by all of this and very disappointed." She unlaced her fingers and sat back. "But I do commend you for your candor. At least you aren't denying your actions."

"I'm not denying what I did last night, no," I said, trying to speak distinctly despite my mouth being so dry it tried to grab ahold of my words. "But I never went in pursuit of Captain Brohammer. In fact, many times I told him quite sternly that I had come here to work and had no interest in being his girl. I explained long ago, beginning back in Paris, that I didn't want any involvement other than friendship. He continued to seek me out everywhere we went, against my wishes."

Dr. Logan looked momentarily puzzled. "If that is true, why did you never tell us?"

Why indeed? Now I wished I had. "It didn't seem important enough to bother you. With all the . . . goings-on . . . I thought I could handle it."

Now skepticism crossed her face. "So you have no interest in Captain Brohammer . . ." She nodded in his direction. "And yet with another man, you've had no qualms about traipsing off into the woods."

I inhaled gravely and said through the release, "That's correct. The feelings I have for the soldier are different."

Dr. Logan leveled an appraising gaze on me, one that made me feel vulnerable and judged. After a few painful, tense moments, she said, "I suppose it's beyond the point now, isn't it? You've admitted to breaking our rules and doing things you knew would shame us. And I have to say it's difficult to believe your account of the association you've had with the captain here, when it differs so much from his account."

I retorted, "Just because he's an officer, it doesn't mean he's truthful."

I heard Brohammer let out a snort, and Dr. Logan turned toward him in surprise. I thought, *Yes, let him lose his temper and reveal his true colors.* But out of the corner of my eye, I could discern that he pulled out a handkerchief and brought it to his nose, as if he'd sneezed instead of snorted. He murmured, "Excuse me."

Dr. Logan's expression eased, and she focused firmly on me again. "I see no reason to believe he isn't truthful."

"From the beginning he wouldn't listen to me. I tried everything."

She just barely shook her head. "This sounds like a misunderstanding between two people that doesn't have much to do with your behavior while here in the service of the AWH, Miss Favier. What you did last night, however—"

"Why do you think he brought my 'behavior' to your attention? Why do you think he wants to hurt me? He feels jilted and jealous. Why, in fact, early on he began to accuse me of having someone else, and at that time I'd run into the soldier only once, and we talked for just a few minutes."

"As I've said already, most of this sounds like a personal matter. Your actions, on the other hand—"

I interrupted. Why couldn't they see? "Why would an officer in the midst of war concern himself so much about two ambulance drivers?"

She paused. "Some people maintain a strong sense of right and wrong."

Now I snorted. Loudly. I couldn't help myself, and I didn't try to mask it as a sneeze. I didn't try to wipe the indignation off my face, either. Dr. Logan's eyes widened. She was probably embarrassed for me, but I couldn't help reeling. *Right and wrong?*

Realization flashed across my brain. Suddenly flushed with excitement, I turned toward Brohammer and made myself look at his smug, satisfied face. "Captain, did you arrive here in your car?"

His face paled. "Yes."

I stared back at Dr. Logan. "We must go down there at once. You speak of right and wrong. Well, I happen to know that this man here"— I pointed jerkily in his direction—"has been breaking military law. In fact, it's the reason that I, at one time, might have encouraged him, so I could obtain proof. Captain Brohammer sells essential tools—wire cutters and barbed-wire gloves—to his own men, making money off them, making a profit for his own self. And I have proof. Right now it's sitting in the back seat of his car. I've seen it there before."

Dr. Logan's face drained. "Miss Favier, you are spinning out of control . . . to make such an accusation . . ."

"All we have to do is go downstairs and check his car. He keeps his contraband there. Trust me."

I studied Dr. Logan, who seemed as if she were considering my suggestion. Heat emanated from Brohammer, but no one spoke for a moment. Dr. Logan said, "You are trying to change the subject."

"This is important. It will reveal everything. Please. Follow me down to his car. Please."

Then Beryl, who'd remained silent, stood. "Let us go and take a look, shall we? No harm in checking, is there?"

I turned to her. "Thank you," I whispered. In her eyes I saw belief, faith in me.

"Very well. Shall we?" said Dr. Logan. I dared not steal a look at Brohammer, although I could imagine his panicked expression and the cool façade he would try to cover it with.

I led our group out of Dr. Logan's office, down the hall and staircase, and outside into the brightest, whitest sunlight that reflected off Brohammer's car, which appeared recently polished.

The light half-blinding me and fatigue in my every bone, I tripped on some pebbles and righted myself. Then I strode to the back of the car, where intense relief fell over me when I saw two crates. I grabbed the lid of one; it wasn't nailed, and I lifted it off.

Then stopped breathing. Inside the crate were the small comfort kits the Red Cross canteen workers often put together and distributed to soldiers; they held candy, gum, cigarettes, and such.

No, no, no. My head suddenly became a hive buzzing with panicked questions.

Gulping hard and trying to gather myself, I waited for an explanation to hit me. Maybe the Red Cross kits had been placed on top of the tools as camouflage. I dug beneath them but found nothing other than more kits. I moved to the next crate, removed the lid, frantically dug again, and found it exactly the same as the first one.

I held on to the fender while my breath failed me altogether. I pulled in enough air to say to Dr. Logan, "They were here before. I promise you. I saw them." I spoke the truth; Beryl and Dr. Logan had to believe me.

Instead, in Dr. Logan's eyes was the kind of fear and dismay one might feel when confronted with a mad person stepping over the line from a state of normalcy into lunacy. I looked at Beryl, whose expression mirrored Dr. Logan's. Clearly I had appalled them. And then I glared at Brohammer, too enraged to even try to speak. Nausea overtook me as the side of his mouth curled into a cruel, ugly smile.

He had done this. He had orchestrated this. He had beaten me. Like a fox that has caught its prey and holds it down with both paws while it prepares to dig in with its teeth for blood. He must have realized that in Neufmoutiers someone had opened a crate. Maybe he figured out I had done it. Or was this retaliation all because I had refused him and chosen someone else? It hardly mattered now; the contraband was no longer in his car, and he'd made me look like a liar and an idiot.

"My office, Miss Favier," Dr. Logan said as she spun on her heel and marched back to the building, Beryl close behind her. At the door she turned around and said to Brohammer, "Thank you, Captain, and you have my sincerest apologies."

He tipped his hat toward Dr. Logan and then smiled at me. Again, like a fox.

She said "Come with us, please" to me, then entered the building.

Still glaring at Brohammer, I came the closest to pure, unfiltered hatred as I ever did for the rest of my days on earth. Although neither of the doctors would hear me by then, I answered anyway, "Of course."

Back in Dr. Logan's office, Beryl sat next to me. Now that I had them alone, I had to try once more to convince them. "Please hear me out. Please."

I pulled myself together as best I could. Sweat had collected on my forehead, and I took a swipe at it while Beryl fumbled about in her pockets for a handkerchief.

"Captain Brohammer is not who he pretends to be," I began. My voice croaked. "He offended me and insulted me back in Paris, and when I refused him, his attention became quite consuming. He wouldn't take no for an answer. And once after we'd spoken, I overheard some French soldiers saying that he was the officer making money off his own men. Then I learned that an American officer was indeed selling life-saving tools to our men in the trenches—"

"I must stop you." Dr. Logan held up her hands. "I'll hear no more of this character assassination. If this is true, prove it! Instead you have taken us on a wild-goose chase. Digging in that fine officer's gifts for his men, after all. You have humiliated all of us."

"I saw them there. He's selling needed tools to our men to make money."

"I've never heard of such a thing."

"I hadn't either, but it's true," I insisted.

Dr. Logan stared beyond her window, which looked out over the courtyard. My claims had fallen on deaf ears, and her mind had traveled elsewhere.

When she turned back to me, she said, "All that remains is to decide what I am to do with you. You have been an excellent ambulance driver for us, but I'm afraid your work here has ended. I'll arrange for transportation to the nearest rail station, where you can make your way to Paris. There you'll stay until I can book your passage back home."

"Please don't, Dr. Logan. I never meant to get involved with anyone. I never sought romance. In the beginning, I met with the enlisted man because he's a friend from home."

She smoothed the front of her jacket. "I can only hope you haven't already found yourself in a . . . family way."

"It never went that far."

She scoffed. "Again, I can't believe you. Your affair has gone on for quite some time, hasn't it? Shortly after we arrived in Neufmoutiers, a member of our team informed me that another member of our team had begun to slip outside at night on the sly. People have heard sounds, found muddied footprints in the foyer, and discovered doors left unlocked—to name but a few things—but no one has had the gumption, I suppose, to find out who had done it all, and so I dismissed these things as . . ." She smiled. "Possibly . . . the result of living in haunted houses." Her face turned serious again very quickly. "But now I know it was you, and . . . you must face the consequences."

"I met him twice, Dr. Logan, twice."

She tilted her head and touched her temple. "So if not you, then who? Am I to believe that someone else has done the same thing you've done? Indeed, come to think of it, one of the rumormongers maintained that more than one person had been heard leaving the building. Are there more without decent sense?"

Cass and Eve. They'd been oblivious, not careful enough. Cass's words came back to me then. *Can you imagine what they'd do if they found out about us? If someone like Dr. Logan knew?* Cass and Eve. Their names lodged in my throat.

I couldn't answer her question. "I left our building three times only—"

"A moment ago, you said twice!"

"Twice I met the soldier. The other time I checked Brohammer's car. That's when I found the cutters and the gloves. That's when I found them and knew. The only reason to possess crates full of non-army tools is to sell them."

Dr. Logan pressed her fingers over her eyes for a moment, then dropped her hands. I could tell she hadn't really listened to much of what I'd said. "I've heard enough. Because you insist on repeating this bizarre, unsubstantiated story, I want you to leave today. You won't have a chance to spread this nasty claim or see your soldier again. It's time for all the forays during the night to stop."

She blamed me for all of them, and I didn't deny it.

She paused for a moment, as if allowing her anger and indignation to build. "And if you dare to make any attempt to see this soldier of yours or contact him in any way, I'll hear about it, and you'll have to arrange your *own* way back across the ocean."

I sat still, then turned to Beryl. Her face looked blank, and I crumbled, utterly ruined. All of my pleas and explanations had come up short.

"Miss Favier," Dr. Logan said, and I turned my head back to her. "Do you hear me?"

At that very moment, cheers and hollering and clanging sounds came from outside. "It's over! It's over!" someone shouted as he banged the bottom of what sounded like a metal pot, and more sounds of glee followed.

"It's over. The war is over!"

Later that afternoon I walked outside, packed and ready to leave. Cass would drive me to the station. Almost the entire original team of the AWH had lined up to see me off, which surprised me and further cracked open my heart. Some of them wouldn't meet my eyes—it seemed everyone already knew about my rendezvous with Jimmy and my accusations against Brohammer—but at least they thought enough of me to say goodbye.

Dr. Logan didn't attend, of course, but Beryl did. She stood at the end of the line, and she *did* meet my eyes. In them I witnessed the strangest mixture of sadness, anger, disbelief, and even some loss.

I breathed shallowly, denying my lungs what they needed. If only I could plead my case to her. If only I could get her to believe in me again.

She could see the question in my eyes and quickly shook her head. "No, Arlene. I don't care about moralizing and following strict rules. I never cared for anything like that. But we made a deal. I asked you for two things: stay till the end of the war, and don't embarrass me."

Beryl thought I was building up to ask about my pay and bonus. Those things hadn't even occurred to me yet. I wanted her to stand by me. I wanted to stay and continue to help along with the others.

"And you did embarrass me," she finished.

Chapter Twenty-Seven

Paris, France

November 1918

Before Cass left me at the train station, she handed me an envelope full of cash that Dr. Logan had asked her to pass on to me. In it was the salary owed to me, all in US dollars.

Cass said, "She'll get reimbursed by the Red Cross."

Grateful, I nodded.

I would not receive the bonus, although I had worked until the end of the war as promised. Worse than the loss of the money, however, was knowing I'd let Beryl down. I thought of myself as a person as good as her word, and it pierced me through that someone I respected thought me capable of deception.

I had *some* money in my pocket now, enough perhaps to give new life to Favier Farm's stud service, perhaps even enough to purchase a long shot of a stallion to replace Chicory. But I didn't have nearly enough money to build the house I'd promised Maman.

"At least she didn't want you to leave here with nothing," Cass said before we parted, her face so full of sorrow and worry I almost couldn't look at her. She didn't know that I'd taken the blame for all of her secret meetings with Eve, and I would never tell her. What could she do besides feel miserable about it?

"Just for the record," I said. "What I accused Captain Brohammer of—profiting off our soldiers by selling them high-priced tools—is true."

"Just for the record," she responded. "I believe you." After another breath she said, "I just wish you'd told me before. I wish you'd told someone."

"I do, too. Now with the benefit of hindsight . . ."

"Just for the record also," she said. "I told them Brohammer had followed you around since Paris and that you'd resisted. But—"

"It made no difference," I finished and then looked about in disbelief. Everything had collapsed because of a jealous man and his ego. "Thanks for trying. It means a lot."

"All I did was tell the truth. I said I found Brohammer a very troubling and odd man, and I would take your word over his under any circumstances."

I shrugged and said to Cass, "What will you do now?"

"I'll stay as long as they want me."

"Please be careful. You and Eve need to be more cautious."

"We are careful. Why are you saying this now?"

I had to warn her without revealing that I'd taken unjust blame for her. "Someone heard me last night when I went out with Jimmy."

Her face reflected a surprised realization.

"Yes, apparently some people on our team listen to every sound in the night."

Over the next few days, I walked the streets of Paris. While I waited to receive notification of my travel schedule, I wandered around a city in full celebratory mode.

I didn't enter any bars or restaurants, instead eating bread and cheese and drinking coffee from a stand so I could hold on to as much money as possible. It surprised me that I could think of tomorrow after all that had happened, that I could form coherent plans, that I could still shape a future. Kentucky called me home, and I could almost smell the spongy grass beneath my feet, hear the horses neighing in the stables. I couldn't wait to watch them trotting about in their paddocks, and listen to birdsong in the air instead of whistling shells and exploding bombs.

On a bridge over the Seine, I stood and imagined all the lovers who had waited here for someone. How many waited for someone who would never come? I could not think of Jimmy. Missing him caught me up every hour of the day, and his face would materialize before me—those charming and dancing eyes, the way he closed them when I touched him. I tried not to think about questions I had no answers to. Had word somehow reached him about what had happened to me? Did he have any idea where I was? How would he find me now?

My lease on France had expired. My tickets showed up at the hotel the next day. I would board the boat and leave in the morning.

That evening, I took what would be my last stroll through Paris. My father walked around in my mind, and for the first time I found it almost a good thing that he was gone. At least he would never learn of the shame I'd brought down on myself in the country of his birth. Would I ever tell Maman?

I doubted it, but the story could reach her someday. I couldn't imagine how, but I'd never imagined any of it. And yet, I'd never regret coming to France. France now ran in my blood like minnows in a stream. Half of my line came from here and sent me forth into the world, and it seemed fitting that I'd walked in its forests, drunk from its waters, and shed tears on its soil.

And peace worked its magic, even on me. The gauzy air of Paris, like filtered light or moonlight, made everything, even the sandbags, streets, and buildings, look softly luminous. The lamplights shone silky, like beacons showing us the way ahead. Paris was made of poetry and power, riches and romance, war and now a glorious peace. At times the boisterous merriment seemed to mock my shame, but lovely memories of France would always wind gently through my mind. Here, I had lived fully for the first time. Here, I'd found Jimmy.

The city swarmed with Allied soldiers drinking, cheering, and celebrating, and I ran into Emile, the French ambulance driver from Meaux. He had worked there at the same time Jimmy had.

He recognized me and asked me to join him for a drink. Even thinner and more disheveled than he'd looked at the front, apparently he'd participated in some full-scale celebrations and perhaps hadn't slept all night. In his eyes, however, I recognized something else, a darkness that told me he really wanted to talk. We sat down at a café. I asked for water instead of wine.

After we'd caught up for a bit, I asked him in French, "Do you remember the American driver, Jimmy Tucker?"

"Yes, of course. Nice guy," he said. "Funny fellow."

I could've asked him if Jimmy was celebrating in Paris, too, but I intended to follow Dr. Logan's last directions and not seek him out. We'd have plenty of time after we both landed back in the US, whenever that might be. In the meantime, I would spend my nights longing for something I'd never before allowed myself to want or even name. And it comforted me to know that Jimmy and I slept under the same stars.

"I'm surprised you asked about him," Emile said.

The brush of a warning came with his words, and my skin tightened. The breeze picked up, and I wanted to hug myself. "Why wouldn't I?"

He shook his head as if disbelieving. "You haven't heard what happened to him?"

My stomach turned, and an image of Jimmy dead on the road flashed in front of me.

Emile must have registered it. "Don't worry. He's alive. But he has gone through a most terrible ordeal."

"What do you mean?"

"He was arrested and almost court-martialed."

Incredulous and blinking, I asked, "Why?"

"Yes. For taking his ambulance on the sly and using it for personal reasons." He glanced away and then back. "To see you."

Emile watched me intently, and I imagined that his statement *to see you* hinted at something of an accusation, but I detected no such malice in his eyes.

I said, "I met with him twice, and both times he was on leave."

"That's not what someone told his CO. Someone said it had been going on for months, and that Jimmy had abandoned his post while on duty and left the area without permission, to go off and meet you. That's dereliction of duty."

I nearly fell on the pavement. My thoughts tangled like vines in my head. It couldn't be. Jimmy had done nothing wrong. They could not have accused him of dereliction of duty. I said, "Until recently we weren't in the same area. It wouldn't have even been possible . . ." Then I remembered when we both worked in Meaux for a short while, and after that, I remained in Meaux and he moved to Charly, not so far away. "Except for one other time."

"Even one time would be enough to get him in trouble. Even one dereliction of duty is dereliction of duty."

I couldn't speak.

He said, "As I said, a bad ordeal." At least Emile didn't spare me from the awful truth of the matter; he didn't treat me like a fragile thing.

Both times I'd met Jimmy in the woods, he had been on leave, and I didn't think any military rules governed matters of the heart while the men were off duty. Of course, another double standard existed there, in that men were encouraged to seek female attention, whereas we women were shunned for doing so—unless the attention came from an eligible officer, that is.

But I'd let Dr. Logan believe all the forays into the night had been mine and Jimmy's, and someone had seen fit to pass that information along. Brohammer, of course. Even though he would've had no way to spell out specific dates and times, apparently a general accusation had placed Jimmy in hot water. Jimmy and I *had* been in close enough proximity before. Emile spoke the truth: How many times did it take?

I hadn't thought it could get worse, but it had, and I'd caused it all. I was nothing, not even worthy of the air I breathed. "What happened?" I asked Emile, surprised I could speak.

"After a few days, they released him and decided against a court-martial. He had some buddies willing to vouch for him, a little bit of an alibi if his friends could be believed, and now that the war's over, it didn't seem so important any longer. But his army career is probably over. He won't go to jail, but he probably won't get an honorable discharge, either."

I shook my head, still trying to believe that the mistaken impression I'd left with Dr. Logan and Beryl had made its way to Jimmy's CO. How had Jimmy reacted? He had no idea why I'd allowed Dr. Logan to believe we'd seen each other for much longer than we actually had. He'd have no clue as to why I would've incriminated him so. He had no idea about Cass and Eve.

I had to stay. I had to find Jimmy's commanding officer and explain to him that I'd protected someone else and that Jimmy and I had never met while he was on duty.

But no one would believe me now. Dr. Logan had warned me that if I made any contact with Jimmy in any way while still in France, I'd have to pay for my passage home. And I had to leave tomorrow. It almost killed me, but the next harsh realization arrived anyway: Jimmy probably thought I had lied, and he'd have no idea why. And the miserable irony: Brohammer had abandoned *his* duty, and he'd gotten away with it.

Paris whirled and tilted around me, and then settled as Emile's face made me see a future I didn't want to see. My tangled reflections turned into dreadful awareness, and the heavens rained down bitter truth: I would never see Jimmy again.

Emile slid his wine glass across the table toward me. "Here," he said. "Take the wine."

My voice cracked. "If I drink enough of it, will it make all of this go away?"

"Who knows?" he said and shrugged. "But I recommend you give it a shot."

In the morning I stood with my bag on the pavement outside the hotel waiting for my ride to the station. From there I would take the train to Le Havre and then the ship home.

I stood there, a husk of my former self.

A messenger on a bicycle pulled up to me and asked, "Miss Arlene Favier?"

"*Oui,*" I answered.

He handed me an envelope and then turned and rode away.

On the outside, my name, and inside, an American bank check in the amount of one thousand dollars, signed by Beryl Rayne. I unfolded the note that came with it.

No hard feelings was all it said.

Chapter Twenty-Eight

PARIS, KENTUCKY

FEBRUARY 1920

In the morning I always took my coffee cup out onto the front porch while Maman made breakfast inside, and Luc, already in the stables, checked on our horses before he went to school. In only a few months, he would have his diploma.

The Sears & Roebuck catalog house had worked well for us. After my return to Paris, Kentucky, I'd purchased the home kit and hired workers to help Luc and me build it. It still required some finishing touches, and we needed more furnishings, but Maman, Luc, and I each had our own room and a comfortable bed on which to sleep inside it. *Petit à petit, l'oiseau fait son nid.* Little by little, the bird builds its nest.

A few weeks after my return, I'd received a very short letter from Jimmy, sent from France. I read it so many times, I knew every word.

> *Dear Arlene,*
> *I hope you're home safely and your family is well. I'm stay-*
> *ing on in Paris, where I hope to decide what to do next.*
> *I have racked my brain trying to figure out why you said*

we'd met many times and not just those two nights while
I was on leave. I kept hoping you'd get word to me, but
when you didn't send a message and I heard you'd gone
home without letting me know, it seemed a clear signal
that you meant for it to be over between us.

Despite it all, you have my best wishes. Take care of
yourself.

Jimmy

There was no return address.

For a while I'd thought I couldn't endure the pain. Of course he felt betrayed, and I couldn't blame him. I'd never had a chance to set the record straight. For a long time the reins he had on me wouldn't relent, even after no other letters came and it became apparent that Jimmy's time in Paris, Kentucky, had run its course and he had washed his hands of all of it, including me. Once, he'd mentioned wanting to live overseas, and I'd seen in his eyes something of a free thing that didn't want to remain anywhere, not even on a horse farm in Kentucky with a woman he might have truly loved at one time. In the end, I realized that my longing for Jimmy wouldn't change the fact that he didn't wish to be found. Jimmy knew where I was. He could've contacted me again at any time.

In France, I'd loved, and I had lost. It seemed to me that love during wartime had required Jimmy and me to run a true course in the present, hauntings from the past and differences about the future be damned. Perhaps that was what made war love such powerful love. Perhaps love born during a time of such pain and suffering, no matter how heartfelt and real it seemed during those moments, was destined to fail. People dearly wanted life to be uplifting and love to be sweet and hopeful. Once love has been tainted by war, maybe it cannot overcome its origins.

Cass and Eve hadn't lasted, either, but Cass now worked back in Cincinnati and had already met someone else, reminding me that time keeps turning and we go on, despite it all. In France, I'd discovered something precious in another person, and also a new side of myself—feelings previously folded up within the layers of my life. My determination, the horses, the farm, and my family—those things had buried it for a long time, but alas, it had lived inside me all along, waiting for me to find it. And when I did, a great load slipped off my back. After all . . . I could love.

Every day the weather allowed, I took a ride on Mary Blue, my dependable mare that my father had purchased and which always reminded me of him. With each ride, with each walk on Favier land, and with each nail hammered into the new Favier house, more of the death-air that had surrounded me in France fell away, until one day, I realized that it had finally departed. I'd never forget France, but I had emerged from the darkness of that war-ravaged land and blinked myself back to life in the place where I belonged.

Our time on earth continued to flow onward, like the streams and rivers I loved. And I began to see that maybe our lives move in just a trickle sometimes or even dry up for a while, but eventually the snows melt, the blocking debris breaks up, and the sweet waters of life surge forward again.

Very soon I purchased a stud horse, a Thoroughbred whose black coat gave off a velvety, almost violet sheen perfectly matched to his name, Twilight. I'd had many good stallions to choose from, and although some stood taller, some had better race records, and some seemed better muscled, I had followed my father's advice. I closed my eyes and listened to my heart and gut and chose the stallion that spoke to me, that moved me, the one whose heart I could feel as true and brave when I laid my head against his neck and breathed in his scent. Only time would tell if I'd chosen wisely.

I offered Twilight for stud service in February 1919, and most of the mares he'd stood at stud for were in foal. Only now had the almost year-long gestational period passed, and the first mare was due to give birth any day. She belonged to a local racehorse breeder, who'd promised to let me know as soon as anything happened.

I looked toward the road, hoping to see signs of a vehicle approaching.

As if I'd beckoned it with my will, a truck pulled into our drive, and I soon saw the breeder I'd hoped to see today. I began to walk toward him and glanced about for Luc. He would want to hear this, too, and he deserved to hear it. We were partners.

Mr. Tomkins, a big man who sported a full beard and was a former friend of my father's, stopped me in my tracks. Wearing smudged overalls, he jumped from the driver's seat holding up a bouquet of blue ribbons. "It's a colt!"

I walked swiftly closer, holding my breath. "How is he?"

"A beauty. Big and strong and stood right away. Nursed right away."

Elated, I looked around for Luc.

"He's the best colt that mare has ever foaled. You may have done it, Arlene," Tomkins said, pulling me back into his gaze. "You just might have your father's gift."

Luc and I spent the rest of the morning with the horses, smiling gratefully and almost shyly at each other, congratulating Twilight, loving him, feeding him special treats, and telling him he was a papa now.

When a cloud of dust stirred on the road between the trees, I feared that Tomkins had come back to give me some bad news about the foal or its mother. I left Luc in the stables when a motorcar headed up the drive.

I didn't recognize the car, and so I remained still and watched it approach and come to a halt. Jimmy stepped out and stilled my heart.

My first thought, my fervent hope: Jimmy had come back to me.

His hair had grown longer, and he looked older wearing civilian clothes—gray slacks and a white shirt—but the face I knew so well hadn't changed. His expression, however, was unreadable.

"Arlene," he said and slowly walked my way.

I didn't know what to do with myself.

Coming closer, he said, "I hope it's alright I came to see you."

I nodded but had to gaze down for a minute. Bewildered by seeing Jimmy's sweet face and not knowing why he'd come, hoping he'd come here for me, I said, "Of course it is."

After reaching into his pocket, he retrieved a small packet and opened it. Inside, my baby locket and chain. "I had to return this."

I said nothing for a while and then, "Oh."

He handed the locket to me and then ran a hand through his hair. "It helped me . . ." He glanced away. "During some dark days at the end of the war."

Still trying to get through the shock of seeing Jimmy again, I wrapped my hand around the locket. "Jimmy," I said, making him look at me. "I have to explain—"

"And I wanted to tell you something. I figured you'd have no means to know . . ." He continued in response to my blank face. "Remember how we feared that scoundrel Brohammer would go unpunished? Well, a couple of weeks after the armistice, while he crossed a street in Château-Thierry, a hit-and-run driver mowed him down. He died an hour later."

At first puzzled, I wondered why he was telling me this. Seeing Jimmy here, standing before me, was already too much to absorb, and now this. Brohammer dead? I hated that man, but . . . did I really want to know about this? "Mowed him down? As in an accident?"

Jimmy answered, "I don't know. No witnesses ever came forward, and the driver was never found. Maybe it was an accident and the driver panicked and ran, or maybe it was murder. We don't know what else he did over there. He probably had a slew of enemies, so my bet is on murder."

"Who would've done it?"

"I can't say. Apparently someone who believes in doling out vigilante justice."

"I'm stunned. I-I've heard nothing." I rubbed my arms.

"At least he didn't get away with it."

"Yes, but I don't know how to feel about him *dying*."

Taking a step closer to me, he said, "That man got his just due. That's how to feel about it."

I nodded and pressed my feet down hard on the earth. It felt like the ground trembled beneath me, and I had nothing to keep me solid and still. Jimmy here. Brohammer dead.

I managed to speak in a normal voice as I lifted my gaze. "Jimmy, please hear me out. When I took the blame for all those nighttime rendezvous, I was protecting someone else. Two people who had truly met at night. For a long time. Good people. And their situation was even more complicated than ours, and their punishment would have been much worse than ours."

He frowned and seemed as if forcing himself to move beyond Brohammer to the two of us, reliving a moment. Something twitched next to his lip, and he appeared to think hard. "People married to other people?" he slowly asked.

"Something like that."

His voice landed on me softly, despite words I didn't want to hear. "And you put them before us."

"I know it must look that way, but I had to let them believe it was us, for the sake of others. I never thought it would make its way back to you and your CO. I never imagined the consequences. The leader of the AWH immediately discharged me the morning after I last saw you. Brohammer had come there. He had been watching me or having someone else watch me. He knew everything—"

Jimmy's face tightened, his eyes dark. "I hate that man. I hate him even more, even as he burns in hell."

"The next day I woke up, and everything in France came crashing down around me. The AWH leader forbade any contact with you before I left. If I'd sent something and they found out, they wouldn't have paid my way back."

I watched him go through a slow realization. "Of course I figured out that something had gone wrong for you because of seeing me. I'd always feared that very thing, but I never imagined they'd force you out like that. And someone told me he saw you in Paris—"

"Waiting for the ship and fighting the urge to contact you anyway. My stay ended because I broke the rules. I did. Not you."

"And you took the blame for someone else who broke the rules, too."

I nodded.

A few long moments that swelled and swelled. Then he shook his head in what looked like resignation and actually smiled, one of those sweet and sad and hopeful but also wistful smiles that only Jimmy could give. "Finally it makes sense. I would never have guessed . . . at least now I can stop tormenting myself."

"You could've written me again and given me your address. I did everything I could to find you so I could explain. I went to see some of our old friends from high school and asked if they'd received a letter or anything. It seems you sent a couple of postcards, but without any return address."

His face slowly fell. "I know, and I'm sorry. I was stumped and then the longer I stayed in Paris, the more baffled I became. Things happened that I didn't want to believe. I got you in trouble, you disappeared, and the army gave me a general discharge, not an honorable one."

Back in Paris, Emile had said something like that might happen, and alas, he had been correct. I laid my hand on my chest, stunned by the unfairness of it. All because of me. "That's just terrible. Oh, Jimmy, I'm so very sorry."

He remained open, still so kind. "I guess I got kind of lost for a while."

"I ruined your military career."

He shook his head gently and spoke to me gently, too. "It could've been worse. I got a blue ticket, a general discharge. I could've received a dishonorable discharge."

"Oh, Jimmy . . ."

He gazed away, squinting into the sun. "I took it hard for a while, but I wasn't formally charged with anything, and it allowed me to get out early and start living again." His face brightened then as he looked back at me. "A couple of my driver buddies and I have opened up a mechanics shop in Paris. We're repairing all the American cars, learning how to fix the European ones, and speaking French . . . well, attempting to speak French. Paris has been good to me." He glanced around the farm, and I could see the admiration hadn't left him; he still loved this land. Twilight pranced around in his paddock, and a smile rose a notch on Jimmy's face, then his eyes swept around full circle. "I see you've gotten all settled here. You have a new house."

I pulled in a long breath, letting it soak in; Jimmy hadn't come back to me after all. He had come because of all those other things—the locket, Brohammer's demise, maybe an explanation—but not for me. I slowly said, "You could've sent the locket in the mail."

"All the way from Paris?" He shook his head. "I couldn't take the chance with something so valuable." The firm line of his eyebrows softened. A pulse throbbed in his neck. "Besides, I needed to come back here and tie up a few loose ends." His tone weakened, and he blinked twice. "And see you one more time."

I managed to ask, "To say goodbye?"

He looked at his feet and then glanced about again. "Yes."

So the love brought to life in a forest in France under moonlight would slowly slip away into nothing more than memory. "Will you write?"

"Sure. I'll splurge on the best postcards in Paris." That gleam, that mischievous way of his that I loved—it was still there. He might have been lost for a while, but he had come back now. "For you."

The same loveable Jimmy. My Jimmy.

"Thank you," I said. But my breath snagged, and my conscience ached. "Please forgive me for implicating you. When our leader accused me of many more nighttime meetings than we'd had, I let it stand. I never thought the tale would spread. I had but one moment to decide—that I could protect the others, and in that moment, it seemed . . . right. I never imagined it would hurt you. Never. Not until later, and by then, the damage had been done."

He said nothing, and then a silence so mournful I forgot to breathe.

"Maybe it was for the best," he said quietly.

My voice cracked, and I shook my head involuntarily. "I don't believe that for a minute."

Then he grasped my hand and held it tightly in his, and his face looked tortured as I'm sure mine did in response to his touch. He lifted my hand and placed it on his cheek, just as he'd done back in France, and my knees nearly unpinned. Agony had tightened his face, his jaw trembled now, and the longing still lived in his gaze. He had not moved past it; he had not gotten over us.

I couldn't pull my hand away, remembering so many things I'd tried to forget. Jimmy wasn't ready to let go, either, despite what he'd come here to say, and perhaps the relief from finally understanding, the knowing now, could open the door to our love again.

He slowly dropped my hand and whispered, "I tried to forget . . ." A regretful smile on his face, and in those words was an understanding of what we'd lost, and it needed no explanation or reply.

But I couldn't lose Jimmy this way. I couldn't let him go without revealing my heart. He deserved no less. "Then give us another chance. Please, Jimmy. I couldn't forget you, either."

Arms at his sides, he turned his palms toward me and started to open up, and there I flew, finding the place where I belonged. Holding me tightly and both of us living through it again. The love and then the loss. He slowly released me, but it took me a long time to move. I made myself take a step back and study his face, where I could still see the dream in his eyes, muddled but still there.

"Please come back. I need you here," I said.

His face revealed hope, but doubt, too. He pulled me close again, sighed heavily, and whispered through my hair. "Don't you see? One thing I did realize was that here with you, I'd always be the stable boy who made good."

He released me again. "You're a war veteran and a hero."

He glanced around for a moment, taking it all in. "This is your place. I'm not sure we could both be happy here."

I swallowed against my dry throat. "There's only one way to find out. You always loved this farm, and you still have friends here. You can work with me, or you can find something else to do—Luc may take over more someday anyway. We can do this; I'm sure of it."

I'd surprised him, and he smiled. "Are you proposing to me?"

"Yes, I suppose I am."

A little laugh slipped out of him. Did I see a hint of joy? "Well, that's a first, and about the last thing I expected to happen today."

"Me too. But we can be happy; I know it."

Turning solemn again, he said, "I want you to be right. Of course I do. I never stopped . . ." Then in an abrupt change, he choked on the words and broke as I'd never seen him do before and bit back tears. Jimmy wasn't one to crumble, but he couldn't hide himself from me.

"Loving," I said for him. "I never stopped loving you, either."

He glanced at his watch. "I have to go now. This was the last thing on my list before I went back, and I almost didn't come. I didn't know if I had the nerve. I had no clue . . . how bad it has been for you. You're right; I should've written, and I'm sorry." I had the sense that he had more to say, but it would have to wait. "I have to catch a train; I can't miss it, and by tomorrow, I'll be at sea."

"Do you have to go back?"

"I do. I have a business with my buddies, and I've made commitments. I have a lease"—a little grin—"and a motorbike, and I can't just simply fail to return. I have to go back, even if it's just to tie things up *there* now."

So Jimmy would disappear again as quickly as he had arrived. But I perceived the plea in his perusal of me, and I knew exactly what he asked.

"You waited for me for years, ever since we were kids," I said. "And you let me find my own way to you. It's my turn to do the same. I'll wait for you now."

I watched a mix of emotions form on his face—some fear and doubt still there—but the most powerful and evident one was love. And then an understanding came together between us, although we had no time to discuss it further. We knew no details, had made no plans, but we would figure it out.

Jimmy had once said something along those lines to me in the woods. We would figure it out.

For the time being, it was enough. The train whistle called; the ocean liner waited. I had to let him go for now. But not without a kiss.

As I stood on my toes, my legs still threatening to give way, our lips and mouths met. Still just as warm and open and sweet and soft and filled with love and desire. After we untangled, I opened my palm and lifted the locket, letting it dangle by its chain like a pendulum, and said to Jimmy, "Please take this back with you."

He didn't move, didn't blink.

I turned to the locket and spoke to it in a whisper. "You brought Jimmy back to me once." I lifted it to my face, kissed it, and said, "Please do it again."

Then I let it fall into Jimmy's open hand.

Epilogue

Twilight and I jumped the fence and landed, fleet-footed, in our far meadow. The sun was setting and painting the western sky in swaths of orange, salmon, and pink. Twilight's coat twitched; he wanted to jump the fence at the far end of the field, but I wouldn't allow it. He was my responsibility now.

I let my eyes roam over Favier lands. Jimmy had left for now, but he would come back. My father's presence, however, was here in every blade of grass, every stone, and every crumb of rich soil. And then my father was gone, too, as he had come, free now to leave it all to me. Free now to find endless peace.

When I turned back toward the stables, Twilight panted from the effort of his run, and I reached down and patted his neck. Tomkins had said, *You just might have your father's gift.* And I finally believed it.

In the dream Jimmy waited for me outside the stables. Of course he had made his way back. He would help me with my wishes and goals as much as he'd made his own come true. Now we knew how foolish it was not to seek all that our lives and time on earth offered. We also knew how other things and other people could step in and tangle everything up. Together, we would make sure it didn't happen again.

I drew closer. Jimmy held a cigarette, and a burning scent seeped into my brain. I opened my eyes to sudden consciousness. I was not riding Twilight; I lay in bed, in the middle of the night, curled up against Jimmy, who slept deeply, peace and contentment on his face.

I lay still, quietly breathing, then turned my face to gaze up at the ceiling. The smell of smoke came from the dream—or from here?

No. Only a few traces of other scents—paint, varnish, sawdust—from a new house that, along with some luck and love and work, I had built.

AUTHOR'S NOTE

The women of the American Women's Hospital believed that their service to the people of France did not end on Armistice Day. They continued to serve the needs of the homeless, poor villagers, and refugees until the spring of 1920 and left behind a fully equipped hospital. Before leaving France, the members of the American Women's Hospital were awarded the *Médaille de la Reconnaissance Française* (Medal of French Recognition), in recognition of those who, without military obligation, had come to the aid of the ill, injured, and disabled of France during World War I.

In the 1920s, the work of the American Women's Hospital continued in Greece, the Balkans, and the Middle East.

ACKNOWLEDGMENTS

As always, my thanks to my agent, Lisa Erbach Vance, for her ongoing support and belief in me. My gratitude also goes to my editor, Jodi Warshaw, and the entire team at Lake Union, who with each novel, continue to make my writing dreams come true. And thanks to my developmental editor, Christina Henry de Tessan, who helped me make the story stronger.

I received generous help from many others, including Ed Vasser and Lynn Kustes for their expertise in historical railroad travel, and Stephen Headley for his assistance with Cincinnati history. Thanks to the guides at the lovely Claiborne Farm for information on horse breeding, Abbe Kesterson for guidance with equine terminology, and Perrine de Seze for her proficiency in the French language and culture. I'm grateful for public access to the Harris and Ewing collection at the Library of Congress, where I ran across the 1917 photo of an ambulance driver used as the cover of this book. Numerous other resources aided me in learning about World War I history in France.

Finally, my inspiration for this novel came from the unsung heroes of the American Women's Hospital and their service during World War I. This group of remarkable women funded, planned, organized, trained, and equipped all-female medical teams to serve in France during the war. Almost unknown and unrecognized, these brave women put themselves at risk, not for personal glory or gain, but simply to help.

RECOMMENDED READING

Paris at the End of the World: The City of Light during the Great War, 1914–1918 by John Baxter

Kentucky and the Great War: World War I on the Home Front by David J. Bettez

Château Thierry & Belleau Wood 1918: American's Baptism of Fire on the Marne by David Bonk

In the Soldier's Service: War Experiences of Mary Dexter, England, Belgium, France, 1914–1918 by Mary Dexter

Three Soldiers by John Dos Passos

Gentlemen Volunteers: The Story of the American Ambulance Drivers in the First World War by Arlen J. Hansen

Battlefields of the First World War by Tonie and Valmai Holt

American Battlefields of World War I: Château-Thierry—Then and Now by David C. Homsher

The Doctor's Duffel Bag by M. Louise Hurrell

Mobilizing Minerva: American Women in the First World War by Kimberly Jensen

Certain Samaritans by Esther Pohl Lovejoy

The House of the Good Neighbor by Esther Pohl Lovejoy

Wounded: A New History of the Western Front in World War I by Emily Mayhew

The Americans in the Great War, Volume I: The Second Battle of the Marne by Michelin and Company

Into the Breach: American Women Overseas in World War I by Dorothy and Carl J. Schneider

BOOK CLUB QUESTIONS

1. Before reading this book, had you ever heard of the American Women's Hospital? Do you feel you learned something valuable while you read this book? Can you think of any other groups serving others today in a similar manner?

2. Tragedy in the form of fire strikes Arlene during the opening of this book; soon after, she faces financial ruin. How would you characterize her responses to the life-altering events early in the book? What about her background and nature gave her the strength to persevere? Were you ever angry at her, or did you ever feel as though her life before had been too sheltered and pampered?

3. When Arlene is presented with an opportunity to go to France as an ambulance driver, she accepts immediately. Was the prospect of earning a lot of money her biggest motivation? What else gave her reason to go? Do you think you would've made the same decision?

4. Cass's friendship quickly becomes important to Arlene. Why do you think they became close? What did they have in common or not have in common? After Cass's revelation toward the end of the novel, do you feel as if they had been close friends all along or not?

5. Brohammer is almost a typical and total villain in this book. Did you ever feel sorry for him? Or wonder why he was the way he was? How well do you think Arlene handled his advances? How did you feel upon learning of his death in the last chapter?

6. On the other hand, Jimmy is presented as one of the best of men. But he also had weaknesses. What about his personal history and place in society made him doubt that he and Arlene could be happy? Did he want to protect her or protect himself? Or both? How did he deal with his doubts, and how did he try to overcome them?

7. Although completely fictitious, the two female doctors/leaders of the American Women's Hospital first medical team have very different personality types. How did their different styles affect the rest of the team? Was Beryl Rayne a good leader? Was Herberta Logan a good leader? Which style of leadership do you prefer?

8. Near the end of the book, Arlene faces a profound decision. She chooses to protect others she cares for, and it turns out to hurt Jimmy and her in ways she'd never expected. How do you feel about her decision? Would you have made the same one?

9. The novel concludes on a strong note of hope, although few details have been worked out. How do you envision the future for both Arlene and Jimmy? Will they be able to get past future obstacles based on the fortitude they developed from serving in the war? How will they deal with problems going forward?

10. What do you see as the theme of this book? Resilience in the face of tragedy? Courage under pressure? The transformative power of love? Or something else?

11. As of this novel's publication date, just over one hundred years have passed since the end of World War I. At that time, women in the US still did not have the right to vote. How have things changed for women over the past century? How would Arlene's life have been different if she'd had the rights women have now?

ABOUT THE AUTHOR

Photo © 2015 Whitney Raines Photography

Ann Howard Creel is the author of the Kindle bestselling historical novel *The Whiskey Sea*, and her novel *The Magic of Ordinary Days* was made into an award-winning CBS Hallmark Hall of Fame movie.

A former registered nurse, Ann writes about strong women facing high-stakes situations and having to make life-changing decisions. Her historical settings have ranged from Victorian-era Galveston to World War I France to World War II New York City. Besides writing, Ann loves renovating old houses, hiking, and all things cat. For more information, visit her at www.annhowardcreel.com.